WICKED

ONCE UPON A VILLAIN

BIANCA COLE

AUTHOR'S NOTE

Hello reader,

This is a warning to let you know that this is a **DARK** mafia romance much like many of my other books, which means there are very sensitive subject matters addressed and dark, triggering content. If you have any triggers, it would be a good idea to proceed with caution and read the warning below.

As well as a possessive and dominant anti-hero who doesn't take **no** for an answer and a lot of spicy scenes, this book addresses some sensitive subjects. A list of these can be found on my website: www.biancacoleauthor.com

If you have any triggers, then it's best to read the warnings and not proceed. However, if none of these are an issue for you, read on and enjoy this dark romance.

WICKED PLAYLIST

"Wake Me Up When September ends"
—Greenday
"Lovely"—Billie Elish (with Khalid)
"Daddy Issues"—The Neighbourhood
"Older"—Isabel La Rosa
"Beautiful"—Bazzi feat. Camila Cabello
"Poison Ivy"— Hemi Morre
"You Put a Spell On Me"—Austin Giorgio
"Devil I know"—Allie X
"I Want To"—Rosenfield
"River" —Bishop Briggs
"Do It For Me"—Rosenfield
"Silk"—Elijah Blond
"When We Get Naked"—FoxTune
"What Was I Made For"—Billie Elish
"Haunted"—Isabel La Rosa
"Die For You"—The weeknd & Ariana Grande

Listen on Spotify

ELLA

Ten years ago…

"Ella!" Dad calls.

I jump to my feet at the sound of his voice. He's been away for two long weeks. He's my favorite person, and I hate that he's away so often. I sprint toward the front door and rush into his arms. "I'm so glad you're back."

He hugs me tightly. Then I hear a soft sigh, warning me he's not back for long. "I'm sorry, sweetie. I can only drop in because I've got to go on another trip right away."

My brow furrows, as he's always home for my birthday. "But—"

"I know it's your birthday, sweetie. I just can't put this trip off. I'm so sorry." He reaches into his pocket and pulls out a small, wrapped gift. "Happy Birthday for tomorrow."

I take it, tears welling in my eyes, because I don't want him to go. He's been here for all my birthdays for eleven years. I know his work is dangerous and has something to do with criminals, which angers me. He does it for the money to keep Mom happy. "Are you sure you have to go?"

He kisses my cheek and wipes away a stray tear. "I'm sorry, but I'll be back before you know it." There's an odd look in his eyes, one that tells me he's not sure he believes he will be back.

"Is there something wrong?" I ask.

He shakes his head, forcing a smile. "Of course not. Why would anything be wrong?"

"The people you work for, I know—"

"Quiet, Ella," he murmurs, shaking his head. "You don't know anything, sweetheart." He hugs me again, even more tightly. "Now, be a good girl for your mom, and I'll call you tomorrow."

Mom doesn't get me the way Dad does. We get on well enough, but I hate that she makes him work for bad people who force him to travel a lot because she wants to live in a fancy apartment and buy designer clothes.

He glances at the present in my hand. "No opening that until tomorrow, got it?"

I smile and nod. "Got it."

"Good girl," he says, patting me on the head. "I'll speak to you in the morning."

He turns and walks out of the apartment, leaving me sad.

I can't help but feel angry at Mom for forcing him to work so hard so that she can spend all his money. She doesn't work. All she does is spend.

The door to her bedroom opens, and her brow furrows. "Did I hear your dad?"

I swallow hard. "Yes, he popped in to give me my gift for tomorrow." I hold it up. "He won't be here for my birthday."

Her brow furrows. "What?"

I shrug. "That's what Dad said."

She looks worried as she shakes her head. "Come on, do you want pancakes for breakfast?"

"Sure!" I say, skipping into the kitchen as I love pancakes with syrup.

Mom follows and starts making the batter. I can tell she's preoccupied, though, making me anxious. I don't like it when she's like this. It feels like she's distant and not really here.

Dad's never like that.

Once she's finished making breakfast, we sit down at the small table in the kitchen to eat. While we eat the pancakes, she keeps checking her phone, a frown on her face.

"Is something wrong, Mom?" I ask, my heart beating faster in my chest, as I don't think she expected Dad to leave.

She glances up, a forced smile on her face. "No, sweetie. Everything's fine."

My brow furrows. "You didn't know Dad was going out of town again today?" I confirm.

She tilts her head. "You, little monster, are too clever for your own good." She sighs. "No, I thought he was back today for your birthday."

I purse my lips. "Dad said he has to go on another trip."

Mom waves her hand in the air and smiles. "I'm sure he forgot to let me know. He'll text back soon enough."

I bite my inner cheek, wishing I didn't feel so worried. My birthday hasn't started yet, but I sense it will be the worst.

IT'S EARLY when I wake the next morning, eager to open the gift Dad gave me. I jump out of bed in my pajamas and rush down the stairs, noticing Mom is sitting in the living room. As I get around the railing, I see two police officers sitting on the couch opposite.

My heart sinks, and dread tightens my stomach.

"Mom, what's going on?" I ask, my voice shaking.

She stands and looks at me, her eyes filled with tears. "Ella, sweetie, I'm so sorry," she says, her voice barely above a whisper. "Your dad... he's gone."

I feel like my world is crashing down around me. "What do you mean, gone?"

"He's been murdered," one of the police officers interjects. "We're here to ask your mother to come to the station to identify the body."

My mind goes blank as I try to process what they're saying. My Dad has been brutally taken away from me on my birthday. Tears stream down my face as I

4

crumple to the floor, unable to understand why or how this has happened.

Mom picks me up off the floor and hugs me. "I'm sorry," she says, tears flooding her cheeks.

"Mam, do you have anyone to look after your daughter while you come with us?"

Mom shakes her head. "No, she'll have to come."

I notice the look that the police officers give each other. "That's not advisable."

"I want to see my dad."

Their eyes widen, and the male officer shakes his head. "That's definitely not advisable."

Mom's chin wobbles. "Why?"

"He's in a bad way," the female officer says. "One of us will wait with your daughter while you identify the body."

The male officer steps forward. "Can you follow us?"

Mom nods. "Go and get a jacket and your shoes on, Ella."

I walk to the front door and slip on my shoes before grabbing my jacket off the peg by the door.

Mom ushers me out and straight into the elevator to the parking lot below. Tears stream down my face like a river. I glance at Mom to find she's no longer crying, just staring ahead.

The elevator doors open, and she marches toward the car without a word. I rush after her, my heart aching as I've never felt so sad. I climb into the car, and she brushes the tears still resting on her cheeks from her face. She turns over the engine and pulls out of the parking lot.

"I can't believe he's dead, Mom."

Her jaw clenches. "Death is part of life, Ella. The sooner you learn that, the better."

The pain in my chest is so intense. "I won't see him again?"

She shrugs and wipes her tears from her cheeks, following the police car onto the highway. "Worry about how the fuck we're going to live."

I stare at her in shock.

Did she even love Dad?

"How can you care about that?"

Her eyes cut to mine, and she glares at me. "In time, you will learn the importance of money. You can't live without it."

I want to tell her that there are more important things in life than money, but I know she'll never agree. Instead, I cross my arms over my chest and look out the window as a feeling of emptiness engulfs me.

The only thing that can make this moment bearable is music, so I take out my iPod and go through my playlist to find something that fits my mood. "Wake Me Up When September Ends" by *Greenday* stands out, and I play it, letting the music ease the pain. The lyrics wash over me as I drift off into my own world, away from Mom, trying to make sense of everything.

I close my eyes and imagine Dad singing along to the words. He always loved Greenday and would play their songs all the time. "Summer has come and passed. The innocent can never last. Wake me up when

September ends," we sing. I never understood the meaning of this song until this moment, and it's September. My birthday will never be a happy occasion again, as it will always be the day I lost my best friend.

The tears come back, and I let them fall, not daring to glance at Mom. I'm not sure I even know who she is anymore.

ELLA

P *resent day...*
Mom's constant chattering fills the back of the limousine as we are driven up the driveway of my new stepdad's home, a stepdad I've yet to meet.

I feel betrayed.

She eloped with a man called Remy Morrone only last week. A man she only met a few days before, and now we've left our hometown of Washington to come and live in Chicago at his home. It shouldn't surprise me, as she's always been like this.

Not only has she forced me away from my life and friends, but from Dad's grave, too. I used to visit every Saturday morning to put new flowers on his headstone.

At twenty-one years old, you'd think I'd have a choice whether I stay in Washington, but you would be wrong. Mom has had control over my bank account since I wrote one hit novel three years ago, which still makes a good living. It means I'm tied to her wherever she goes.

I tried opening another bank account a year ago, but she found out and hit the roof. Tearing up the documents and burning them. She said I was trying to leave her destitute after everything she'd *done* for me. I laughed when she said that, as all she's ever done for me was be absent and care more about money than her daughter.

My new stepdad has five kids, so I've got brothers and sisters overnight, but only two live at his home.

"Who is this guy?" I ask as we travel up the longest driveway I've ever seen.

Mom beams at me. "I told you, Ella, He's rich as hell. We're going to be fine now."

I sigh, as Mom has always been shallow. It's one of the things I can't stand about her. Money means the world to her, and it's why Dad worked for the people he did and got killed. And yet, she's gotten worse since he died and has been driven by a need to become rich. It looks like she's finally succeeded as we stop in front of an enormous mansion.

As I step out of the limousine, I'm struck by the grandeur of it. It's huge, with towering columns and a large porch. It's impressive, even if material things have never interested me.

Mom nods toward the entrance of the house. "Come and meet your new family."

I can feel my nerves creeping up on me.

What if Remy is a complete asshole?

What if his kids hate me?

I take a deep breath, trying to calm myself down.

"What are you waiting for?" Mom asks.

I shake my head. "Nothing, I'm just nervous." I

follow her up the steps to the front door, where she rings the bell.

The door opens and we're greeted by an insanely tall, muscular man with a square jaw and stunning dark brown eyes. He has to be almost seven feet tall, possibly the tallest man I've ever seen. My stomach churns as I wonder if this is my mom's new husband, who is unbelievably handsome for an older man. Mom said he's in his fifties, but this man looks forty years old and is wearing a well-tailored suit.

His eyes flash with something undetectable when they land on me, but it's gone quickly. "Hey there, you must be Ella," he says, his voice deep and smooth.

I feel my cheeks heat at the sound.

"I'm Remy. Welcome to our home." There's something a little sinister about the way he says that.

Two equally handsome men stand behind him, arms crossed over their chests. The expressions on their faces are far from friendly as I step into the entryway, feeling a shiver race down my spine.

Remy's jaw clenches. "These are my two youngest sons. Leo and Luca. Both are yet to fly the nest despite being over twenty-one." He glares at them, and I sense it's a sore subject despite this man living in a mansion with plenty of room.

"Hi," Luca says, smiling, but it's not a kind smile.

Leo grunts and continues to look at me like a piece of meat.

"Isn't this lovely?" Mom asks, completely unaware of the tension in the air. "A new family for you, Ella."

As if I wanted a new family. For ten years, it's been

Mom and me, and while she has her vices, we've been fine as we were, even if I miss Dad daily.

"We've got dinner prepared if you'd like some," Remy says, his eyes boring into me like lasers.

"Yes, that would be lovely, wouldn't it, Ella?"

I'd rather escape to a room and lock myself inside.

"Sure," I say, shrugging.

Remy's eyes finally leave me, and he leads us through the huge, pretentious home toward a lavish dining room. The grandeur of the place strikes me as I step into the dining hall. The dining table is so long I'm sure it could seat at least twenty people surrounded by expensive ornate backed chairs. Three crystal chandeliers hang from the ceiling, bathing the room in a welcoming glow even if nothing about this place feels welcoming. It's intimidating.

I don't fit in here.

"Take a seat," Remy says, his voice clipped as he gestures to one.

Mom sits to the right of him. Thankfully, I'm as far as possible from him, sitting opposite Luca and beside Leo. A shiver skates down my spine as Leo's arm brushes mine.

Remy and Mom chat together and she laughs, squeezing his arm at something he said.

Two women dressed in server uniforms enter carrying lots of food trays, setting them down. It's a heinous amount of food for five people, but Mom's eyes light up.

"So, Ella, tell us about yourself. What do you enjoy

doing in your spare time?" Remy asks, eyes fixed on me intently.

I swallow hard, feeling as though I'm being interviewed as his two sons stare at me. "Reading. I enjoy reading and…"

"And?" He presses.

"Writing, too. I'm working on my second novel."

Mom scoffs. "How often do I have to tell you that authors are poor? Set your sights higher."

I glare at her. "That's not what you said when it was our only income." I grab a spoon of vegetables and put them on the plate.

My cheeks burn with heat at the way she dismissed my writing in front of people I don't know, especially as she never complained when it was our main source of income.

"What kind of novel is it?" Leo asks, leaning toward me. "Is it erotic?"

I glare at him. "No, a thriller."

He scrunches his nose up. "Sounds boring."

"What are you two muttering about?" Luca asks.

"Boring fucking books," Leo says, making me dislike him even more.

Luca smirks. "He's only saying they're boring because he can't read."

"Bullshit," Leo says, but there's some weight behind his retort, suggesting Luca is on to something.

"You've got to be pretty smart to write a book," Luca says, giving me the kindest smile yet. "And I love thrillers, so if you need anyone to read it, count me in."

I smile as it's kind of him to offer, although my book

is nowhere near ready to be seen by anyone's eyes but my own. "Thanks, it's not finished yet. But I might take you up on that," I say, not wanting to reject him immediately.

He nods, and a silence falls between us.

Leo clears his throat. "You will get on with Camilla and Mia, I'm sure."

I swallow hard, assuming those are my two stepsisters. "Where are they tonight?"

"They couldn't make it. Camilla lives in Maine, and Mia is out of town with her husband and son for the weekend."

I nod in response. "I see."

Luca's eyes shift toward my cleavage. "So, little sister, do you have a boyfriend?"

My stomach churns as it's gross how he looks at me. He's my stepbrother, but it's clear both of these guys don't give a shit.

Remy clears his throat, drawing everyone's attention to him. "Enough polite chit-chat, and let's cut to the chase, shall we?"

I swallow hard as my eyes meet Remy's, and it feels like my whole world is on fire. "The chase?" I question.

He nods. "Yes, you're a Morrone now, so you'll act like one." His eyes narrow. "Women in the Morrone famiglia don't write books. They aspire to be a good wife to their future husband, and that's all." He sounds just like her.

Mom beams. "Indeed, a very rich husband, of course."

I feel like murdering her, as she has lost the plot.

The last thing that matters to me in this world is money. I want happiness and a partner who cares about me, not some rich businessman who couldn't give two shits.

"That's chauvinistic and old-fashioned. I intend to marry a man who loves me, and I don't care how much money he has."

Luca chuckles. "Clearly, you have no idea what world your mom has married into."

My brow furrows. "What do you mean?"

Leo snorts. "You can't be serious? Are you saying you have no idea who we are?"

I swallow hard as everyone looks at me like I'm an airhead. "I don't know who you are."

Remy glances at Mom. "You didn't tell her?"

She shrugs. "It's a difficult thing to bring up."

"We're mobsters, Ella," Remy says so casually it takes me a while to register what he said. When it finally does, it feels like my entire world tilts on its axis.

"Mobsters?" I repeat. The same kind of people that killed Dad. Rage coils through my gut, directed entirely at my pathetic excuse of a mother. She makes me sick.

"How could you?" I ask, glaring at her. "Especially after what happened to Dad."

"Quiet, Ella. I don't want to hear a word about it." Her eyes narrow. "You'll be a good girl and fit into this family, which will probably involve an arranged marriage."

"Arranged marriage?" I can't keep the shock from my voice.

"Yes, you're a Morrone now, and who you marry is

15

important." Remy's dark eyes look almost black in the dim light of the dining room.

This is going worse than I ever could have imagined. When Mom said she'd married someone rich, I assumed he was a businessman, not a criminal.

"Are you alright? You're looking a little pale?" Luca asks, a teasing lilt to his voice.

I glare at him, already developing a dislike for both of my stepbrothers. "It's not every day you find out you've been forced into a fucking mobster family, so no, I'm not okay."

Luca chuckles. "She's feisty, I'll give her that."

"I think you'll fit right in." Leo's tone is humourless.

I clench my fists beneath the table, holding back a retort.

"You'll accept it in time." Remy brings his glass of whiskey to his lips, taking a sip. "They all do."

I want to question who *they* are, but the man is so intimidating I'd rather keep my mouth shut. His eyes don't leave me, and his intense gaze makes me feel mixed emotions. All I want is for this night to be over so I can plan how to escape this hell Mom dragged me into.

As dinner progresses, I feel like I'm trapped in a nightmare. The conversation is heavily laced with innu-endos that make my skin crawl. Luca and Leo keep making inappropriate comments, while Remy is the epitome of a grumpy older man. Mom is as bad, encouraging their behavior with her silence. It's like I don't even know her anymore.

In the middle of the meal, one of Remy's men enters and whispers something in his ear. Remy's expression darkens, and he excuses himself, leaving the rest of us to finish dinner. I can't shake off the feeling that something bad is happening, and I'm stuck in the middle.

As soon as dinner is over, I rush to my room, eager to escape the suffocating atmosphere of this family. I turn on the light and take a deep breath, trying to calm myself down. I can't believe this is my life now. I dreamed of being a writer, traveling the world, and meeting new people. Now, I'm trapped in a mansion with criminals who insist I will be forced to marry one.

As I'm lost in thought, I hear a knock on the door. I open it to see Luca standing there, a sly smile on his face.

"Hey, Ella," he says, leaning against the door frame. "I thought I'd come to say goodnight."

I roll my eyes, not in the mood for his games. "Goodnight, Luca. I'm tired."

He cocks his head to the side. "Are you sure? We could have some fun."

My blood runs cold at his words. I take a step back, feeling my heart rate spike. "What do you mean?" My voice is barely a whisper.

Luca steps closer, scanning my body with his dark eyes. "You know, fun. We can escape this boring reality and enjoy a bit of excitement. I could show you a good time."

I shake my head, my eyes narrowing. "You're my stepbrother, Luca. Leave me alone."

He chuckles, stepping closer. "Come on. Don't be so uptight. I promise you'll enjoy it."

I reach for the doorknob. "I said leave me alone. I'm not interested."

He grabs my wrist, pulling me toward him and into the corridor. "I don't think you understand, Ella. You're part of this family and will do as you're told."

I try to yank my wrist out of his grip, but he's too strong. "Let go of me!" I hiss.

He leans in, his lips almost touching my ear. "You know you want this," he whispers.

I grit my teeth, feeling a surge of fury. "Let go of me, Luca!" I repeat, louder this time.

Remy appears behind him, his eyes dark with anger. "What the hell is going on here?" His angry gaze is directed at Luca.

Luca drops my wrist, taking a step back. "Just having a little fun, Dad."

Remy's expression darkens. "That's not how we treat family." He steps closer. "She's your stepsister, and you'll stay away from her. Got it?"

Luca's smirk disappears. "Fine." He holds his hands up. "I knew you'd destroy my stepsister fantasy." He winks at me and then walks away.

My stomach churns as Remy faces me, his expression softening.

"I apologize for my son." His jaw clenches. "He's an asshole."

I chuckle, but it doesn't ease the tension. "You could say that again."

His eyes narrow. "Get some rest. You look like you

need it."

This guy is acting like a jackass. "What's that supposed to mean?"

His jaw clenches and eyes drop to my lips as he leans closer.

They part instinctively, even though the way he makes me feel is fucked up. He's married to Mom! And old enough to be my dad.

"It means you look tired. Make sure you always look your best if you want to fit into your new life."

I glare at him. "I've been traveling all fucking day. What do you expect?"

He grabs my wrist, and the skin-to-skin contact makes me gasp. "I expect you not to talk back to me."

Even when he's a jerk, I can't stop my mind from running wild with sick fantasies. The thought of him pushing me against the wall and kissing me drives me crazy. And it's as if he can sense it as his nostrils flare and eyes light up with what looks like desire.

"Now get some sleep." He releases my wrist and turns to leave, pausing mid-stride. "And I'd sleep with the door locked if I were you."

I can't tell if he's telling me to lock it because he thinks Luca will try something or he might come into my room, but that's probably wishful thinking.

"Fine, I will."

"Goodnight," he grunts before walking away.

I step into my room and close the door, locking it. I sink to the ground, feeling like my world is spinning out of control.

How did I end up in this mess?

REMY

*E*rin sits opposite me, beaming.

She's completely unaware of the tension in the air.

My five children weren't impressed with my decision to remarry and not tell them until my new wife showed up at my door. I made her sign a prenup to protect the *famiglia's* assets from outsiders, but they're still pissed.

It's been two weeks since they moved in. Camilla has returned home for the first time in over a year since she married her professor, which I still haven't recovered from. Especially as it happened while I was being treated for stage three bowel cancer. They didn't think I'd survive it. Thankfully, I'm rich and could afford to pay for treatments not yet available to most people, and that's what saved me. It's taken a while to forgive Camilla enough to allow her to return home, but she's my daughter at the end of the day. Blood is blood.

"So, Erin…" Massimo starts, moving food around

his plate in disinterest. "How long have you known my father?"

She smiles at Massimo and grabs my hand, squeezing. "We met in Vegas two weeks ago. One week together, and we were married."

"Sounds like a stupid fucking thing to do if you ask me," Camilla says, glaring at me. Ever since she married Gavril, she's been more insolent.

"No one asked you," I reply.

However, she's right. Marrying Erin was a snap decision fueled by lust and nothing else. We had a whirlwind romance over one week, and we were married. One thing is for sure: I've been far more impulsive since I recovered from cancer.

"Yeah. Only a dumbass marries someone they've known for a week," Luca adds, smirking at me, as he knows I don't like being belittled.

"Enough," I growl, slamming my hand down on the table and making everyone jump.

As I sit opposite my wife, I wonder what the hell I was thinking. Sure, Erin is gorgeous, and we were attracted to one another. At the time, it made sense because I was fed up with being alone and without a woman to warm my bed. However, I knew my mistake when I saw her daughter. She's something else. A temptation I don't need living under my roof. From how my two unmarried sons look at her, they're tempted, too.

She's a rare beauty. And I can hardly keep my eyes off her, which is sick on many levels. The main problem is that I'm not the kind of man who gets bogged down over morals and what is right or wrong.

Erin notices my gaze and clears her throat, snapping me from my thoughts. "Remy, is something wrong? You seem... distracted."

I shake my head, forcing a smile. "No, just thinking about work. You know how it is."

She nods, but I can tell she doesn't quite believe me.

Throughout the rest of the meal, I make snide comments directed at Ella and ignore her when possible. She's only twenty-one and my stepdaughter, for fuck's sake. But the more I try to push her out of my mind, the more I find myself fantasizing about her.

Mia smiles. "Ella, how are you finding Chicago?"

Ella sinks her teeth into her bottom lip. A move that is entirely innocent but makes my pants uncomfortably tight. "I haven't had a chance to explore yet." She shrugs.

Mia shakes her head. "We'll have to change that. Maybe we can go shopping sometime?"

A genuine and beautiful smile lights Ella's face. "I'd love that." While Ella doesn't strike me as the kind of girl who loves shopping, I sense she craves companionship.

Camilla rolls her eyes. "Good luck to you. The girl can shop for hours."

Ella looks a little worried. "It would be nice to get out of the house and see Chicago."

Erin nods. "Yes, no good for you mopping around the house with a book. You're twenty-one years old, not seventy."

Ella's eyes flash with hurt at her mom's comment.

I clear my throat. "Nothing wrong with reading." I

don't know where that came from, but I hate myself for coming to Ella's rescue. Her eyes land on me, wide in surprise. "However, your mom is right. It's important to get out of the house more. You're acting like a loner."

The surprise vanishes as I return to offending her at every opportunity.

Mia clears her throat. "I like reading, just not as much as shopping."

Camilla laughs. "There's nothing in this world you like as much as shopping. It's a surprise you haven't bankrupted the Callaghans by now."

Mia glares at her. "Don't be an idiot. They've got billions of dollars."

"Luckily," Massimo adds. "I must admit I've never met someone who can spend like you, Mia."

Mia takes Ella's hand and squeezes. "Can you believe they're all ganging up on me?"

Ella shakes her head. "No, very mean."

She smiles widely. "We're going to get on well, I can tell."

The joy on Ella's face is almost enough to undo me entirely. She's too fucking beautiful. I clear my throat, deciding I need to change the subject. "Shall we have a sensible conversation tonight? We're here to get to know each other and integrate as a family."

Camilla scoffs. "What family?"

I glare at my youngest. "Our family. A family you have no loyalty to after you had your thug of a husband rain hellfire down on us. So, don't question the rest of us. We're loyal to each other and have always been."

Camilla's eyes flash with hurt. "I would do it a thousand times over."

I'm about to tell her to leave, but Massimo speaks, "Let's not get into this when meeting our new family members for the first time."

Erin looks confused as her brow furrows. "Massimo. What interests do you have?"

Massimo glares at her. "I hardly have time for interests when I'm practically running the Morrone empire."

"I've told you I'd take back the position if it's too much for you." He's always trying to rub in the fact he does all the work.

Massimo's jaw clenches. "No. I've got it handled."

He knows I could take back the position of Don in a heartbeat, but it's been good for him. He's grown up. Become the man I always knew he could be. And Paisley is partly to thank for that. She has made him a better man.

I told him he could bring her tonight, but I think he wanted to shield her from the chaos that's likely to ensue.

"And you are married, is that right?" Erin asks.

Massimo nods. "Yes, Paisley couldn't make it tonight."

"That's a shame." Erin takes a swig of wine. "Do you have children?"

I wince, and so does Massimo, as it's a difficult subject for him and his wife. They've been trying but haven't had any luck.

"Not yet," he says, meeting my gaze with annoyance.

I should have told her not to ask him about kids.

We all fall quiet until Massimo stands. "I'm going to head back home."

I can tell he's agitated, so I don't try to stop him.

"Thanks for coming," I say, standing too. "Let me know if you need anything."

Massimo nods and then leaves without another word.

Luca and Leo continue cracking jokes, but everyone else is quiet, including Ella.

Erin speaks quietly to me. "Was mentioning kids a bad idea?"

I nod. "Massimo and his wife have been trying to get pregnant for a while. They're on their fourth attempt at IVF."

"Oh, shit." She places a hand over her mouth. "Sorry."

I shrug. "He's a big boy. He'll get over it." Massimo is being difficult because he hates that I've moved on from his mother. I'd do anything to bring Giada back for our family. While I'm not sure I know how to love, we had mutual respect for one another. We were a team. And she was taken away from my children far too early.

Her death broke me. It changed the way our lives were forever. We had happy memories together, and they were tarnished because I couldn't protect her and failed to keep my family safe. It's haunted me ever since.

I gaze across the table and sigh heavily, knowing my wife would hate the discord I've brought into the family.

Not just marrying Erin, but falling out with Camilla. She'd hate it. Hell, I doubt it would have happened if she'd been here. Giada was a force to be reckoned with, that's for sure.

My eyes land on Ella, and something sharp twists in my chest. I hate that she's so alluring, and I want her more than any other woman I've wanted. The sooner I get her married off and out from under my roof, the better.

4

ELLA

hree pairs of dark eyes land on me as I enter the dining hall.

A month has passed since I moved here, and the men of the house have done nothing but make me feel like shit. The worst part is that my self-esteem is so low that I still can't help but fantasize about my stepdad. A man who treats me no better than trash.

Mom's out tonight, God knows where. She's rarely here, leaving me at the mercy of my two stepbrothers and stepdad.

"Evening, sis," Luca says.

He's the least terrible of the three but he still joins in.

"Evening," I mumble and take my seat, trying not to look at them in the hope they'll leave me alone.

"You're late," Remy says.

I meet his gaze, and my heart thunders. It's the same every time I look at him, even when he's an asshole.

Butterflies erupt in my stomach, and heat floods my veins like lava.

"Sorry, I got caught up in—"

"It's not acceptable, Ella. All you do is mope around in your room all day. You can keep to a schedule and arrive at dinner on time." His jaw clenches. "Go and get me a drink."

I stand up, my gaze darting to Leo and Luca. Their eyes are glued on me like a piece of meat ready for slaughter.

I walk over to the bar to pour Remy his whiskey. As I place it on the dinner table, my hands tremble.

Sitting back down, I ignore the snide comments, sneering faces, and lewd remarks hidden in their mundane conversation. Their words are like daggers, cutting through the heavy silence.

"So, Ella, how was your day?" Leo's voice brings me back to reality.

"Fine," I shrug, focusing on my plate.

"Just 'fine'?" Remy's voice holds a subtle edge as if he's challenging me.

"I helped out in the garden," I add, trying to provide a topic that wouldn't give them a chance to twist my words.

"Oh, I bet you looked so pretty, all hot and sweaty, working those muscles," Luca chimes in. His words make my skin crawl.

"I... I was pulling out weeds," I stammer, the room suddenly feeling too small, their laughter echoing in my ears. I try to keep my composure, the taste of my dinner turning bitter in my mouth.

The laughter dies down, but it's still ringing in my head, each echo a fresh wave of humiliation. A knot forms in my stomach. My heart pounds a lonely rhythm in my chest, a constant reminder of the isolation that has become my reality in this house.

"Well, at least she's useful for something." Remy's comment slices through the uneasy silence like a well-aimed arrow. His words sting, a harsh reminder of my value in their eyes.

The room fills with their laughter again. I keep my gaze down, focusing on the barely touched food on my plate as I swallow my pride and the bile rises in my throat.

Remy's gaze is heavy, his eyes burning into me. He lifts a single eyebrow, daring me to say something. But my throat is tight, and the words won't come out. I look away as heat creeps up my neck, hating myself for still feeling attracted to him despite how wicked he can be. I find the confidence from somewhere to speak out.

"What exactly have I done to the three of you to treat me like this?"

Luca leans back in his chair, a smirk playing on his lips as he meets my gaze. "Oh, don't act so innocent, Ella. Remember when I offered to show you a good time? You shot me down like I was nothing," he says, his tone mocking.

"Because you are my stepbrother! For fuck's sake. What is wrong with you?"

Remy clears his throat. "She's right. You shouldn't have tried it on with her."

I'm surprised to hear him back me up.

Leo chuckles. "No, because she's too fucking frigid." He pauses, running a hand through his hair. "Although I've seen her looking at you, Dad, like she wants a ride."

The room falls silent at Leo's words. I can feel my cheeks burning, embarrassment searing through me like wildfire. I wish I could deny it, but the truth was plain for all to see. I've been caught. "That's... that's not true," I stammer, but the conviction in my voice is lackluster at best.

Remy chuckles, a low, throaty sound that sends shivers down my spine. "Are you sure, angel?" he teases, but beneath his joking tone, I can see a dangerous glint in his eyes. "Maybe you'd like me to put you over my knee."

Leo and Luca chuckle.

Any appetite I may have had is gone now. All that's left is shame and disgust at myself. Because he's right, I want him even though I shouldn't.

"Certain," I say, shaking my head. "I'm not attracted to old men."

His eyes flash with dangerous rage as he clenches his jaw.

Luca laughs out loud. "Good one, sis."

I can't look at him. I can't take my eyes off Remy as the look in his eyes is like a warning. I've seen that look before when he's been pushed too far, and his brutal nature takes the reins. That look spells trouble, and I find myself caught in the crossfire, a helpless moth drawn to the flame of his dark desire. He doesn't speak, but I feel the shift in tension in the air.

My heart hammers so hard it feels like it'll bruise my ribs.

Leo clears his throat. "I think we'll make a Morrone out of her yet."

The fact is, I don't want to be a Morrone. I don't even want to be here.

"Ella," Remy says my name, his voice as cold as the Antarctic.

"Yes?" I squeak.

"I'm dry. Get me another drink." He holds up the tumbler in his hand.

I hate that my nature is to do as I'm told. It always has been. And when Remy commands me, I'm powerless. My mind wants to tell him to fuck off, but my body is on autopilot.

I take the glass, but our fingers brush together, pulling an involuntary gasp from me.

A whisper of a smirk twists Remy's lips upward, and he grabs my other hand, pulling me close.

"You, Ella, are a liar," he purrs into my ear. "Don't think I don't know the truth."

I swallow hard and step away from him when he releases my wrist.

"What did you say to her? She's turned the color of beetroot," Luca points out.

I walk as fast as I can away to pour him another glass of whiskey.

"It's not important," Remy replies.

Am I that obvious?

It's embarrassing if it is. Remy knows that I want him.

Trying to push the thoughts away, I pour his glass and return to the table. I clear my throat instead of sitting down. "I'm not hungry. Can I go to bed now?"

"What the fuck, it's eight o'clock! Who goes to bed that early?" Leo asks.

Remy's jaw is clenched as he nods. "Yes, we don't need you dragging us down and moping about here. Leave."

The sting of his words slashes through me like a serrated knife, raw and unrefined, sending me reeling. I choke back a sob, drawing on every ounce of self-control I possess to keep the tears at bay. I can't afford to show weakness, not in front of them.

I escape the room, the echo of their laughter following me. The tears threaten to spill over as I rush upstairs, but I blink them away fiercely. The last thing I need is for those bastards to get to me.

I slam the door to my room shut, leaning against it as a wave of despair engulfs me. My stepfamily is tormenting me. I need to get away from here, from them. The room suddenly feels too small, the walls closing in on me as I slide down the door, the tears streaming down my face.

I glance around the luxurious room that has served as my prison cell, the stark reality of my situation hitting me hard. I can't live like this, trapped in this house with these vile people who enjoy my pain.

My mom probably wouldn't care if I left anyway, even if she said I must marry a mobster. If I disappeared, she'd probably forget my existence entirely. The knife of pain in my chest twists harder.

There has to be a way out. There must be. I need to escape before I become more of a broken shell than when I arrived.

5

ELLA

"*P*lease don't leave me alone with them," I beg, clutching Mom's hand.

Ever since she married Remy Morrone, she's changed for the worst. Mom was always cold and obsessed with money, but she's become more distant. Focused on her obsession with being a socialite.

"Don't be so silly, Ella. I'll be home before you know it. It's only a week."

Perhaps I'm being silly, but my new family isn't exactly thrilled to have me here, and I'm not thrilled to be here. Leo and Luca are assholes toward me, especially after what happened outside my room. And Remy is as much of a jackass as the day we met whenever he opens his mouth.

"I miss it being the two of us."

She shakes her head. "Ella, we could hardly put food on the table most nights. Your stepdad saved us from ruin; be more grateful."

Grateful to Remy Morrone? The guy is wicked

beyond compare. He's horrible, and I don't know how she overlooks what he and his family are involved in. While I don't know the specifics, the mafia normally means guns and drugs.

Not to mention, we couldn't put food on the table because she was off buying designer handbags with my money! I had to get a part-time job at a pizza place in between working on my next novel to supplement our income while she did nothing.

"You keep leaving me here alone with them, and it's awkward." This is her fifth trip in the three months since we moved in. I don't know why she keeps going away to Vegas. I can only assume she has some kind of gambling problem that she's kept under wraps.

Mom's expression turns irritated. "Grow up. You're twenty-one years old."

I swallow hard, realizing that she's never going to change. She's always been obsessed with money, but now she's unrecognizable. Lost to the lifestyle of the mafia world. "Fine. See you when you get back."

She puts her sunglasses on and grabs her clutch. "Behave for your stepdad."

I feel like making a smart remark, but I hold my tongue. "Have a good trip."

I let out a deep breath as soon as she's out of sight. The house feels empty and cold. For three months, I've tried to make myself feel at home here but I can't. A part of the reason is because the other people sharing this house don't make me feel welcome.

Leo probably creeps me out the most as he's quiet but also looks at me with a darkness that scares me. And while relations have been strained between Luca and I since I refused his advances, he's still more relaxed and easygoing.

Remy, on the other hand, scares and excites me in equal measures. He's grumpy and quiet, always glaring at me with an intensity that makes me shiver. I hate how attracted I am to him.

Despite Mia suggesting we'd go shopping, I have only seen her in passing a couple of times, which is a shame. However, she's a busy mom to Ronan, her son. I'm sure we will get on well if we find the time to go out.

I hear Leo and Luca chatting in the living room. My heart sinks. I don't want to deal with them right now, but I don't want to be rude. I take a deep breath and walk down the hall. As soon as I step into the room, I regret it when Leo's eyes fall on me and drag down my body.

"Hey, Ella," he says, his voice cold.

I try to smile, but it comes out as a grimace. "Hi, Leo."

Luca grins at me. "Come join the party, little sis."

I hesitate, but then I remind myself to be polite. They'll never accept me if I don't at least try. "Sure."

I walk over to the sofa and sit down awkwardly. At that moment, I realize Remy is in here. His intense gaze shoots lasers through me. The man is as cold as ice, and he's also insanely gorgeous.

"Not going to say hello to your stepdad?" he asks, eyes flashing with amusement.

"Sorry I didn't see you there."

His jaw clenches, and his eyes flash with irritation. He stands and walks closer. "Do you need glasses then,

Ella? As I was sitting right there the entire time." His eyes narrow as he glares at me, holding a whiskey tumbler. "I'm dry. Can you get me a drink?"

My lips purse as he often treats me like a server at a bar, and I can't help but obey him. He has this commanding presence I can't put into words. It doesn't help that I've been a people pleaser all my life; it's one of my biggest vices, especially since moving into the Morrone Mansion. "Sure," I say, grabbing the glass from his hand and accidentally brushing my fingers against his.

Our eyes meet for a second, and my body blazes with heat.

Fuck.

Anytime I accidentally touch my stepdad, it's the same. He's so damn attractive, and it feels like there's electricity flowing between us whenever we're near.

I walk over to the dresser to put space between us as the three men snicker behind me, making me self-conscious.

Grabbing the bottle of scotch, I pour him a large tumbler full. I've learned that no one can get through scotch like Remy. He drinks a lot, probably to help him live with what he does for a living.

It shouldn't have shocked me that Mom married a mobster. She's never really cared about anything but money, but marrying into a family of criminals is a step too far. When I questioned her about it, she shrugged it off and said at least he's rich.

I return to Remy's side and place the tumbler in his hand, turning to walk back to my chair. He grabs my wrist hard and yanks me back. "What the fuck is this?" He holds up the tumbler.

I frown. "Whiskey."

"Yeah, half the fucking bottle. Do I look like an alcoholic to you?" His eyes narrow.

My honest answer would be *yes* because he's an alcoholic. He drinks far too much. However, I shake my head. "I thought it would save more trips."

"Getting up and down to get my drinks is good exercise for you. It'll keep you fit and toned for your future husband."

I glare at him. "I've no intention of getting married." I've never dreamed about a big white wedding, like some girls do. I'd only get married if I was truly in love.

Luca laughs. "Good luck with that. You're a Morrone now. Morrone women get married by arrangement."

"I'm not a Morrone. My second name is Kelly and always will be."

Remy's hand tightens around my wrist, drawing my attention back to the fact he hasn't let go yet. "No, you're a Morrone. The moment your mom married me, you became one of us."

"I'll never be one of you because I don't agree with what you do for a living."

Remy's grip on my wrist tightens further, and it's starting to hurt. "Careful, Ella." His tone is deep and full of warning. "You live under my roof, which means you must show me respect. I provide for you and your mother."

I grit my teeth and try to pull my wrist out of his grasp, but he doesn't let go. His eyes spark with dangerous rage, making my heart pound. The way he looks at me makes something illicit and taboo flutter to life between my thighs. It's not the first time he's been like this with me, but it's the first time it's happened in front of Luca and Leo.

Luca clears his throat. "Dad, let her go. You're hurting her."

Remy releases me, and I stumble back, rubbing my wrist.

"I wouldn't hurt her if she didn't talk back," he says, his tone clipped. "I get so tired of her insolence."

"Insolence?" I regret my tone instantly as those dark eyes find mine. "I got you a drink and poured you too much. How is that insolent?"

"Questioning me is insolent," he replies, glaring at me. "But perhaps that's because you want Daddy to put you over his knee and spank you."

My stepbrothers laugh.

"Probably. She's always looking at you like a horny teenager with a crush," Luca says.

My entire body flames with heat. "No, I'm not," I say, despite it being a lie, as Remy Morrone does something to me no other man has. He turns me into lava with every look or touch, and I hate it because he's married to my mom for God's sake. Not to mention he treats me like trash.

Even so, the thought of him spanking my bare ass while I call him *Daddy* does something to me that no other fantasy can. I'm ashamed to admit the amount of times I've made myself come picturing him between my legs.

"She's flushing bright red. Maybe it's true," Leo says, walking toward me. "Maybe we should all have a go at you and see who makes you come hardest."

"Leo!" Remy shakes his head. "Don't be disgusting. She's your sister, now."

"Stepsister," he says, looking at me like he wants to feast on me. "Doesn't count, does it?"

Remy's eyes flash, and he stands, keeping his attention on his son when he says, "Go to your room, Ella."

I can't look him in the eye because my body is on fire, considering the turn this conversation took. "Okay." I turn away, thankful for an escape.

Luca snickers as I walk past. "Try not to dream about the three of us fucking every one of your holes."

I shudder at the thought, as Luca and Leo don't appeal to me. Remy, on the other hand...

What the hell am I thinking?

All of their eyes are on me as I make my way out of the room. I can feel tears prickling at the corners of my eyes, but I blink them away. I refuse to allow them to fall, as I'm stronger than that.

Once I'm safely in my room, I close the door, lean against it, and take deep breaths. I hate that I can't get the image of Remy's dark brown eyes out of my mind or how he makes me feel.

The first thing I do in my room is strip and grab my vibrator from my nightstand drawer. I jump onto the bed, and turn it on. Remy Morrone has been the star of my sick fantasies since we met.

He's a God of a man. Built like a man half his age, and his facial lines only add to his pure masculine beauty. I bite my lip as I picture him grabbing me with his huge hands and hoisting me onto his lap, both naked, as he orders me to ride his cock.

My back arches off the bed as my pleasure heightens, and I know it won't take long for me to come. I can feel the phantom pressure of his hand wrapped around my wrist.

"Fuck, Daddy!" I cry as I come apart, hit with a wave of shame the moment my high crashes.

What the hell is wrong with me?

I bury my face in the pillows on the bed and try to ignore the voice of shame telling me I'm fucked up. No matter how much I try to ignore the sexual attraction I feel around Remy, it won't go away.

6

REMY

I enter the library and immediately freeze in my tracks. Ella sits on the couch with her legs tucked beneath her and a book in her hand, looking unbelievably beautiful.

If I'd met her before I'd eloped with Erin, then there's no way Erin and I would be married. Ella is kind, innocent, and not cut out for the world her mom dragged her into.

Erin is an entirely different story. A gold digger through and through. We met, and the attraction was hot and fiery, and yet the moment I put a ring on it, she decided she couldn't be bothered to suck my dick anymore. We haven't had any sexual contact since she moved in, and part of me knows it's because I can't imagine having sex with her while thinking of her daughter.

Erin's constantly leaving and writing me notes despite the fact I told her she needs security wherever she goes. I was furious this morning when I woke to find a note in the closet pinned to my suit. She doesn't understand the danger that follows her now she's a Morrone.

As I watch Ella from the doorway, I envy how young and untainted by the darkness she is. The darkness that breathes within me wants to corrupt her. I've wanted her since the moment I set eyes on her. A rather questionable desire, considering she's my stepdaughter and younger than my two daughters.

The only way I know how to handle it is to treat her like shit to make sure she doesn't get too close. I'd easily lose control if she did.

Luca and Leo are utterly rotten to her, probably because they want her too.

It's no surprise. She's an innocent and beautiful goddess that men like us long to defile. I'm not a good man, and I don't fucking pretend to be. If I got my hands on that sweet, innocent thing, I'd destroy her, utterly consume every part of the good within her until she'd be nothing but a husk.

"Remy," Ella says my name suddenly, breaking my perverse train of thought. "Sorry, do you want me to leave?"

I shake my head. "No, I was going to select something to read." My eyes move to the book she's holding. "What are you reading?"

Her cheeks flush, and she hides it out of view. "Nothing much."

Her embarrassed reaction makes me want to know what she's reading even more, but I don't push it.

"Fine." I shake my head. "You spend so much time here. Have you got any recommendations?"

"What do you like reading?" She asks, her eyes alight with hope that perhaps we've found some common ground.

I sense that Ella would have liked me to be a father figure to her, but that was unlikely to happen even if I wasn't disgustingly attracted to her to the point I couldn't be in the same room as her without a semi-hard cock. Since I got married, I've had to take matters into my own hands more than ever.

"Thrillers. I like a good thriller when I have time to read."

Her brow arches. "Because your life isn't thrilling enough?"

I can't help the small smile that creeps onto my lips. My life is more than thrilling. Every day, I live in danger, and I love it. "I guess not."

She sighs, walking over to me. The moment she's within a foot of me, I smell that sweet strawberry scent of whatever hair product she uses. It makes it even harder to keep my sick fantasies at bay when she smells so damn divine.

"Have you read Gillian Flynn?" she asks, searching a bookcase nearby.

I shake my head. "No, should I have?"

"Definitely." She grabs a book off the shelf. "Have you seen the movie?" The book she's holding is *Gone Girl*.

I shake my head. "No, I rarely have time to watch movies. It's not often I get a chance to read either."

Rubbing a hand across the back of my neck, I realize I shouldn't be sharing any of this with her.

She laughs. "The movies are usually faster than the books, but never as good."

I swallow hard, knowing our friendly conversation can't happen often. I'm too much of a liability.

My moral compass is practically non-existent, and so it's taking all the strength within me not to slam this pretty little thing against the bookcase and force my cock deep inside of her tight virgin cunt.

God Damn it.

I can't be around her without my mind diving into the gutter.

"Are you okay?" Ella asks.

Her voice brings me back to the present, and I shove my hand in my pocket to hide the disgusting bulge. "Fine," I say simply, grabbing the book from her hand. "Thanks." And then I turn to leave.

"You're welcome," she says, sounding a little discouraged. "I wondered if you wanted to go out for dinner tonight."

I freeze at the invitation as it sends my mind to all the wrong places.

"With Luca and Leo, too, of course. It may be a good chance to get to know each other better." The hope in her voice is enough to shatter me, as I can't agree. Turning to look at her, my resolve crumbles because she looks so sweet and hopeful. "You want to have dinner with us?" I ask, shocked because we've been nothing but assholes to her since she arrived three months ago and even more so when her mom's out of town, God knows where.

She nods. "Yeah, there's this nice little Mediterranean restaurant I've wanted to try for a few weeks. It's near here, and I don't know anyone in town."

I narrow my eyes. "What's it called?"

"Calypso," she says.

I grind my teeth, wishing it had belonged to one of my enemies as I could have refused. "Sure. What time?"

"Eight o'clock?" she suggests.

"Book a table for four. I'll have a car meet us at a quarter to eight."

She smiles, and it's such a fucking beautiful smile. "Thank you, Remy."

I nod. "No problem. See you at eight."

I leave the room before I do something I regret. I can't be around Ella, yet here I am with a raging hard-on for her. My dick is about to punch a hole through my pants at the thought of fucking that pretty little virgin.

I have to go and get my tortured mind off of the beautiful creature and work out my frustrations probably multiple times before tonight, or I'll be trying to eat dinner with a fucking boner. Something tells me I'll probably have one throughout dinner, regardless.

Clutching the book she recommended, I head upstairs to go and grab a shower. Knowing that all I will be able to think about is the sweet little virgin reading in my library and know I can't do a fucking thing about it other than fantasize about her sucking my cock.

Once I reach my bedroom, I strip off my clothes and

turn on the shower. Steam fills the room as I step inside, letting the hot water run over my body. My mind races with images of *Ella*, those sweet lips wrapped around my cock. Her soft skin against mine as she begs me for more. Her innocent eyes and rosy cheeks as she moans out my name.

I stroke myself, hardening at the thought of being inside her tight little body. I fantasize about what it would be like to have her completely at my mercy.

I imagine pressing her against the wall and fucking her hard as she screams *Daddy*, begging for more. Her tight virgin pussy grips me as I thrust faster and harder. She starts to tremble around me, and I know it won't be long until we both reach our climaxes.

"Ella," I growl her name as my orgasm rips through me. I press my arm against the shower wall, still stroking long after I've climaxed. It takes me a few moments to catch my breath before I grab some soap and wash properly, hating the way my cock is hard again in no time. The fantasy of having my stepdaughter is impossible to chase away, no matter how hard I try.

Dinner with her at a restaurant is a bad idea, even with my two sons. I don't know how long I can keep my hands off her. The thought of her curves pressing against me and her lips begging for more is too much to handle.

Feeling the heat of the water recede, I turn off the shower, step out, and retrieve a towel from the rack, wrapping it around my waist. As I stare at my reflection in the foggy mirror, I hardly recognize the man staring back. My darkness has ruled me for as long as I can remember, but wanting to fuck my stepdaughter is wrong.

Ella.

She's a vortex threatening to pull me under, and I'm unsure how long I can resist her.

Tonight's dinner could be a tipping point, a precipice I'm too aware of. It's a dangerous game we're playing, teetering on the edge of the taboo. And I've never been good at resisting my urges.

7

ELLA

I sit across the table from Remy, trying my best not to look at him. Every time I do, he's staring at me as if he can see right into my soul.

Leo sits on my left, giving me that hungry look that makes my heart race for all the wrong reasons. Luca is the only one talking as he sits on my right, mainly making stupid comments. Remy is his usual grumpy self, not saying a word.

"Has everyone decided what they'd like to order now?" The server asks, breaking the tension at the table.

I smile at him. "Yes, I'll—"

"Men first, Ella. That's the rule in our household," Luca says, smirking at me. "I'll have the shawarma."

Remy's jaw clenches, but he doesn't reprimand his youngest son. "Ella, what will you have?" he asks.

"The falafel, please."

The server nods and writes down my order.

Remy orders the Kleftico, and Leo orders a chicken dish. The server leaves, and a more awkward silence issues. Seriously, what was I thinking when I invited them to dinner?

"So, Remy, what are your interests?" I ask, wanting to break the ice.

Leo and Luca both snicker. "Yeah, Daddy, what do you like doing in your spare time," Luca says, trying to imitate my voice and failing.

I now know what it feels like to have annoying brothers.

Remy takes a sip of his whiskey, puts the glass down, and says, "I don't have any."

I arch a brow. "None at all?"

He shakes his head.

Leo leans toward me. "So interested in your step*daddy*, but what about your two stepbrothers? We're more likely to bite."

Luca laughs and waves his hand dismissively. "It's no use. I've tried." He winks at me. "She flatly refused a wild night with me."

Heat radiates from the pit of my stomach across my skin. "You two are disgusting. I'm your stepsister, for God's sake."

I can't help but look at Remy when I say that and notice the odd look in his eyes.

My stepbrothers may not tempt me, but my stepdad, on the other hand... I'm so fucked up for thinking about him in that way.

"Taboo sex is the best sex around," Leo teases.

I swallow hard, sipping my cocktail and tearing my eyes away from Remy. I will need a few of these to make it through dinner. "Fine. What interests do you have,

Leo?"

"Fucking," he says, as if that constitutes a hobby.

I wrinkle my nose. "You need to get a life, then."

Luca laughs. "Right. He spends far too much time in the strip club. It's pathetic."

"Screw you, Luca. At least I'm not wasting my life teaching."

"Teaching?" I ask.

Luca nods. "Yeah, I teach math at a mafia academy in Maine. It's summer break, so I'm here with this asshole." He nods his head at Leo.

I'm surprised to hear that Luca is a teacher. He comes across as far too immature. "Wow, I never would have guessed you'd be into teaching."

Luca shrugs. "I've always been good at math." He meets my gaze. "The principal needed a new teacher and asked me to fill in. It turned into a full-time thing."

"Pathetic," Leo says, shaking his head. "We're meant to be mobsters, not teachers."

I tilt my head. "You know what they say, those who can't do, teach."

Leo laughs and nudges me in the ribs. "You are not so bad, sis." He winks.

Luca growls softly. "You two are idiots."

I smile. "I'm only joking. I think it's great you're teaching. You've found what you like and aren't being forced to do something you don't want to."

Luca's expression softens. "Thanks, sis."

Remy's eyes are like lasers on me. "That's the stupidest thing I've ever heard."

I glare at him. "How is it stupid?"

"He's my son. He should be working in the family business." His attention moves to Luca. "It's his responsibility."

That's fucked up. "Massimo is already taking the reins, so why does it matter what Luca does?" I can't believe I'm defending my asshole of a stepbrother right now.

"Because he's a Morrone and should act like one."

"Which means acting like a fucking criminal?" I confirm. I still can't get over the Morrone family being mobsters. My mom has forced me into the world I've spent half of my life loathing.

Remy's eyes flash with dangerous rage. "Shut up," he snaps, nostrils flaring. "You may know what we do, but we all follow one key rule. Our business is never discussed in public."

My stomach churns, and I heat. "Well, if someone had told me the rules, then I'd know that wouldn't I?"

Luca nods. "Right. You can't blame her if you didn't tell her."

Remy cracks his knuckles. "It's common fucking sense." He glares at me. "Something your stepsister lacks."

I hate how much his words wound me. Luca and Leo can spend all night attacking me, but one nasty comment from Remy and I can feel the tears threatening to claw their way out of my eyes. I'm pathetic.

"I didn't think."

"No, you didn't. I'm not sure why you even suggested this dinner."

I swallow hard, struggling to remember what

possessed me to suggest it in the first place. Breaking the ice seemed like a good idea with a dinner while Mom was away. An attempt to get to know the people I'm living with and end their ceaseless teasing. "Neither am I. It was a mistake."

Luca clears his throat. "You two need to cool it. I don't care what Dad thinks about my teaching, and I don't need my little stepsis to defend me."

Remy doesn't take his gaze away from me.

I glare at Luca. "I know what it's like when people don't support what you do."

Luca's expression softens, and he clears his throat.

Thankfully, the server brings our food, breaking the tension. An awkward silence settles between us as we eat. It's the one time Luca isn't messing about when he has food in front of him.

We all eat silently, and Remy's intense gaze is off me for once. It's a welcome reprieve.

"That was delicious," Luca says, breaking the silence as he drops his cutlery with a clang to his plate.

I look up, shaking my head. "You eat way too fast."

Leo laughs. "No, it's you who eats too slow. The three of us have finished, and you're eating like a fucking mouse."

I narrow my eyes at him. "I'm sorry that I like to savor my food."

Luca throws his serviette onto his plate. "Well, while this was lovely, Leo and I have to get going to Secret Obsession."

My brow furrows. "What's that?"

"A strip club," Leo says.

I wrinkle my nose. "Gross."

"Dad, are you coming?" he asks Remy.

I look at him to find he's staring at me *again.*

He doesn't take his eyes off of me. "No, you go ahead. I'll take Ella home."

I swallow hard at the thought of being in the car alone with him. My mom has been away a couple of days, and I can't stop thinking about my stepdad's hands on me.

What is wrong with me?

"You got the check?" Luca confirms.

Remy nods. "Yeah."

Luca and Leo leave me alone with the man I've been having illicit fantasies about since we met.

I stand. "I'm going to use the restroom."

"Fine, I'll pay the check and meet you out front."

I can hardly breathe as I rush into the ladies' restroom and lean over the wash basin. "Fuck," I say, running a hand through my hair.

"Are you okay?" A lady asks.

I shake my head and smile. "Yes, sorry for my language. I just had some bad news," I lie.

She doesn't look convinced but leaves me alone.

I splash some cool water on my neck, trying to cool the inferno that Remy Morrone keeps stoking inside me with his dark gaze. Mom doesn't give a shit about him, just like she didn't give a shit about my dad.

I look at myself in the mirror, straighten my blouse, and head out of the restroom. I walk through the restaurant and toward the exit. The sudden coolness of the night air hits me as I step outside the restaurant. I see

Remy in the back of the town car, his silhouette outlined against the dim interior light. The sight of him sends a shiver down my spine that has nothing to do with the chill and everything to do with the anticipation of being alone with him.

I walk toward the car, my heart pounding. The door is held open for me. His intoxicating scent engulfs me as I slide into the plush leather seat. I glance at Remy. His eyes are a dark abyss, full of dangerous desire. The tension between us is palpable, a pulsating electrical charge that I can almost taste in the air.

"Ella," he says, his voice a low growl that sends a delicious thrill through me. "Is there anywhere else you need to go?"

I look at him, utterly lost in those intense eyes. "No, you?"

He shakes his head as the town car pulls away from the curb, and we're left in silence, the only sound being the soft hum of the engine and the erratic beat of my heart.

I feel like a moth drawn to a flame, which scares me as much as it excites me. God, what is happening to me?

I look away from him, fixating my stare on the dark window as we drive. The windows of the town car are tinted black, and I feel like I'm in my own little world with Remy, a place where anything could happen. It's a dangerous notion.

The music coming through the speakers is soft and melodic—some classic rock I've never heard before. I can feel Remy's eyes on me, like an invisible rope between us.

"What music do you like?" I ask, wondering if this is his preference.

His jaw tightens. "I thought the getting to know you was over."

I swallow hard because he doesn't make this easy. "Do you enjoy being a grump?"

The whisper of a smile graces his lips. "A grump?"

I nod. "Yeah, you know—a grouch. A grump."

He leans forward in his seat, our faces inches apart. "Yes, I enjoy it, especially when it irritates you, Ella." His lips pull into an amused grin.

The lump in my throat hurts. "Right, because you hate me and want to piss me off as much as possible."

"No," he breathes, eyes flashing. "I don't hate you. And I like to irritate you because you're beautiful when you get flustered and flushed like you are right now."

My heart skips a beat. Did my stepdad call me beautiful?

I swallow hard, wondering if he feels this electric connection, too. "What?"

His jaw works. "It's just an observation." He sits back, his expression turning hard. "You are beautiful, Ella. Like your mom."

I swallow hard, wishing he wouldn't compare me to her. I'm nothing like her. She's coldhearted and cares about nothing but herself. I strive to be everything she's not. "I'm nothing like her."

He nods. "On the inside, no. You are innocent and pure. Your mother is..." He trails off as if unsure about speaking his mind around me.

"A cold-hearted bitch."

His brows raise. "I was going to be a little less to the point..."

"What's the point of beating around the bush? Just say what you mean." I glance out of the window. "I hate it when people skirt around things. It's annoying."

"I couldn't agree more."

I look at him again, and our eyes meet, making my heart beat so hard it feels like it will beat out of my chest.

Is it possible that my soul mate is my stepdad?

It would be a cruel and vicious joke, as he's off-limits. I've never felt this way around anyone before. As if one look in his eyes could tear me apart. I want him with every fiber of my being and know I'll never have him.

It's a difficult pill to swallow.

8

ELLA

*M*ia opens the door and rushes into the library, stopping still when she sees me. "Oh, I'm sorry." She shakes her head. "No one's ever in here normally."

"No need to apologize," I say, smiling at her. "It's your home."

Her lips purse together. "I haven't spoken to you much since the dinner three months ago. How is my dad treating you? I hope he's treating you well." She approaches hesitantly.

I shrug. "He's okay."

Mia slumps beside me on the couch. "He can be a bit of an asshole."

I laugh. "Yeah, a bit."

Mia sighs. "Ever since he managed to defy death and got over his cancer, he's been worse than ever. It's like he believes he's a God because the doctors all told him he was terminal."

I nod as Mom mentioned he'd had a pretty serious

cancer scare before they met. "It must have been hard on you, thinking he would die."

She nods. "I'm not going to lie. It was. We didn't think Dad would pull through." There's a tense silence between us before Mia grabs my hand and squeezes. "If you need a friend, I'm happy to meet for coffee or have a meal together. Whatever you want. And don't forget our shopping trip. I need a prior warning to ensure I have a babysitter for Ronan, or we can do it when he's at preschool." She draws in a deep breath. "It sucks that Camilla is so far away, living in fucking Maine. She has her hands full, though, with her twin baby girls, Avery and Callie."

Out of the siblings, Mia is by far my favorite. "That would be good. All of my friends are so far away."

Mia sighs. "It must have been tough moving here." Her brow furrows. "But you're twenty-one. Why didn't you stay?"

"My mom made it impossible."

"How?" she asks.

I swallow hard. "I self-published my first novel a few years ago, and it does quite well. We had little money, so Mom took control of my bank account. I have no way of accessing it."

"That's just wrong." She runs her fingers through her hair. "Now that she's married, surely she can give you the money back, and you could live wherever you want, right?"

"You'd think it was that simple." I sigh. "She told me your dad will force me into an arranged marriage."

Mia rolls her eyes. "God, Dad really can't drop this

arranged marriage shit. Tell them to shove it up their asses."

I laugh. "I wish I had the guts to say that to your dad. He's pretty intimidating."

"Hmm, I guess he might be to someone who doesn't know him." She shrugs. "I'm used to him."

I clear my throat. "Speaking of your dad, what exactly does the Morrone family do for a living?"

Mia gives me a look that worries me. "You don't want to know the details. Crime. That's all you need to know."

I don't push, as I don't know Mia at all. "Fair enough. And your husband, too, right?"

She nods, a soft smile on her lips. "Yes, Killian is the brother of the leader of the Irish mob in Chicago."

"And it doesn't worry you?"

"Worry me how?"

I press my lips together. "The danger to you and your loved ones."

She frowns. "I've grown up around it, so it seems normal."

"Fair enough. How old is your son?"

Her face lights up. "Ronan is three years old. He's at preschool right now." She glances around the shelves. "It's why I rushed over here to come and get a few books and return these." She holds up a couple of romance novels, both I've read.

"How did you find them?"

Her brow furrows. "Good, but a little..."

"Too cutesy?" I suggest.

She nods. "Yeah, I think I need a thriller or something now."

I get up and search the bookshelves. "With romance or without?"

Mia's brow furrows. "Not sure."

"Verity is a good book. It's a thriller, but romance elements are mixed in." I pull it off the shelf and give it to her.

"Perfect." She takes the book. "You saved me about half an hour trying to work out what to read."

I laugh. "Anytime."

She tucks the book into her Louis Vuitton purse. "Do you want to get out of here and come for a coffee with me round the corner from Ronan's preschool?"

I smile. "I'd love to get out of this house."

"Perfect. You can meet Ronan after when I pick him up."

My mood picks up as I love kids. Also, getting out for a while will be a godsend. "Can't wait."

I stand, and she hooks her arm with mine. "My car is parked out front."

We walk in comfortable silence to the front door, but it opens before we make it.

My heart flutters when I see Remy standing there, his eyes finding mine instantly.

"Where are you going?"

I haven't seen him since our awkward car ride from the restaurant.

"Ella is joining me for a coffee before we pick up Ronan. She is his step-aunt."

It's wild how my mom's decision to marry this man

brought so much family. I'm a stepsister to five siblings and a step-aunt to three toddlers.

"I haven't seen Ronan in a while. Will you be bringing him back here?" Remy asks.

Mia's brow furrows. "I'll be dropping off Ella. I guess I can pop in with him."

Remy nods, eyes still fixed on me. "I'd like to see him."

I break our prolonged eye contact and squeeze Mia's arm. "Let's go."

She nods, and we head out and get into her car. An awkwardness swirls between us after the encounter with her dad.

"Do you get on with your father?"

Mia frowns. "We have a strained relationship after I went behind his back and chose to be with Killian. Although it's not half as strained as Camilla's relationship with him."

She turns out of the driveway toward the city center. "How about you? Where is your dad?"

I clench my jaw. "He's dead. Murdered when I was eleven years old."

Mia's mouth drops open. "I'm so sorry, Ella. I had no idea."

We fall into an uncomfortable silence as my mind races back to that day when my world changed forever.

"My mom was murdered when I was six, so I don't have many memories of her."

I swallow hard. "That's terrible. Did your dad find out who did it?"

Her jaw tightens. "Yes. He made them pay."

I shudder at the tone of her voice as I sense she has darkness in her, just like the rest of the family. It's impossible not to be touched by it when she's been around it all her life. It makes me wonder what Remy is capable of.

She pulls up in front of a cute bohemian cafe and parks the car. "Here we are. They do the best caramel macchiato."

I smile. "I love a good caramel macchiato."

We head inside, and the smell of freshly brewed coffee hits me as soon as I enter. Mia orders both drinks, and we choose our seats at the corner table. As we sip our drinks, we finally have a chance to talk without distractions or judgment from other family members.

We get lost in conversation, discussing our favorite music, books, and films. Mia has a wicked sense of humor, and before I know it, we're laughing hysterically at her jokes. I can't believe how quickly we've connected, like I'm talking to an old friend.

I look at Mia, and my heart swells with hope. Maybe this family won't be so bad after all.

Mia grins. "We've had so much fun that it's time to pick up Ronan!" She looks at her watch. "Are you ready?"

"Yes, will he be alright with me tagging along? I know some toddlers don't like strangers."

She smiles and shakes her head. "Ronan is as social as they come. He'll be so excited."

We link arms and walk around the corner to his preschool, where we wait at the entrance for the teacher to bring him out. I see a little boy with dark hair and eyes come out, and when he spots Mia, he beams.

"Mommy." He runs into Mia's arms, and she picks him up and twirls him around. "Hey, how was your day?"

"It was great—" He stops when he notices me watching them. "Who are you?"

Mia sets him down on his feet. "This is your step-aunt, Ella."

He beams widely. "Oh yay, I've always wanted a step-aunt."

Mia and I both chuckle, and I crouch down to be on his level. "It's lovely to meet you, Ronan." I hold a hand out for him to shake, but he hugs me instead.

I can't deny that he is adorable.

We leave the preschool and head back to the car, Ronan skipping between us as we chat about his day. Once we're in the car, I sit in the back with him, and he shows me pictures he drew in school, pointing at all his favorite things.

My stomach churns when Mia pulls into the drive of the Morrone mansion. I'd had such a good time away from this place, but it's not the only reason for my nerves. Remy is waiting to see his grandson. I don't know why the thought of seeing how he is with a kid makes me feel nauseous.

Mia helps Ronan out of the car, and we enter. Remy is waiting for us in the foyer, and his face lights up when he sees Mia holding his grandson's hand.

"Grandpa!" He shouts, rushing forward and jumping into Remy's arms.

My stomach flips as he twirls him around and plants kisses on his cheek.

Ronan giggles and shakes his head. "Your beard tickles!"

He doesn't have a beard, just stubble.

"Good," he replies gruffly. "How has my little man been?"

I can't believe the difference in Remy around his grandson. The way he smiles makes butterflies take flight in my stomach. It's sick the way seeing him with a child makes me feel broody.

"Are we staying for dinner, mommy?" Ronan asks as Remy sets him down on the ground.

I heat when his dark eyes find mine. It feels like he can read my thoughts.

"No, sweetheart," Mia replies firmly. "Daddy will be waiting for us at home."

Remy's jaw clenches. "Can't you stay for some milk and cookies?" he asks.

Mia looks unsure, but Ronan's face at the mention of cookies is priceless.

"Yay, cookies! Please, mommy."

She glares at Remy. "Well, I can't say no now, can I?"

He shrugs. "That was the point. I don't see my grandson enough."

"I'll see you later, Mia."

She grabs my arm. "Join us. You're family."

I swallow hard, unsure my ovaries can handle watching Remy doting over his grandson. My sick ass self can't help my mind from disappearing into the forbidden gutter. "I've got some writing to do," I lie because I haven't put words on the page for months.

Mia pouts. "Okay, well, we'll arrange that shopping trip soon."

I smile. "Can't wait."

I watch Remy lift his grandson into his arms and carry him toward the kitchen, Mia trailing behind. I need to stop thinking of my stepdad in the most illicit and forbidden way. Mom will be back home tomorrow.

And yet, I can't stop the dirty thoughts from flooding my mind whenever I'm near him. The only option is to avoid him at all costs, which shouldn't be too difficult in a giant mansion, right?

9

REMY

*R*elationships have never been my forte, even when I presumed myself in love with my first wife and the mother of my children.

I don't think I've ever truly believed that love exists.

As I listen to my man explain how my current wife has been found brutally murdered in Las Vegas, I can't muster an ounce of emotion. I never loved Erin. While she was beautiful like her daughter, there was something rotten about her on the inside. A complete contrast to her daughter, who is pure innocence.

"Find the people responsible and bring them to me," I say, ending the call.

I have to tell Ella that her mother is dead, but I hate being alone with her. A difficult task as now it leaves her in limbo.

Where will she live?

She can't stay under my roof, especially now that Erin is no longer an obstacle between us. I'd have her calling me Daddy while I fuck her into oblivion before I could think straight if she lived permanently under my roof without her mom, but she has nowhere to go and no one.

"Fuck," I growl, knowing that this is the most twisted situation I've found myself in, in a long time. My cock is semi-hard in my boxer briefs mere minutes after discovering my wife has been murdered, thinking about her daughter calling me Daddy.

Someone needs to lock me in a fucking mental asylum fast and throw away the key because I fear I won't be able to control myself around that girl.

I take a deep breath and head to Ella's room, bracing myself for the task.

The door is ajar, and I glance through the gap to see her sitting on her bed with a book in her hands. Her long blonde hair falls over her shoulders gracefully, and she doesn't notice as I push the door open further.

"Ella," I say her name more sternly than I intended.

She practically jumps a mile at the sound of my voice. And then she glances at her attire, blushing as she's only wearing a skimpy pair of pajama shorts and a top with no bra underneath.

"R-Remy, what are you doing in here?" She crosses her arms over her chest to hide her hard nipples.

Fuck, what am I doing in here?

I should have asked her to get dressed and come downstairs. "I've got some bad news," I say, knowing I should be sensitive about this, but it's not in my nature.

Her eyes widen. "What kind of bad news?"

"Your mom, she got killed in Vegas."

The color drains from Ella's face, and her eyes widen

in shock. I can see tears forming behind them, but she's trying to hold them back in front of me. "How?"

"Someone murdered her. My men are trying to track down who. It was likely a rival trying to get back at me for something."

Her lip wobbles, and then the floodgates open as she collapses onto her bed, sobbing. A part of me wants to go to her, wrap my arms around her and pull her into my lap, but I know I can't go near her.

"I'm sorry," I say simply, turning to leave.

"Wait," Ella says, her voice so small and broken. "I-I don't want to be alone, can you..." she trails off because she knows I've been fucking terrible to her since she arrived here. She shakes her head. "Never mind."

"Do you have any friends I can call for you?"

Her throat bobs. "No one within a few hundred miles." Tears stream down her face. "What's going to happen now?"

The one question I *didn't* want her to ask me. "I haven't figured that out yet." I cross my arms over my chest.

"Are you going to kick me out?"

My lips purse as kicking her out on the street is tempting to ensure I don't cross the line with her. However, I couldn't. It would be like throwing her to the wolves, as what happened to her mom might happen to her. Or they might sell her into sex trafficking because she's so young and beautiful.

My possessive side roars to life at the thought of any other man touching her.

"Remy?" Her soft voice pushes me for an answer.

"We'll discuss what happens in the following weeks. First, let's grieve your mother and bury her."

"What am I going to do?" Ella asks, and her entire face crumbles, and she starts sobbing again. "Please," she gasps.

I clench my jaw, knowing she's asking me to console her without outright saying it. And I can't help myself. I stride across the room and sit beside her on the bed, pulling her against my chest.

She clings to me as if I'm her lifeline, and I wrap an arm around her, trying to keep my mind out of the gutter. Ella just lost her mother; all I can think about is stripping her and making her mine. My cock is as hard as stone as she sobs into my shirt, clawing at me like a crutch.

"I don't know how I'm going to go on," she mutters.

I'm tense, trying to control my sickening urges. "Are you sure there's no one I can call?"

She pauses and looks at me, and goddamn, I've never seen a woman cry and look this fucking angelic doing it. "W-Wait." She sits up, pulling out of my arms. "Mia said if there's anything I need to call her." Her throat bobs as she swallows. "Maybe she could come over."

Best idea yet.

I need to get out of this room right away. Standing, I nod. "I'll ring Mia for you and send her up when she arrives."

I turn toward the door, but Ella grabs my hand. Her soft skin against mine sends an electric shock through my veins. "I've got her number on my cell. Please don't leave. I can't be alone right now."

Motherfucker.

"I hardly think I'm any use, am I?" I ask, glancing at her.

Her lip wobbles. "You don't need to be, just be here." She's so damn vulnerable, and my dark heart sings seeing her like this, easily malleable. If I kissed her, she'd undoubtedly melt into me, desperate for a distraction and someone to support her. But I wouldn't support her. I'd take full fucking advantage of her.

"Okay, give her a call." I sit down, ignoring my crotch straining against my pants.

She dials the number and then glances at me. "Can you…" she holds the phone out.

I snatch it, praying my daughter will pick it up.

"Hey, Ella. What's up?"

"Mia, it's your dad."

"Why the fuck are you calling me off of Ella's phone?" She gasps suddenly. "Don't tell me you killed her."

"Don't be ridiculous. I'm calling you because Ella isn't up to telling you this." I clear my throat. "Her mother was killed in Vegas today, and she wondered if you could come over." I pause, glancing at Ella. "Be a support as I'm no use."

"Oh my God, of course. I'll be over in half an hour tops. Killian is here so he can take care of Ronan."

I hear a deep voice grumbling in the background.

It takes all of my strength not to tell her to hurry. "Okay, great. See you soon." I end the call.

"Is she coming?" Ella asks, tears still streaming down her face.

"Yes, she'll be half an hour at the most."

She sighs in relief. "Okay." She moves toward me again, placing her head on my shoulder. "Thank you."

"No problem," I reply.

"Can I lie down?" She asks, staring at me with those big, innocent eyes. And then I realize she means she wants to lie with her head in my lap.

"Is that appropriate?"

Her brow furrows. "Why wouldn't it be?"

I grind my teeth, realizing she doesn't see me that way. Lying with her head in my lap is nothing more than paternal. For me, it's so fucking wrong. And yet, I find myself nodding.

She settles down, her head against my crotch, which is throbbing and hard. I can feel precum leaking into my briefs. If Ella notices the hardness against her face, she doesn't react. Perhaps she's too distracted by her grief.

Her breathing turns deeper within minutes, and I realize she's fallen asleep. Which only makes my perverse thoughts run wilder, imagining sliding my fingers into those tiny shorts and fingering her virgin cunt. Her mom mentioned she's a social pariah, has never had a boyfriend, and is still a virgin.

I grit my teeth, trying to stop the images of my cock tearing through her unfucked pussy from forming. If I don't think about fucking her, I can endure this. I have to. I have to keep my desires to myself.

She shifts her head and murmurs something in her sleep. Her face scrunches up, and she looks so damn cute. Her cheeks are pink from the crying, and her lips glisten from whatever balm she's wearing. She's so fucking beautiful, and I'm so fucking hard for her. Fuck, I've never been this hard for a woman before.

"Dad?" Mia stands in the doorway, an accusing expression on her face.

I clench my jaw. "Thank fuck you're here," I hiss, wondering if I should move out from under Ella. "She wouldn't let me leave."

Mia moves closer. "It looks like you're pretty comfy," she says, her eyes landing on my hand, alerting me that it's on Ella's ass. "Please don't tell me that you intend to—"

"Don't be sick, Mia. She wanted consoling and asked to lie down in my lap. It's not my fucking fault."

She shakes her head. "Unbelievable."

"Do you think I'd be that sick?"

She arches her brow, as we both know I have no morals. Instead of arguing, Mia comes over and gently wakes Ella. "Ella, sweetie, wake up." She shakes her.

Thankfully, the arrival of my daughter has killed the raging boner I had.

Ella jolts up, her head almost slamming into my chin as I try to steady her, grabbing her arms.

"Don't panic. You fell asleep," Mia explains as I get up off the bed and put some distance between us. "I'm here now."

Ella starts sobbing again as reality hits her that her mom is dead.

"I'll leave you both to it," I say, walking away.

And then I hear her voice again. "Remy,"

I turn to gaze at her, wishing I hadn't, as the gratitude in her eyes makes me sick. "Thank you for staying with me."

I nod and walk out without another word, knowing that if I don't get that girl out from under my roof soon, I'll do something irreversible.

10

ELLA

I feel lost, staring at Mom's coffin in the deep hole.

I have no blood family left on this earth. Dad died ten years ago, and now my Mom is dead too early. Criminals took both of them. I stand by the side of her resting place while a flood of anger coils to life inside me.

The crazy thing is I'm grieving when all she did was make my life hell. She never loved me. Her affair with money was far too important to her. And yet I loved her because she was my mom. Out of obligation, in a sense.

Remy Morrone is to blame for her death. He knew that she would be a target for his enemies, but didn't provide her protection. And yet, I can't voice that anger because I'm at his mercy. He has no reason to keep me under his roof. Since he announced my mom's murder, I've been waiting with bated breath for him to kick me to the curb or worse…

I know he's powerful. And I know he could easily force me into an arranged marriage.

The service is long finished, but I stand by the grave's edge, unable to walk away. And for some reason, Remy is right by my side.

I feel his hand on my shoulder and flinch at his touch. "Ella, I know this is hard for you. And I'm sorry for what happened to your mom."

I turn to face him, anger simmering beneath the surface. "You're sorry? You could have prevented this by giving her more security, but you let her die."

His jaw clenches. "Your mother went off on a fucking bender with my cash, so she wasn't traceable. She didn't tell me where she was going and just went. Are you saying I should have somehow read her mind and stopped her?"

My eyes widen. "She didn't tell you she was going to Vegas?"

He shakes his head. "No, I got a note pinned to my suit saying she needed a break. Nothing else."

"Oh..." I say, unsure what else to add since I practically accused him of not protecting her when she didn't want his protection. Mom was stubborn like that.

"I don't take the protection of my famiglia lightly, Ella. I had men looking for her the moment she left. As it wasn't the first time that Erin kept her location from me." He rubs a hand across the back of his neck. "It was foolish of me not to ask you if you knew where she'd gone."

I purse my lips as I underestimated him. Even

though I know he didn't love my mom, he didn't want her dead. "Sorry, I just assumed—"

"Assumed that because I'm a mobster that I'm a monster who doesn't care if his wife lives or dies?"

"No, I don't think you're a monster," I murmur, knowing I've never seen him like that despite who he is and the terrible things he does for a living.

A dark smirk twists his lips. "You should do because I am a monster, Ella. A dark and sadistic one."

My stomach churns at his words, but even as he tells me he's a monster I struggle to see him as anything other than a strong, protective man I want with every part of my soul.

"What's going to happen to me now?" I breathe, finally asking.

His expression hardens. "It's no use thinking about it now."

I lick my dry lips. "But—"

"But nothing. We're burying your mother right now. The future isn't important."

A flood of tears rush down my cheeks as my mom just died. The last thing I should be thinking about is whether my stepdad will kick me out. "I'm sorry." I shake my head, trying to wipe the tears away, but they keep falling.

"Don't apologize for showing grief. It's natural." His voice softens, and he's closer when I glance at him.

"I'm not good at this, but come here," he murmurs, his voice barely a whisper as he opens his arms to me.

I practically run into them, burying my face against his chest. He smells of musk and pine and home. His

BIANCA COLE

arms wrap around me, and This doesn't feel like a platonic embrace which makes me feel guilty. My feelings toward him have been inappropriate since the day we met.

I want to stay wrapped in his arms and never leave. And I hate myself for it, especially thinking that here, of all places.

Remy clears his throat and releases me. When I look at him, I'm sure I see desire in his eyes for a moment, but it's gone like an illusion. No doubt my fantasy is bleeding into reality. I need to get a grip.

"Are you still intending to marry me off?"

"What did I say, Ella?"

"Not to think about the future right now."

He nods. "Come on. The wake is being held at our home."

I scoff. "It's not like anyone will be there. Mom's friends are all back in Washington, and none of them bothered coming." I feel a tinge of pain in my chest, wondering if that'll be my fate.

I may be young, but I've no idea how long I'll last in Remy's world.

"It was short notice, and we're far away," he says, touching my shoulder. "The car is waiting." He leads me to a black town car parked nearby, and I get in.

Remy slides in next to me. The rest of the family has already left in other cars.

It's only a twenty-minute drive back to the mansion, and yet it may as well be an eternity trapped with this God of a man. He sits with his arms crossed over his broad chest as he stares out the window. Remy has this dark, brooding older man vibe, which I can't resist. I guess I should be glad he's not talking to me because I struggle to draw breath into my lungs whenever he looks at me.

"Why are you staring at me, Ella?"

I swallow hard and tear my eyes from him. "Do you have eyes in the back of your head?"

He glances at me. "I can see your reflection in the window."

I heat, clearing my throat. "I was just thinking."

"About what, exactly?"

I shake my head. "Nothing important." He doesn't want to know the thoughts that were going through my mind.

"I prefer it if you don't lie to me."

I clench my jaw. "My thoughts are my own. I don't need to tell you them."

He leans closer to me, his musky scent invading my senses. "Is that right? Shall I tell you what I've been thinking?"

I lick my lips. "Yes," I breathe.

His nostrils flare, and his jaw clenches. "I've been thinking you're so damn beautiful, Ella." He cups my face in his large hands. "I can't stop thinking about you in the most inappropriate fucking ways."

I hate that hope flares to life inside me. "What kind of ways?"

"Don't ask questions you don't want to know the answer to." He drops his hands and turns to look out of the window again.

I tug at his jacket softly. "What if I do want to know?"

His jaw clenches. "Ella…" His voice is breathless and low, a hint of warning in his tone.

"Please tell me."

His eyes flash with something hot and illicit. "I think about you the way no stepdad should ever think of his stepdaughter, let's leave it at that."

I lick my lips, wondering if he means he has the same fucked up thoughts about us together. "Maybe I think the same things."

His jaw clenches. "Careful, angel."

I tilt my head, forgetting everything but the two of us in this car. As if the back of this car is all that exists in this world. "Or what?"

He grabs my throat suddenly, his rough palm forceful. "You're treading a dangerous path, baby."

When he calls me *baby*, it feels like I'm going to combust. I'm not in my right mind right now.

I just buried my mom.

This is so fucked.

"Remy, I…"

His eyes dip to my lips and they part under the attention. I've never wanted to be kissed by someone as badly as I want to be right now. "You what?" he asks, eyes still fixated on my lips.

There're only inches between us now as we walk a line that shouldn't be crossed. So close and yet so far. "I want to know."

He groans, eyes clamping shut as if he's trying to gain control. "You don't, Ella. I know you think you do, but fuck… This is hard."

"Stop resisting then," I murmur.

His eyes fly open and a soft growl escapes his lips. And that's when the car comes to a stop, snapping whatever spell had fallen over us. It's as if a light switch flicks.

Remy turns stiff and removes his hand from my neck, shaking his head. "Shit. I don't know what I was thinking. Sorry." He runs a hand through his hair. "Forget what I said."

I bite my bottom lip. "But—"

"Forget it, Ella," he growls.

My chest clenches painfully as I don't want him to return to the grumpy, broody stepdad he's been since I met him. "Can't we talk about—"

His hand wraps around my throat again and he squeezes, sending my heart rate spiking. "You're playing with fire."

I lick my lips. "Maybe I want to burn."

His eyes flicker with a mix of desire and anger. "I won't be the one to burn you." He releases my throat and opens the car door, leaving me in the back.

A flood of guilt, grief, and disgust hit me simultaneously. I sit there for a few minutes until the driver clears his throat. "Apologies, miss, but I've got to get going."

I shake my head. "Sorry," I mutter, climbing out of the back of the car.

Mia rushes over to me the moment I step out. "There you are." She pulls me into a hug I didn't know I needed. "I'm so sorry."

I hug her back tightly. "Thank you."

"Don't thank me. Come on, let's get you inside."

She laces her fingers with mine and drags me into the house. My grief is odd. It's different from what I felt when Dad died. Mom and I never saw eye to eye. We couldn't have been any different from each other. However, it doesn't make what I feel toward her husband okay.

Remy was her husband, and we buried her today. I shouldn't be disappointed that he didn't kiss me. Although his words have just made everything more complicated.

I think about you the way no stepdad should ever think of his stepdaughter.

I hate myself for wishing that he'd just fuck propriety and give in to what he wants.

REMY

I've lost the plot.

I think about you the way no stepdad should ever think of his stepdaughter.

While I didn't tell her I wanted to fuck her, I might as well have.

The question is, what the fuck came over me in the back of that car?

A very good question, and I don't have the answer. As I stand on one side of the room, pretending to listen to Massimo prattle on about another deal he's struck with the bikers, all I can focus on is *her*.

The angel living under the devil's roof.

My cock took control of my fucking brain for a moment of insanity. And the craziest thing is that Ella was into it. Hell, she was goading me to cross the line and speak the truth out loud. Truth that should never be spoken.

I can't stop replaying the moment.

The way her lips parted, and she let out a barely

audible moan when I squeezed her throat. If the journey had been longer, I would have had her naked and riding my cock with her tight virgin cunt before we made it to our destination.

I rub a hand across my face.

"Are you even listening?" Massimo asks, glaring at me.

"I'm distracted," I admit, shaking my head. "This is my wife's funeral."

Massimo laughs. "Let's be honest, you didn't give two shits about Erin."

I narrow my eyes. "I didn't want Erin dead if that's what you are suggesting."

He purses his lips together. "Considering how you stare at her daughter, it wouldn't surprise me if you did."

"What the fuck is that supposed to mean?" Since Massimo took over as Don during my illness, he's far more cocky.

"It means you look at her like a lion staring at a juicy steak."

I growl. "Don't be an idiot, Massimo. She's my step-daughter."

He laughs. "Let's be honest with each other, shall we?"

I glare at him. "What do you mean?"

"You don't give a shit that she's your stepdaughter. You have no morals, so don't give me that excuse."

"Be careful how you speak to me, son. You may be Don for now, but I can snatch the crown back if you test me."

He stiffens. "I know that," he replies through gritted teeth. "But that doesn't mean I can't call you out on your shit. I've known you all my life. You look at her like I've never seen you look at a woman."

"She's twenty-one years old," I say.

He arches a brow. "And your point is?"

I'm not sure what my point is. I've fucked young women her age before, but I know that if I went there, there'd be no going back. Ella is the most beautiful, pure, innocent angel I've ever seen, and I'm the opposite. Rotten darkness that continues to fester.

I'd drink her in, and she wouldn't survive me.

"What's holding you back, Dad?" Massimo asks.

I clench my jaw, hating that my son knows me so well. "I'm not holding back. Ella will be sold to the highest bidding mafia family at auction in six weeks, and that will be the end of it."

Even as I say it, I don't know how I'll go through with it.

"Really?" Massimo asks. "That doesn't give us any control over the family we create ties with."

I shrug. "It's the best option. Ella's not a blood relation, so the standard is to offer the marriage contract at auction."

Massimo nods. "Right... Are you sure you can let her go?"

"Massimo, stop acting like a child. I've told you—"

"Yeah, Dad. You've told me lies. If you'd excuse me, I'm going to find my wife." He turns and walks away, leaving me reeling.

Am I that fucking obvious?

I won't tell Ella about the plan to auction her marriage contract until the last moment. I know she will fight me over it.

Searching the room, my eyes land on her at the bar, getting a drink. When I set eyes on her full, curvy figure, my cock hardens.

She's wearing a satin black dress that hugs her in all the right places, pushing her full breasts up. Her blonde hair is curled and cascading down her back like a waterfall, and the neckline of her dress is cut low enough to reveal just the right amount of cleavage. She may not like the glamorous life, but she suits it.

She looks gorgeous, like an angel sent from Heaven. A dangerous angel, one I'd do anything to have in my bed. My jaw clenches as I imagine slipping off that dress she has on and exploring every inch of her body with my lips until she screams *Daddy*.

No.

I can't have her. She'll be auctioned off to the best family for her. Once she is, I'll forget about her and move on with my life. The auction isn't for six weeks, so I don't need to tell her yet. I think she will fight me at every turn when I tell her.

Someone clears their throat behind me, and I see Mia glaring at me. "Why are you staring at Ella like that?"

I run a hand across the back of my neck. "I don't know what you're talking about."

"Dad, you are obvious." She shakes her head. "But Ella is too sweet for you. You can't go there."

I clench my jaw. "I'm not going there, Mia. She's younger than you, for fuck's sake."

She puts her hands on her hips. "I'll repeat. I know you. Her age doesn't matter to you." She draws in a deep breath. "Don't hurt her, I like her."

"I've already put her marriage contract up for auction. She'll have a husband within six weeks."

Mia's eyes widen. "Does she know?"

I shake my head. "Not yet. I only agreed on the retainer yesterday." My eyes narrow. "And you won't dare tell her until I'm ready. There's no use in her stewing over it for six weeks."

Mia looks furious. "Are you going to tell her the night before?"

My jaw works because I would do that if there weren't four pre-auction events that she must attend. "No, I'll tell her two weeks before the auction."

Mia rolls her eyes. "Classic Dad, always putting off the inevitable. So for the next four weeks, I've got to pretend I don't know she's being sold off?"

I ignore her sarcasm. "Yes, and if you care about her like you say you do, then I suggest you keep it to your-self until the time comes for me to tell her."

Mia doesn't say anything, staring at me with a cold glint in her eye before turning and walking toward the bar.

I watch Ella stand by the buffet with an empty plate. She's been standing there since leaving the bar, staring at the food.

"Dad," Camilla says my name, and I turn around. "I'm sorry for your loss."

I look into my daughter's eyes, wondering where the time went. I remember her as a baby. It feels like it was merely a blink of an eye, and she's grown up and fled the nest to marry some sadistic professor. "Why are you here, Camilla?"

Her eyes flash with hurt. "Because you invited me."

I clench my jaw. "And your husband?"

"He's with the twins."

I forgot that she has had two babies, neither of whom I've met yet. "Right, the grandchildren you won't let me meet?"

She presses her lips together. "It's Gavril... He—"

"He took you from me, and now he's withholding my grandkids, right?"

She sighs heavily. "Gavril doesn't trust anyone and believes you might try to..." She trails off as she knows it's ridiculous. "Give it time."

I'm not one for being patient. Mia practically did the same thing, but at least her husband had connections and brought something to our family. Gavril stole Camilla and then acts like we're the fucking assholes.

"I don't like being treated like a cunt, Camilla. And you know it. So, I want to meet my grandchildren soon."

She looks into my eyes and nods. "Okay, I'll make it happen."

I run a hand over the back of my neck. "Family is everything to me, you know that. I'd never let any harm come to them."

"Of course," she replies.

"I'll see you later." I walk away from her and toward

my study, noticing I don't see Ella anywhere. I need space to clear my head.

As I walk toward it, I hear soft sobs from the library. I know who it is without even looking.

Ella.

She's taken her mom's death hard. I still can't believe she tried to blame me when Erin disrespected my rules and took off without a word. I may not be a good guy, but I always protect my family, which included Erin, the moment she became my wife.

I should walk by and leave her, especially after what I said in the back of the car. Instead, I knock on the door.

Ella's eyes widen, and she wipes the tears away frantically as if she's scared of me seeing her crying. She looks just as beautiful, even with her puffy eyes and red face. "Sorry, I needed some space."

I swallow hard. "Me too."

A flash of hope enters her eyes. "Do you want to sit?"

I shouldn't, but I can't walk away when she looks this vulnerable. I don't trust myself to speak. Instead, I sit with her.

"I find it hard to believe she's gone."

"You and your mother had a strained relationship, didn't you?"

Ella nods. "Yes. She never treated me or Dad well when he was alive."

My heart breaks for her even though I was sure I didn't have one. I don't know why I take her hand, but I do it and regret it immediately. Sparks fly between us,

and Ella's eyes darken with lust. I can't believe this innocent creature wants me the way I want her.

It's taboo. It's forbidden. Not to mention, I'm no
good for her.

No matter how often I repeat that mantra, I still
want her like nothing else. We both know we should pull
away, but neither of us does; instead, we look at each
other with a dark desire burning between us.

"About what you said in the car—"

"No, Ella."

Her eyes flash with hurt. "But—"

I pull my hand from hers and shuffle over on the
couch as we enter dangerous territory. "I told you. It was
a mistake to tell you that, and we should never talk
about it again."

She places her hand on my thigh, excruciatingly
close to my straining cock. "What if I want to talk about
it?"

"We buried your mom today, and look at the two of
us?" I growl, unable to remove her hand from my thigh.
"Do you realize how fucked up this is?"

Her throat bobs, and she nods. "I know." I notice
how she starts to doubt herself, making me feel guilty.
Because this girl has nothing to feel guilty about, it's all
on me. I told her what I'd been thinking since we met.

"Fuck." I run a hand through my hair, searching
those big sapphire blue eyes. She's looking at me in a
way that makes me crazy. As if I'm the best fucking
thing she's ever seen. As if she craves me as badly as I
crave her.

"I'm sorry," she murmurs, moving to stand. "I think I'm going to go to my—"

I grab her wrist and pull her onto my lap so she's facing me, grabbing her face. "You're not going anywhere."

A tiny gasp escapes her lips before I capture them with my own, tasting her for the first time. It's better than I imagined as her lips part willingly for me, allowing me inside. A heat so intense coils through my veins. It's burning me from the inside out. Driving me crazy. For three months, this girl has been under my roof, and I am like a fucking teenager, jerking off constantly.

Ella moans into my mouth as I tangle my tongue with hers, a burning bonfire raging to life between us. Her hands claw at my shirt like she never wants this to stop. I could die a happy man with this girl in my arms.

I can't believe the way she drives me wild. All I can think of is striping and fucking her until she comes all over my cock with her tight virgin cunt, while my family are just down the hall.

She can feel my hardness as she begins to rock herself against it, moaning as her fingers tug at my hair. I give her lip a warning tug between my teeth and grab a fistful of her hair, yanking her mouth away.

"Such a dirty girl and so needy for her stepdaddy's cock," I breathe, feeling like a man possessed. "Have you thought about it, too, Ella?"

"Yes."

I pull her bottom lip between my teeth and suck.

"Yes, Daddy," I instruct, despite knowing that only adds to how fucked this is.

She swallows hard and squirms more on my lap. "Yes, Daddy."

I stare into those innocent blue eyes, trying to claw myself back from the edge. "This is wrong."

She shakes her head. "It doesn't feel wrong."

I grit my teeth. "It is."

She looks at me with those beautiful blue eyes, and I'm torn. "Why deny ourselves what we both want?"

It's a damn good question, and I'm struggling to find the answer when she's this close to me. I know she wants a distraction from her grief. Maybe that's all this is, and who am I to deny her? Her strawberry scent is intoxicating, and it's making my mind hazy.

"Fuck me," she breathes into my ear. And I can't believe how hot it is hearing her say that.

A clatter outside the library breaks the stupor I'd fallen into, and I shake my head. My hands wrap around her hips, stopping her from moving. She's so wet beneath her dress that she's leaving a patch on the front of my pants, making my cock harder than steel. "No, Ella. You're a virgin."

A flash of hurt enters her eyes, but she tugs her lip into her mouth. "I want you to be my first," she murmurs.

God. I didn't know I had this much restraint. Hearing her tell me that is like waving a dead rabbit in front of a starving wolf. "Do you know how fucked up that is?"

I'm holding on to my control by a thread, but I know fucking her isn't an option.

"Please," she begs, ignoring my question.

I lift her off my lap and shake my head. "I can't fuck you."

The disappointment and sheer embarrassment written across her face are unmistakable. It makes me feel bad, but I've put her marriage contract up for auction in six weeks. It states she's a virgin. I can't fuck her. No matter how badly I want to. Before I can say another word, she runs out of the room.

12

ELLA

*I*t's been a month since we buried Mom. I've spent a month holding my breath, waiting for Remy to kick me out. He hasn't touched me again since we crossed the line and kissed in the library.

I could get a place of my own now I have access to my bank account again. Something is holding me back, and I sense it's the man of the house. Even though I've only had one taste, I crave more.

I head out of the library and slam straight into a hard wall of muscle. Before I look up, I know it's Remy. The masculine scent of him makes my heart pound faster and harder.

When my brain catches up, I realize he's got his hands on my hips to steady me. I glance up, and those dark, chocolate-brown eyes are gazing at me with an unreadable expression.

"Sorry, Remy. I didn't see you there."

His grip tightens, sending that unwanted, illicit thrill to my core.

I think about you the way no stepdad should ever think of his stepdaughter.

Heat floods my body as I look into those dark, almost black eyes.

"I was coming to see you," he says, releasing my hips and stepping back.

My stomach flips as I sense this is the moment I've been dreading. "Oh, what did you want to see me about?" I ask, nervously moving my hair out of my face.

"I want you to have dinner with me. We've got some important things to discuss."

I swallow hard. "Okay, sure."

"Meet me in the dining room in an hour." He turns and marches away from me without another word. Stoic and grumpy, as always. He didn't crack a smile at all. I'm unsure why I'm so attracted to him when he's so cold toward me ninety percent of the time.

I head to my bedroom and into the adjoining bathroom, turning on the shower. I need a cold one after bumping into Remy, let alone sitting at dinner with him.

He didn't say whether Leo and Luca would be there. Hopefully, they will be a buffer between us. While they drive me insane, it does help to have them there. It's awkward when I'm alone with Remy, especially after the incident in the library.

I slip off my shirt and pants, hanging them on the back of the door. Tiptoeing into the shower, I turn the dial to cold and wash myself.

Even with the cool water, I can't stop my mind from running wild with fantasies. One dream I can't stop having is that we're both in the home gym. He's on the weights bench but stops to watch me run.

He's watching me intently, eyeing my body up and down. He leans over, his face in line with my breasts. He licks his lips, and his hot tongue flashes out to lick my nipple through the fabric of my workout top. I gasp. I can feel it in response, that all too familiar ache.

And then he turns the machine off and yanks me back with my hair, kissing me. I moan as I imagine him taking me on the treadmill. I imagine him holding my hips as he drives his hard cock right into me viciously. My finger is joined by another, even though I'm unsure when I slipped another one in. I'm rubbing my clit and imagining that he's fucking me. I imagine him dropping me onto my hands and knees on the treadmill, holding my hips with his huge hands as he pounds into me relentlessly.

I grip the side rails of the treadmill as he fucks me like an animal. I make these desperate sounds as I come hard on my fingers, imagining they're Remy's dick. I lean against the wall because my legs are jelly and shaking. I bite my lip to stop myself from crying out his name.

Fuck.

I need help.

My stomach is full of butterflies. I sense Remy is more likely to kick me out than fuck me tonight.

I dry myself and my hair before putting on some makeup. Then I head into the closet, select a burgundy full-length Givenchy dress from the rack, and slide it on, smiling when I look in the mirror. It's tight and hugs my body like a second skin.

Time to face the music.

I walk down the stairs and turn left toward the dining room. Remy is already in there, pacing up and down with a glass of scotch.

When I walk in, his eyes snap up. They darken as they travel the length of my dress.

I notice we're the only two here. No sign of Luca and Leo.

"Are Leo and Luca not joining us?"

He shakes his head. "No." He doesn't say anything else as he drinks me in with his eyes. I wish he would stop holding back and grab me like he did in the library.

"Shall we sit?" I ask, noticing the appetizer is already on the table.

He nods and walks to his usual seat.

I sit where I normally do, a few seats away from him.

He clears his throat. "Sit closer," he demands.

I swallow hard, wishing that the way he commands didn't turn me on. "Okay." I take the seat to his left.

An awkward silence falls between us. "Have you found Mom's killer yet?" I ask, knowing his men have been trying to track down who did this ever since it happened.

He shakes his head. "No, all the leads were dead ends."

I sigh heavily, wondering if he'll ever be able to get justice for her.

"Don't worry, I'll find the bastard." He clenches his fists.

I nod. "What exactly did you want to talk to me about?"

He doesn't look at me as he forks some cold meat and cheese onto his plate. "Your future," he says.

"I can leave if you're worried about me being around too long. I have my income from my book and savings." I shrug. "I'll get my own place."

His eyes snap up, burning with a darkness that frightens me. "You won't be going anywhere. At least not until you're married."

"Married?" I roll my eyes. "I don't want an arranged marriage to a mobster."

"Too bad," Remy says, sipping his scotch. "You're my last chance to create a meaningful alliance with a powerful family, Ella. My two daughters were fucking idiots and fell in love with the wrong men."

"I'm not a Morrone," I say.

His jaw clenches. "It doesn't matter. Your hand in marriage will be up for auction in two weeks."

"Auction?" I question.

He nods, jaw clenched. "Yes, your marriage contract is up for auction. It's a common way to make alliances. You'll attend a few pre-auction dinners where you'll meet the possible buyers."

I stare at him in shock, as while I thought he might try to arrange my marriage, this is fucked up. "You're selling me?"

He tilts his head. "Don't be so dramatic. I'm selling

your hand in marriage. The man that buys the right." He grinds his teeth. "Will protect you."

I clench my fists on the table. "I'm not being dramatic. You're essentially selling me like a slave."

"The man who buys you will be rich and powerful. You'll want for nothing."

I stand and glare at him, knocking my chair to the floor. "If you didn't realize, I don't give a shit about either of those things." My rage is insurmountable. "I'm not my mother."

He remains calm, staring back at me. "No, you're not," He breathes.

The air between us shifts, and I hate that instead of wanting to storm away from him for breaking this shitty news, I want to kiss him.

"What's your next move, Ella?" He tilts his head. "Are you going to run to your bedroom and sulk like a brat?"

I laugh. "A brat? I'm not one of the rich, spoiled kids you raised. Goodnight." I turn around, but he captures my wrist before I can walk away.

"No," he breathes, his voice softer.

"No, what?" I ask, glancing at him as he stares at his hand around my wrist, conflict waging war in his eyes.

"You're not spoiled," he murmurs, raising his eyes to meet mine. "However, when your mother married me, she sealed your fate." He releases my wrist. "I told her the terms before we married, and she said it was the only way to stop your stubbornness."

I let out a dark laugh. "I should have known Mom was aware of this from the start." I glance at the food on the table and back at Remy. "Excuse me, I think I've lost my appetite."

Remy's jaw clenches, but he doesn't stop me. Instead, he watches me as I walk out of the dining hall and shut the door behind me.

I rest my back against it and draw in a shuddering breath, tears in my eyes. Remy's an asshole for putting me up for auction.

I know it hurts all the more because I want him. But his actions speak louder than words; clearly, it's all one-sided. He wouldn't sell me to the highest bidder if he wanted me. I need to escape and start afresh somewhere new before he sells me.

13

ELLA

"*T*hat one looks so hot on you," Mia says, playing with the satin tulle on the navy blue Gucci dress she made me try. It's a fortune, so there's no way in hell I'm buying it.

I think Mia forgets I don't come from a billion-dollar family.

While my earnings from my book allow me to live comfortably, a five-thousand-dollar dress is certainly out of my price range.

"It's nice, sure. I'm not buying it, though."

Mia groans. "Why not?"

"I can't afford it."

She waves her hand dismissively. "Don't worry, I've got you. My treat."

I clench my jaw. "I'm good, but thanks for the offer."

Mia sets her hands on her hips, and I know from the look in her eyes we might end up spending the entire afternoon arguing about this. "You get lunch. I get this dress. Deal?"

"Right, because they have the same monetary value."

Mia's jaw clenches. "It doesn't matter about the money. You look fucking gorgeous in it, and it's a crime to fashion if you don't have it."

"That's a bit dramatic." I laugh. "I don't even know where I'll wear it."

Mia's lips purse. "Well, there's the pre-auction dinner at the weekend."

A dinner I have no intention of attending. I'll be gone by then. I've paid for my plane tickets to take me to Texas. As far as fucking possible away from Remy. I feel a little bad leaving Mia, as we've become good friends, but I won't be sold off. Once I'm gone, I doubt Remy will put too much effort into finding me.

I shake my head. "You're not going to drop it, are you?"

Mia shrugs. "If we don't leave here with the dress, I'll come back and buy it on my own and put it in your room."

I sigh. "Fine. Deal."

Mia smiles. "Great. Now get dressed, I'm starving."

I return to the cabin and change into my blouse and skinny jeans. There's no point in Mia buying this dress, as once I'm in Texas, I won't attend any fancy dinners or events. Maybe I can leave it, and she'll return it.

I place the Gucci dress back in the garment bag and place it carefully over my arm.

Mia takes it from me when I step out of the

changing room. "Vivian is going to hold it for us while we have lunch. We've still got lots more time to shop."

I groan. "I'll drop dead if we shop much more."

"Now, who is being dramatic?" Mia asks as she goes to put it behind the counter.

As we walk out of the store and into the bright sunshine, I can't help but feel a sense of relief. While I'm grateful for Mia's generosity, I don't like feeling like I owe anyone anything.

Mia links arms with me. "What do you want for lunch?"

"Sushi?" I suggest.

Her eyes light up. "Great choice. I know a good place around the corner that serves the best sushi in town."

We make our way to the restaurant which is a short walk down the street. The sun beats down on me, and a light breeze rustles through my hair. Chicago is very different from Washington; busier and louder.

"There it is," Mia says, nodding toward a fancy-looking restaurant called Roka Akor. It's not the kind of place I'd normally go, as I know it will be expensive.

"Wow, it looks fancy."

She stops walking. "Oh shit, it isn't cheap. Did you want to—"

I place a hand on her arm and shake my head. "It's fine. I'm not that broke."

She laughs, and we walk inside.

We're led to a table by an attentive waiter. We order the sashimi and maki rolls to share, and both arrive

117

beautifully plated and topped with edible flowers and crisp vegetables.

As soon as I take my first bite, I instantly know why this place is so popular; everything tastes fresh and delicious.

"So, what do you think?" Mia asks as I finish my last maki roll.

"It's probably the best sushi I've ever had."

She smiles. "Good. Now you'll be suitably recharged for an afternoon of more shopping."

"Your siblings weren't kidding when they said you can shop."

"No, they weren't. Tell me more about the next book you're working on?" She takes a sip of her cocktail. "It's pretty impressive. You've already written and published a book at twenty-one."

I shrug. "Mom didn't think so. It's a thriller. I've been working on it for a while, but..." I trail off, unsure how to explain why I haven't been able to put any more words down.

"What is it?"

"My mom put my writing down so much I've lost confidence in it." My throat bobs as I feel guilty that a part of me is relieved she's no longer here. She's no longer got me trapped, yet it's like her ghost is still trying to trap me in a life I don't want through Remy.

"That sucks." Her brow furrows. "It's a shame you didn't have a better relationship with her."

"Yeah," I say, looking down at the table.

"Do you think your dad would have supported you if he were alive?" Mia asks.

It's something I've thought about a lot in the past. "I think so. He was different from her."

"Did they ever catch who murdered him?"

I shake my head. "No, but I know it was his employers. I don't know who they were, but they were mafia. It's why I was so angry when I learned what your dad does for a living."

Mia sinks her teeth into her bottom lip. "That makes sense. God, that's pretty insensitive of her."

Insensitive is the perfect word to describe how she was. All my life.

"Yeah, shall I get the bill?"

Mia nods. "Yep, and then we shop until we drop."

"I hope that's not meant in the literal sense."

She wiggles her brows. "Maybe?"

I roll my eyes. I won't be in a rush to go on another shopping trip with my stepsister. Lunch, yes. Shopping, no thanks. I should have heeded Massimo's and Camilla's warning.

I catch the server's attention and ask for the bill. He brings it, and I give him my card. The total is eighty-five dollars. He tries to put it on the card, but it makes a beep.

"It's been declined, miss," he says.

My brow furrows. "That's not possible. There's more than enough for the bill. Try it again."

He does the same thing. "Sorry, miss. It's not working."

Mia gives him her card. "Don't worry about it. I got it."

I pull out my cell and open my banking app. All the

money is still in there, but it states the account is on hold. "What the hell?"

"What's wrong?" Mia asks.

"My account is on hold. I've got the cash in there, but there's a hold on the funds. I'll ring the bank, and then I'll transfer you the money."

Mia waves her hand. "Don't worry about it. You can get the next lunch."

I don't mention that there won't be a next lunch. Tomorrow I'm flying away from Chicago and not coming back for a while. I excuse myself to call the bank.

"Hello, Northerntrust customer service. How can I help?"

"Hi, I just tried using my card, which was declined. I checked the banking app, and the account is on hold. Can you tell me what's going on, please?"

"Sure, can I take your account number?"

I give her the number and wait for her to 'investigate.'

"Thank you for holding, Miss. So it appears that the second account holder put the account on hold."

"What second account holder? It's my account."

She clears her throat. "No, we have a signed document dated a month ago adding Remy Morrone as a full-access member. Are you saying you didn't authorize this?"

"No, I didn't."

"Do you know Remy Morrone?"

"Yes, thank you for letting me know. I'll be in touch once I get this misunderstanding ironed out."

"Of course."

"In the meantime, can you unfreeze the account?"

"No, I'm afraid I can't because I need both the account holders' permission."

I growl. "You didn't have my permission to freeze it, so why would you need it to unfreeze it?"

"We did have your permission. Yesterday afternoon, we had a call from both you and Remy. The person who called gave all of your security answers."

Motherfucker.

I end the call, too angry to speak.

Mia's hand lands on my shoulder. "Is everything okay?"

I spin around to face her, shaking my head. "No, everything is not okay. Your dad has frozen my bank account."

Mia's eyes widen. "Shit. Why would he do that?"

It dawns on me then that he must know I paid for the plane tickets yesterday. And then he froze the account to make sure I couldn't leave.

That bastard.

I won't sit by while he controls my entire life.

14

REMY

"*A*re you serious?" Ella says, barging into my office while two of my men, Edoardo and Gino, explain how they plan to increase our profits at Secret Obsession.

I glance at them. "Excuse me, gentleman. We'll discuss this at a later date."

They both nod and exit my study. I sit back in my chair, placing my fingers together. "Am I serious about what, Ella?"

I know why she's pissed. She tried to use her card at lunch with Mia. I had a notification on my phone from the banking app.

"You can't take control of my bank account."

I tilt my head. "I can and have, Ella." I stand and move around the desk. "Did you really think you could book those tickets and run away before the pre-auction dinner this weekend?"

She squares up to me and holds my gaze. "Unfreeze the account and let me go," she growls.

My eyes narrow. "Careful how you talk to me."

Her eyes flash with fire. Fire that I'd love to play with, but I need to keep a level head. Two weeks and she'll go to live with whatever lucky son of a bitch buys her hand in marriage.

"Do it, or I'll call the police," she threatens.

It's amusing that she thinks that will get her anywhere. "Go ahead, see if it helps."

Her brow furrows. "Don't tell me you have the cops in your pockets?"

I shrug. "What do you think?"

Defeat slumps her shoulders. "Please, Remy," she begs, eyes dazzling with unshed tears.

Fuck.

Hearing her beg me is not good. I've wanted to hear her beg me since the second I set eyes on her. My cock is a steel rod in my pants. It's been hard since she stormed in her like a tornado, but when she begs me... No, I can't back down on this.

"There's nothing that can be done. I've entered you into the auction with a ten million dollar reserve."

Her mouth falls open. "Who the hell will pay ten million dollars for me?"

Is she really that blind to how gorgeous she is?

"Many men would. It's a payment for you and the alliance with the Morrone famiglia."

Her throat bobs. "Remy, you've got to do something. I don't want this. I want..."

She trails off, and I wonder what she was going to say.

"What do you want, Ella?" I ask, intrigued to learn more about her wants despite my better judgment.

She sucks in a deep breath. "Love."

One simple word, but it makes my stomach clench. Love. Of course, that's what this sweet, innocent creature craves. Something I could never give her.

"Explain," I say.

She looks into my eyes. "My parents didn't love each other." Her jaw clenches. "Well, Dad may have loved Mom initially, but he fell out of love with her. And I don't think she ever loved him. I don't want a marriage like that."

I shake my head. "You're too innocent, believing love even exists."

Her brow furrows. "Are you saying you don't believe in love?"

I take her chin and force her to look at me. I shouldn't touch her as it draws my attention to how close we are. Her eyes are filled with so much emotion that my chest aches because I will crush her with my answer. "Love is a fairy tale, Ella. It doesn't exist in the real world. The quicker you learn that, the easier it'll be to accept your fate."

She looks me in the eye. "Just because you've never known love doesn't mean it doesn't exist in this world." Her jaw clenches. "You can't make me believe otherwise."

I release her chin, shaking my head. "Poor, naïve Ella. Your innocence will be your downfall."

Her eyes flash with hurt at my comment. I don't normally give a shit if I hurt people, but when I see that vulnerability clear in her beautiful bright blue eyes, it makes me feel something I haven't felt in a very long time. *Guilt.*

"You're a monster," she breathes, her voice quiet and broken.

I can't let her hurt get to me. Ella staying under my roof is not an option, and letting her go into the world with nothing and no one to protect her isn't either. As ridiculous as it sounds, selling her hand in marriage to a mobster is for her safety. She'll be protected and given a good life.

"I know you don't understand this, Ella, but it's for your own good."

She shakes her head. "My own good? How in the world is any of this benefitting me?"

"Your mom was married to me for three months and ended up dead at the hands of my enemies. What do you think will happen if one of them gets their hands on you?"

Her eyes narrow. "I'm no one to you. Why would they bother?"

"The moment your mom married me, she tied you to the famiglia for life. My enemies will be well aware of your existence, and if you're unprotected, they'll go for you."

She sinks her teeth into her bottom lip and looks at me as if trying to decide whether to say something. "Can't I stay here? Maybe I can be like one of the staff or something?"

"One of the staff?"

She nods. "Yeah, I'm not a bad cook or could clean."

I may have considered her proposal if I wasn't damn near obsessed with her. The idea of her prancing around my house in a maid's outfit drives me to despair. Keeping her under my roof isn't an option. "It wouldn't work."

"I promise I'm a good, hard worker and—"

"No, Ella. It's not up for discussion."

Unshed tears fill her eyes and her lip wobbles. "Why not?"

I clench my jaw, knowing we're moving into dangerous territory. "I can't have you under my roof."

Her eyes widen. "Because you hate me that much?"

I look into her eyes, wondering why she would think I hate her. "Hate you?" I shake my head. "I don't hate you, Ella. I crave you in a way no stepdad should ever crave his stepdaughter." My jaw clenches as hope ignites in her eyes. "You can't stay here, as I don't trust myself."

She closes the gap between us, and I stiffen when she places a hand on my chest, looking up at me with those beautiful blue eyes. "Please, Remy. I don't want to be anywhere else but here."

Fuck.

I don't know how to read that comment. Is Ella suggesting I cross the line and have her for myself? Something other than our stepdad and stepdaughter relationship is holding me back. It's fear. Fear I might learn what it means to love. I've never felt this way about a woman, and I haven't even fucked her. And anyone married to me always winds up dead. I can't let that be Ella's fate.

"Ella," I breathe her name, gazing down at her.

Her lips part, and her eyes dilate. "Please, Daddy," she says in a seductive tone.

That snaps my resolve as I grab her hips and yank her against me, kissing her for the first time since the library. One month I've kept a level-head, and she comes in here and breaks me down so fucking easily it's embarrassing. My veins light on fire as intense heat floods through me. I lift her into my arms and place her on the edge of my desk.

My brain is no longer in control, and I'm thinking with my cock. I keep kissing her and lift the hem of her skirt to her hips.

Ella doesn't try to stop me. Instead, she kisses me harder. Her tongue eagerly tangles with mine as we lose ourselves in each other.

Lightning would have to strike me down to stop me. She feels so damn right, as if she was made for me.

I let my fingers inch up her exposed thighs, making her moan into my mouth before I touch her. And then, when I get to her panties, I groan as I feel them soaked through. "You're wet for me, angel," I breathe, struggling to think through the lust-filled fog in my brain. "So fucking wet." Pushing aside the soaked fabric.

"I'm always wet for you," she murmurs.

"God damn it," I growl, thrusting two fingers roughly inside her. "You're driving me crazy."

Her head falls back, and she releases the sweetest moan I've ever heard. "Remy."

"I want you to call me Daddy. Can you do that for me?"

Her eyes find mine, and she plays with her nipples through her dress. "Yes, Daddy."

"Fuck, that's right. Touch your perfect tits for me." I stoop down and lick her nipples through the fabric, making her moan. All the while, my fingers build a rhythm in her tight virgin pussy.

Her fingers lace through my hair to tug my lips back to hers, kissing me as if she's needed this her whole damn life. I kiss her back hungrily, our tongues dancing as her hips move toward me, seeking more from my fingers.

I can feel her orgasm building as her muscles contract.

Fuck.

I can't believe we're doing this. I'm going to make my fucking stepdaughter come on the edge of my desk.

"Sir."

We both freeze, and I realize we didn't even shut the door to my office.

"I'm busy, Salvatore. What is it?"

"Urgent business. I wouldn't want to say in the company of others."

Ella tries to jump down from the desk, but I hold her firmly in place. My fingers still deep in her cunt.

"Give me a few minutes, and I'll be with you." I glance over my shoulder at my man. "And shut the door."

Salvatore nods and leaves.

"Oh my God," Ella says, trying to get down from my desk. "I need to go."

"No," I growl. "I'm finishing what I started, but know this, Ella. This is the first and last time I touch you."

Her eyes flash with hurt, but I can't dwell on what that look means. Instead, I thrust my fingers deeper, making her gasp as her back arches.

I fuck her with my fingers and use my other hand to play with her clit. That makes her moan louder as her muscles spasm around my fingers, making her already tight pussy tighter. The thought of her strangling my dick like this is almost enough to make me come in my pants.

"Come for me," I command.

Her orgasm rips through her body as I watch with satisfaction.

And then it's over.

She jumps down from my desk and adjusts her panties. And then she looks at me, eyes shining still with desire. "Thank you," she murmurs.

I grab her throat and squeeze softly, moving my lips to within an inch of hers. "You're welcome, but remember what I said."

She pouts slightly. "The last time you'll touch me, right?"

I nod in response as we hold each other's gaze, the electricity zapping through the air impossible to ignore as I release her throat.

She steps away from me and glances back at me over her shoulder. "We'll see," she says, a devious glint in her eyes. "See you later." She goes to walk away, but I'm too fast as I grab her wrist and pull her to a stop.

"I meant it, Ella. This is the last time. Understood?"

She purses her lips together as if she doesn't quite believe me but nods. Hell, I don't know if I believe myself right now.

I release her arm, and she leaves the room without a word.

My fingers are soaked with her arousal, and I suck them clean, groaning at the taste and the throbbing of my cock in my briefs. Before I can wrap my head around what happened, Salvatore knocks on the door again.

With a heavy sigh, I stand and put on my mask. It's time to go back to business.

But as the day wears on, all the depraved things I want to do with Ella play in my mind like a porno. I want her, and making her come for me on my desk only made me want her more.

All I know is I can't have her. In three days, she will attend the first pre-auction dinner. And then, in two weeks, her marriage contract will be purchased by another man for a minimum of ten million dollars.

Our wicked desires can never go further. But, in my darkest moments, I can't help imagine Ella by my side —forever.

15

ELLA

I play with the hem of the Gucci dress Mia bought me, my hands trembling.

Mia stands to the side, watching me. "Are you okay?"

I shake my head, scared about attending this event.

She moves closer. "It's okay to be scared, Ella," Mia whispers, placing a hand on my shoulder.

"Is this how you found Killian?"

Her lips purse together. "No, we knew each other at the academy we attended. Our match wasn't exactly one my father supported."

I clench my jaw. "Same with Camilla, right?"

Mia nods.

"But I have to be sold? I'm not even a *Morrone*."

She gives me a pitying look. "Don't think of it as being sold. Think of this as an opportunity to find the nicest and hottest guy on offer and snag him."

I laugh. Mia has a way with words. "Only you could see the positive in being auctioned off."

Mia shrugs. "Seriously, you can find someone decent. You have some control over this. If you aren't friendly to buyers that don't interest you, they'll be less likely to buy you."

I consider her suggestion, as she has a point. I hope to find Prince Charming to rescue me from a terrible existence. I can hardly imagine how many men in this line of work treat women as second-class citizens. "Fine. Shall we get this over with?"

"Yeah, I'll be by your side the entire time." Her brow furrows. "And Killian is here tonight. You'll get to meet him."

I've heard so much about her husband but haven't met him in the few months since I moved here. He's busy with the Callaghan clan business, for the most part. "Finally. I was starting to question if he exists."

She shoves me. "Are you suggesting I'm crazy enough to believe I'm married to an imaginary man?"

I smile. "Perhaps."

We walk with our arms linked down the stairs and into the main hallway, where Remy, Luca, and Leo are all dressed in their finest suits. And another man, who must be Killian.

I swallow hard when Remy notices me, his eyes darkening as they always do. His gaze moves up and down my dress in a predatory way, heating me from the inside out. I hate how confusing my feelings for him are, even more so since his office three days ago. We haven't spoken since. I wanted him so badly. I wanted him to be the one to take my virginity.

"Killian!" Mia calls.

He glances up, and I notice the tattoos that stretch up his neck and the flash of his green eyes when he sees Mia. "Hey, baby girl." His voice has an Irish lilt to it. He steps forward and wraps an arm around her, giving her a kiss. Killian isn't exactly how I imagined him, as he's more of a bad boy than I expected. "Is this the infamous Ella?" He gives me a handsome, friendly smile.

I hold out a hand. "It's good to meet you, finally."

He takes it and shakes. "Yeah, same. Sorry it wasn't sooner. I've been fucking busy."

I laugh and so does Mia.

"Ready?" Remy asks in a low voice.

I glare at him. "Not exactly. I'd rather be going anywhere else." While I understand his twisted logic and why he's doing this more, it doesn't mean I'm happy about it.

He could protect me. I know how sick it is to want that. The man who was married to my mother, but I'm coming to think desire isn't straightforward. It's confusing and twisted. I can't explain why I have felt so drawn to him since we met, but it feels like fate.

Mia pulls me away from him. "Come on, let's not waste our energy on him."

I nod in agreement and walk away, emboldened by Mia's encouragement.

Even so, I can feel his gaze like lasers at the back of me. I'm thankful when we walk outside into the cool fall air for some reprieve from the heat my stepdad inspires.

I get into the back first, followed by Mia and then Killian. I'm glad to sit next to the window and hope that the others will be a buffer between me and her dad.

Remy is next to join us, but instead of sitting by Killian, he sits directly opposite me, eyes fixed on mine. Luca and Leo are the last to get in, chatting about something vulgar and disgusting.

I glance at Mia. "Do you know the kind of people that will attend?"

She shakes her head.

"Mafia bosses of all ages," Killian says.

"You could end up with a guy your age or a seventy-year-old man," Luca interjects, smirking.

I put my fingers down my throat. "I'm not marrying a man old enough to be my grandpa."

Leo looks me in the eye. "What's your limit then? Would you be happy with someone like your stepdad?" His eyes flicker with amusement as I, no doubt, turn the color of beetroot. "I think you'd like calling your husband *Daddy* while he fucks you."

Mia growls. "Don't be so crass, Leo." She leans across and punches him hard on the shoulder.

"Ouch. I'm only messing about." Leo glares at her.

I'm on fire and can't look at Remy or I'll die. At least, that's how it feels right now.

"Ignore him. He's an asshole." Mia smiles at me. "You're beautiful and will snag a hot young man." Her brow furrows. "Or older, if that's your thing."

Oh my God.

I could kill Leo right about now for being such a dick.

"No," I practically squeak like a mouse. "My age or a little older is good."

Luca chuckles. "You're practically as red as my Ferrari right now. Don't lie, little sis."

I glare at him. "I'm not your sister."

Mia sighs heavily. "Lucky for you. I've had to put up with these two my entire life."

"You love us, Mia," Leo says.

She glares at him. "Sometimes, I'm not so sure."

Remy is silent as always, but when I look at him, he's staring at me.

I can't stop thinking about what happened in his office three days ago.

He tears his eyes off me and glares at Mia and Leo, who are bickering. "Would you two quit it? It's hard to believe you're both adults when you act like this."

Both Leo and Mia fall silent.

"But tell the truth, Ella. You like older men. That's why I wasn't good enough for you, right?" Luca asks.

I glare at him. "No, I just don't fuck idiots like you two, and you're supposed to be my stepbrothers."

Mia makes a fake vomiting sound. "You two are sick for wanting to bang your stepsister."

Killian nods. "Got to admit that's pretty fucked up."

"It's not like she's a blood relation. If her mom hadn't married Dad, I could have met her somewhere, and it wouldn't be an issue." Luca shakes his head. "It's not sick."

Luca has a point, but it still is taboo, no matter what he says.

Mia throws her hands in the air. "It's messed up, and you know it!"

Leo laughs. "No, what would be messed up is if Dad and Ella got together."

My heart nearly stops beating at his words.

Mia shakes her head. "She's going to be auctioned off, you idiot."

Remy's eyes turns dark, and he glares at Leo. "Shut your mouth, or I'll make sure it's shut for good."

A chill runs down my spine, and my heart races. I can feel chemistry sparking between Remy and me.

"Thank fuck we're here. This conversation has taken a weird fucking turn," Luca says as the town car stops in front of an elegant hotel in the center of Chicago. Luca and Leo get out, followed by Mia and Killian.

I'm about to follow her out when Remy grabs my wrist. "Don't listen to them, Ella. Us can't happen, you know that, right?" He sounds like he's trying to convince himself more than me.

I nod in response. "Of course. I'm here to be auctioned off to the highest bidder, and you're the one selling me. It's crystal clear."

His jaw clenches. "I told you, I'm not selling—"

"Call it what you want. It feels that way to me." I get out of the car.

Mia holds her arm out, and I link arms with her. "Come on, let's go and find your prince charming."

I chuckle. "Not sure I'll find him amongst mobsters."

"You'd be surprised how charming some mobsters can be. I know first hand."

We walk behind Leo and Luca into the huge hotel with a large ballroom where the pre-auction dinner is being held.

The ballroom is a spectacle of opulence and grandeur. Frosted chandeliers dangle from the ceiling and cast a soft glow upon the polished marble floor, reflecting the glimmer of a hundred twinkling lights.

Majestic columns rise from the floor to meet the intricate crown molding wrapped in golden filigree that glints as the light hits it. Crimson velvet drapes cascade down the enormous windows, offering glimpses of the moonlit city beyond.

Amidst this elegance, clusters of silk-draped tables are scattered, adorned with crystal glassware and white roses.

The hum of hushed conversations and the faint strain of a string quartet reach my ears as we step further into the room. The atmosphere is tinged with anticipation and an undercurrent of danger, a stark reminder of the darkly forbidden nature of this event.

The room falls silent as I cross the threshold. All eyes turn to me, and a chill runs down my spine. Even though I know I'm nothing more than a commodity, being the center of such attention is unnerving.

A young man not much older than me steps toward us. His black suit fits him like a glove, emphasizing his broad shoulders and powerful build. His sharp features, dark hair, and penetrating gaze make him a masterpiece of virile beauty. But there's an aura of danger that surrounds him.

"Remy, it's good to see you," the man says.

Remy's jaw clenches. I can tell he's trying to keep his temper in check. "And you, Alex. What brings you here?"

Alex turns his gaze to me, and my skin prickles with awareness. "I'm here to find a wife. My father insisted."

I smile at him. "Looks like we have something in common."

His serious expression melts, and he grins. "Glad to hear it. I wasn't sure what kind of woman to expect, but I didn't expect to find one as beautiful as you."

Remy growls softly. "Careful Vishekov."

"Is there a problem? She's one of the assets, and I'm one of the buyers. This event is for us to get to know each other."

I watch Remy's eyes darken. "Of course not," he says gruffly.

If he were so worried about who I'd be speaking with, he never would have entered my marriage contract into this auction. Now, he has to deal with the consequences.

Alex offers me his arm. "Let me get you a drink..." He pauses and shakes his head. "I'm sorry, I'm so rude. What's your name?"

"Ella," I say, taking his arm. "I'd love a drink. Thank you."

I glance briefly at Remy and see his eyes darken with barely contained rage.

We stroll across the room, arm in arm, and I can feel Remy's gaze on us every step of the way.

Alex orders me a drink, and I take it with shaking hands. He's attractive, young, and exactly the kind of man I should be drawn to. And yet here I am, listening to him speak but unable to get my mind off my stepdad.

I'm playing with fire, and I know it.

16

REMY

I'm going to kill him.

Sitting at the dining table across from Ella, I watch Alex fucking Vishekov make her laugh. It sends liquid fire through my veins.

He's young, charming, handsome, and fucking perfect for her.

Although his family is questionable, the Vishekov Bratva have been trying to push their way into Chicago for years. I sense this is their play to get me to allow them in, but there's no space for them. Too many wolves are fighting over territory, and after the war a couple of years ago, I won't start another.

I didn't expect to feel *this* possessive watching her with another man. She smiles at him. A genuine, warm smile that makes my heart ache.

She's too good for anyone here—too pure.

And certainly too fucking good for me.

I down another glass of scotch and stand from the table, marching toward the bar.

Ella hasn't torn her eyes off him since he sat beside her. I hold the tumbler so tight I'm surprised it doesn't shatter in my fingers.

"Scotch on the rocks," I order.

The lady smiles at me in a flirtatious manner. "Of course, handsome." She winks.

I clench my jaw as while she's pretty enough, she's not Ella.

Fuck.

My stepdaughter has done something to me. Corrupted my mind and turned me into a raving lunatic. I want to kill Alex Vishekov with my bare hands even though he's completely within his rights to talk to Ella because I put her hand in marriage up for auction.

As the bartender returns with my drink, I run a hand across my neck. "One scotch on the rocks." She bats her eyelashes at me. "Can I get you anything else?"

I shake my head. "No." And then I turn around and lean against the bar, my eyes instantly drawn to Ella, who is still talking to that piece of shit.

Luca comes over to me and claps me on the shoulder. "Surprised she's picked such a young guy, considering how she looks at you, Dad."

I narrow my eyes. "What's that supposed to mean?"

"Ella wants you, and you want her. The two of you are fucking obvious." He sighs. "I would have hit that if she wasn't so hooked on you."

I growl softly at the thought of any man going near her, my sons included.

"Why did you put her marriage contract up for auction?" Luca asks.

144

I shake my head. "I don't want Ella."

"Right. And that's why you are staring at her and Alex like you want to rip his head off and drag Ella into a cave to have your way with her."

"You've got it wrong. I merely want the right business deal for our family."

He snorts and pats me on the shoulder. "You've been smitten since you set eyes on her, Dad. Don't even try to deny it."

"Smitten?" I growl, turning on Luca. "I'm not a fucking teenage girl, and you shouldn't forget who you're talking to." I grab the lapel of his shirt and yank him an inch off the floor.

He pales as he knows he's been overstepping the mark. "Calm down. I won't say another word about it."

I drop him to his feet. "Good. Now shut up and do what you are here to do. Find out which one of these sons of bitches we want to sell her marriage contract to, and look into Vishekov's motives."

He nods once and walks away, leaving me alone to sulk by the bar.

I turn back to Ella and notice her hand on Alex's forearm. She's barely spoken to anyone else since he approached us like a fucking viper waiting to strike.

He singled Ella out immediately, and I need to know why. The dark lust in his eyes when he looks at her brings me to the brink of violence. Luca is right. I want to tear his head off and feed it to the wolves just for looking at her like that. And yet all I can do is observe from the sidelines because I'm the fucking idiot that put her marriage contract up for auction.

As I stew, a voice pulls me from my internal turmoil. "Your stepdaughter is quite the enchantress, isn't she?" Gregor Vishekov, Alex's father, approaches with a sly grin. His remark instantly ignites my anger further. "Alex seems quite taken with her. He mentioned something about making her his wife," he continues, his eyes glinting with satisfaction.

His words hang in the air, stoking the inferno within me. I clench my jaw, trying to maintain my composure. The thought of that man, that boy, touching Ella... It's unbearable, sickening. But what can I do? She's my step-daughter, for God's sake. Forbidden fruit. The very thought is maddening.

As much as I wish I could, I can't have her.

"Whether he's worthy remains to be seen."

Gregor chuckles. "I think money talks in this game. It's an auction. Worth doesn't come into it."

I narrow my eyes at him. "What exactly do you want from a marriage between our families?"

He smirks. "Power. What else?"

"There's no room for another player in Chicago. You know that."

His eyes narrow. "Do I?"

"The truce we've had between the Volkov Bratva for the last few years would be shattered if we allowed another Russian family to encroach on Chicago terri-tory. But you already know that, so what are you playing at?"

Gregor shrugs. "I believe my son merely finds your stepdaughter attractive." He glances around the room. "She's the most beautiful girl here."

A soft growl rumbles my chest, making Gregor raise an eyebrow. "Enjoy the rest of your evening, Morrone." He walks away, leaving me even more pissed off than before.

I want nothing more than to drag Ella out of her seat and kiss her right here where everyone can witness *who* she really belongs to.

But I can't do that. All I can do is stand here and watch as the men who wish to buy her hand in marriage get to know her. Well, one man since Alex is monopolizing all of her time.

Ella gets up and heads toward the restroom, so I approach Alex.

"What are your intentions toward my stepdaughter, Vishekov?" I demand.

Alex's eyes flicker with dark intent. "She's an asset at the auction, and I'm getting to know her. It sounds like you've trapped her into a life she doesn't want for herself." He smirks widely. "Perhaps I'll be the one to rescue her and set her free."

"Set her free? You mean enslave her as your wife?"

He shrugs. "Semantics. I sure as hell won't be freezing her bank account, though."

Ella has been talking too freely with Alex, which irritates me. I remain seated in the chair on the other side of her when she returns.

She turns to me as she sits. "Remy, what are you doing over here?"

"Making sure you don't badmouth me to every buyer in here." I glare at her. "You've been telling Alex a lot of bullshit."

Her jaw clenches. "I've only told him the truth,"

I place a hand on her thigh beneath the table and squeeze, leaning closer to her. "Have you told him that your stepdad made you come on his desk no more than three days ago?"

Her cheeks flush. "Remy," she hisses, grabbing my hand to pull it away from her thigh.

"Yes?"

"Stop it."

I let my hand move further up her thigh over the fabric of her dress. "Why? Is it because you're wet?"

She leans toward me. "This auction was your idea. Now get your hands off of me before someone sees."

I'm not used to people talking to me like that, but her reaction snaps me out of it. I remove my hand from her thigh and, without a word, head toward the terrace at the back, needing some fresh air.

What the fuck is wrong with me?

I'm a grown man, acting like a possessive man-child. Ella brings the worst parts of me to light. Another reason why I need to take a step back and let her speak to whoever the fuck she wants.

In a fortnight, she'll live with her fiancé, whoever that may be. And in the meantime, I need to hold it together and stop touching my stepdaughter. I think that will be easier said than done.

17

ELLA

"*I*t's time to go," Remy's dark voice speaks behind me.

I turn around, my hand still entwined with Alex's. "Okay." I turn back to Alex and smile. "I had a great time."

His bright blue eyes flash with desire. "Me too. I'm looking forward to seeing you again next week." He smiles and squeezes my arm. While his smile is handsome and his touch is warm, neither invoke the fire I've grown used to when Remy smiles or touches me.

This handsome man, only a few years older than me, who looks like a male model, doesn't stir half the desire in me as Remy does. A man who is old enough to be my father.

I need to see a shrink.

Remy leads me out of the hotel in silence, the tension in his back evident with each step he takes. He's angry. I'm not sure why considering this was all his fucking idea. The air between us is thick with dark desires that we're both trying to fight.

He holds open the car door for me, and I slip inside. I hear him saying something to the driver but can't make out the words. And then he enters and sits opposite me. I'd rather he sit next to me, as his gaze is too intense.

The door slams shut, and the engine starts, driving us away from the hotel. I gaze out the window and watch as the hotel disappears from view.

As the city lights of Chicago blur past the window, a nocturnal tapestry unfolds. Skyscrapers pierce the night sky, their illuminated windows twinkling like stars. The neon signs of bars and clubs pulse with life, adding splashes of color to the urban landscape.

I have to focus on what is out there to distract myself from the man in here.

"Ella." His commanding voice makes my heart rate spike.

I look into his dark eyes, noting how they look almost black in the back of the car. "Yes?"

"You need to be careful around Alex Vishekov. I'm not sure what his motives are for singling you out."

I laugh. "I need to be careful around every man at that event. They're all mobsters."

He clenches his fists by his sides. "Pick someone other than him."

I search his eyes and realize he's jealous. "I like Alex."

His eyes flash. "I don't care."

"If you're going to force me into a marriage I don't

want, you can at least let me pick someone I like." The man I want to pick is sitting before me. I don't say that, though.

"No. Stay away from Alex."

I shake my head. "If I'd be fawning over Bennet instead, that would have been fine?" I spoke with Bennet for a short while when Alex went to get us drinks. He seemed nice enough, too, for a mobster.

There's a dangerous flicker in his eyes. "No."

I sigh. "I'm wondering what you want from me. You expect me to marry one of these men, but I can't talk to them, is that it?"

"Fuck's sake. Stop it."

"Stop what?"

He moves toward me and wraps his huge palm around my throat, squeezing softly. Remy's size is intoxicating as he takes up all the space in the back of the car. "Stop trying to make me jealous."

I shake my head. "Make you jealous? For God's sake, I'm doing what you told me to do." I narrow my eyes. "If you don't want me talking to anyone else, do something about it."

He tightens his grasp on my throat. "You know I can't."

"Can't or won't?" I push because even though I spent an evening with a charming, handsome man who is far more suited to me, it doesn't stop me from wanting the man before me.

"Ella," he practically growls in warning.

"Yes, Daddy?" I tease.

"Fuck." He yanks me toward him and kisses me hard, his tongue sliding into my mouth.

I moan, my body burning for his touch. It has been ever since he made me come on his desk.

He finally pulls away, his eyes dark with lust. "I told you in my office that was the last time," he says gruffly.

I tilt my head, unsure where I get the nerves to do what I do next. Dropping to my knees before him, I grab the zipper of his pants. "But I didn't take care of you, it's only—"

He grabs my wrist, eyes as black as obsidian as he stares down at me. "What are you doing?"

"Just let me taste you in return," I breathe.

His jaw is so hard set it looks like it's made from granite before he releases my wrist with a silent nod. I unzip his pants, and my heart kicks into overdrive as I find he's not wearing any underwear. Feeling the velvety hardness of him as I pull his cock through the fly in his pants.

I moan when I see it, as it's far bigger than I'd imagined. "How come you aren't wearing any underwear?"

"Because I've been like a fucking horny teenager lately. It makes it easier to jerk myself off in the bathroom." His voice is hoarse.

I lick my lips. "Why have you been so horny?" His cock jerks in my hand.

"You know why."

I return my attention to his cock. "So big." I move my hand up and down his shaft, watching as a bead of precum pools at the tip.

"Can I have a taste?" I whisper.

Remy looks like a God above me. "Just this once. After this, nothing can happen between us ever again."

I move my mouth toward his cock, but Remy grabs my hair and stops me.

"Tell me you understand."

"I understand, Daddy," I murmur. As deep down we both know that's not true. He keeps insisting nothing can happen one second and then touching me the next. It's clear he's as out of control as I feel.

"Have you ever had a cock in your mouth before, angel?"

Heat spreads through my body and rises to my skin as I shake my head. I have no experience whatsoever with sex. Besides a few crappy kisses in high school, I've never done anything with a guy.

"No," I breathe.

Remy groans. "Good, I'm glad mine will be the first."

I moan and lower my mouth over his cock, swirling my tongue around the tip and coaxing a deep growl from him as I do.

Remy thrusts his hips, forcing the huge size into my throat. I gag, and tears collect at the corners of my eyes as he starts to dominate the moment, fucking my face hard. Saliva spills from my mouth all over his pants, making a mess.

"That's it, baby. Take my cock in your throat just like that." He thrusts again. "You're doing so well. You're such a good girl."

The pulse between my thighs heightens at his praise, and I've never felt more desperate. I slide my fingers under the hem of my dress and touch my clit, moaning around his cock.

I'm so sensitive; I know I'll come in no time. I want to straddle Remy and sink every inch of his thick cock inside me.

"God, Ella," he growls above me as his movements become more erratic. "I'm going to come down your throat, and I want you to swallow every drop. Okay?"

I nod in response, knowing any second, I'll come too.

"Good girl," he says moments before his cock swells and releases, shooting his cum into the back of my throat.

The sensation shocks me, and I gag and choke, trying to swallow but unable to keep up. Remy's release forces mine as I shudder on my knees. An intense orgasm tears through me as I lick and clean his cock. Finally, once he's clean, I move away and draw a deep breath of oxygen.

"You missed a few drops, angel." He swipes the cum from my face with a finger. "Open wide."

I moan as I open my mouth, and he slips his fingers inside.

"Suck them clean," he orders.

I suck on his fingers with the same eagerness of his cock, wishing it wasn't over.

"So naturally submissive, cleaning my fingers like a good girl," he breathes, eyes still darkened with desire.

Reality slaps me in the face hard once we both recover from our highs. Remy tucks his cock back into his pants, and his expression hardens. "I meant it. That's the last time."

My stomach dips as I sit back down opposite me. "But why does it have to be?"

"Don't push me. You'll be engaged to someone else in two weeks and you have to be a virgin." He runs a hand through his hair. "I'm just warning you to be careful around Alex."

I grind my teeth. "What if I want you instead?"

"You don't want me, Ella. You know nothing about me." His fists clench by his sides. "I'm dark and rotten and broken. You are light and life and pure fucking innocence. Do you know what happens when the two clash?"

I don't reply as it's rhetorical.

"Darkness always infects, and I'll corrupt you."

"Maybe I want to be corrupted," I breathe.

He laughs, but it's humorless. "You don't know what you're talking about. Do you know what one of the Morrone family's businesses is?"

Despite my research and probing Mia, I have no idea what exactly they do. I shake my head.

"We traffic women."

He says that as if he told me he works for fucking McDonalds. "What?"

"You heard me. We've been doing it for years."

"How can you sell women like me, Mia, and Camilla into a life of slavery?"

He shakes his head. "That's what I'm trying to get you to understand. I don't have any morals. It's business. Plain and simple."

"No, you can't believe that." I hate that my chest feels like it's being torn in two. I knew Remy wasn't a good man, but this... It's sick. After feeling so hot and desperate for more from him, his admission curdles my stomach. Trafficking is completely and utterly wrong. And I can't condone it.

"The Morrone family has built its name on sex trafficking of women. I don't have any issue with it. Do you still want me, Ella?"

I can't even speak. Instead, I turn away and focus on the lights flashing past the window. Tears prickle my eyes as somehow I could accept or perhaps ignore the fact he sold drugs and arms and did terrible things, but this…

His confession makes me sick to my stomach. And my brain screams, no, I don't want him, but my body. I still crave this wicked man's touch. No matter what he's done or does. It's sick, and I want to scream at myself for it.

"Answer me, baby."

That nickname. Shivers travel up my spine as I look into his eyes.

"I wish I didn't because what you do makes me sick."

There's a fire in his eyes as he leans closer. "But you still want me?"

"My body does, but my mind..." I shake my head, not sure how to put it into words. "I want you to stop trafficking women."

He stares at me for a few moments as if contemplating it. "I'll think about it."

My brow furrows. "Really?"

"Don't look too much into it. Massimo has been on to me about nipping it in the bud for a while. It's messy, dangerous, and not as lucrative as it used to be."

I swallow hard as he's only thinking about stopping trafficking because it doesn't make him enough money. "You're a monster."

"I think I told you that before. You decided not to believe me." He moves closer again and grabs my throat. "Instead, you've romanticized me. Haven't you?"

I hate that he's right.

"Answer me," he demands.

"I don't know."

"The fact is, baby, there's nothing romantic about me. I decimate everything in my path, and if I had you." His eyes clamp shut as if he's struggling to continue. "Fuck, you'd be mine forever. I'd never let you go, no matter how hard you begged me. I'm obsessed with you, Ella. And that can never end well. It's better for the both of us that you move on, and we forget about this silly infatuation we both have for one another."

Somehow, his words make me forget he's a monster. "What if I want to be yours forever?"

An animal-like growl tears from his chest, and just as he's about to speak, the car stops.

My brow furrows because that was too fast for us to be home. When I glance out, I see we're not at the house. "Where are we?"

"I've been meaning to show you this place for a

while. Come on." He gets out and turns around to offer me his hand.

I take it, sparks of electricity igniting the moment we touch.

I'm surprised when he doesn't let it go. Instead, he laces our fingers together and walks through huge stone pillars. It feels so natural, and all I want is to hold on and never let go, despite his disgusting confession about what the Morrone family does.

We walk into the dimly lit garden in silence until Remy speaks. "I found this place after I survived cancer. It's fittingly called the Cancer Survivor's Garden."

Her eyes widen slightly. "Why are you showing me?"

"Because I realized you've lost a lot, Ella. And this place brought me peace after surviving cancer, but also from the loss I've felt in my life." His dark eyes find mine. "I thought it might do the same for you."

I squeeze his hand as no one has cared about my feelings, not even my mom. Losing my dad at eleven years old changed me. And my mom's insensitive reaction didn't help.

"Thank you," I breathe.

It's all I can say.

Remy nods and leads me further into the garden. We walk around in contemplative silence, and I reflect on Mom's death and why I've been struggling to work out my feelings over it. Grief but guilt too at being relieved initially to have my freedom back. My bank account and my life, all for it to have been snatched away by Remy.

The moon is high in the sky, casting a glow across the city when we return to the car. It's been a beautiful night, and Remy's hand still encases mine. He opens the door to the car, and I slide in, waiting for him to join me.

This time, he sits next to me, slides an arm around my shoulders, and pulls me into his chest. I rest my head against it, knowing that as soon as we get home, this spell he has cast upon me will be shattered, and reality will come rushing back in.

18

ELLA

"*R*eady?" Mia asks, standing in the doorway of my bedroom.

I smile at her. "Yes, let's do this."

We walk down the stairs and out the front door to the limousine waiting for us. I find Luca and Leo in the back, but there's no sign of Remy.

"Where's your dad?" I ask.

"He can't make it."

I swallow hard, wondering if he's staying away because he can't stand watching me with another man. A part of me wishes he'd cut the crap and accept that we both want each other, consequences be damned.

But the car is already pulling away, and I can't dwell on it anymore. We drive through the city, taking in the sights and sounds of Chicago.

Mia clears her throat. "So, are you sticking with Alex?"

I look at her and smile. Alex Vishekov is sweet,

handsome, and charming I should want him more than I want Remy. "Yeah, he's nice."

She smiles. "Alex is handsome. I think you two will make a great couple."

Leo clears his throat. "Still time to try out your two stepbrothers before you seal the deal." He winks.

I stick my fingers down my throat. "I'd rather ram skewers into my eyes."

Luca laughs, and so do Mia and Leo. "I've got to admit, you fit into this family like a missing piece," Mia says, squeezing my hand. "I'm so glad you're my stepsister."

Guilt slides through me like a viper, twisting around my heart until it squeezes painfully as I look down at our hands.

Would she still say that if she knew the things I've done with her dad?

We've crossed the line too often. The thought of kissing Alex doesn't inspire the toe-curling desire that kissing Remy does. Maybe it's the taboo and forbidden aspect. A novelty I need to forget and move on from.

But no matter how hard I try, Remy keeps sinking under my skin.

The car finally pulls up outside the restaurant, and I take a deep breath. Lunch without him staring at me like a predator waiting to pounce should provide an escape from my tangled emotions. Mia squeezes my hand again before we climb out of the car and head inside.

I'm surrounded by luxurious decor and glittering crystal, but as I try to focus on my surroundings, all I can think about is Remy. Even when he's not here it's like he's always there in the back of my mind.

I shake my head and force a breath between my lips. I need to focus on the present and the man I'm likely to get engaged to in less than two weeks.

As we step inside the main dining room, the familiar notes of the recent pop hit, "Levitating" by Dua Lipa, fill the air. The drumbeat syncs with my racing heart, a rhythmic backdrop to our entrance. Despite the internal war waging within me, I can't help but tap my foot to the tune.

But the further I try to push Remy from my mind, the more the thoughts of him push back. He's everywhere: in my thoughts, in my dreams, and even in this restaurant, as if his presence is haunting me from a distance.

"Ella," Alex's deep, alluring voice speaks from behind me.

I force a smile and turn to face him. "Alex. It's good to see you."

He takes my hand and kisses the back of it. I hate that I make comparisons. I don't feel that spark when our hands touch or when our eyes meet. There's nothing there. Not like there is when Remy looks at me.

"Shall we take our seats?"

"Sure," I respond, and we walk toward the elegantly set table.

Alex's piercing blue eyes are fixed on me. "How have you been since we last met?"

I shrug. "Fine. I've not been up to a lot. What about you?"

There's an odd flash in his eyes as he clears his throat. "Working mostly."

"Your father keeps you busy in the family business?" I ask.

He admitted to me that his family is mafia, like all of them here, and they mainly make money through arms. It made me feel a little sick. And yet, finding out Remy traffics women for money didn't stop me from craving his touch, his kiss.

I need to be put into a mental health facility as clearly I'm not in my right mind.

"Yes, I'm learning the ropes, ready to take over as pakhan."

My brow furrows. "pakhan?"

"I forget you're new to the mafia world. It's the word for a leader in Russian."

"Oh." I nod. "And you will take over from him soon?"

He shakes his head. "I hope not. My dad isn't dead, and until he is, I won't step up as pakhan."

I suppress a shudder as I imagine what growing up in the mafia world must be like. The violence and corruption play on my mind, but I try not to let it show.

"Have you always known what your dad does?" I ask, changing the subject.

Alex nods. "It wasn't kept from me when I was a child."

"That must have been odd to know that at such a young age."

There's a pause as Alex watches me. "It's all I ever

knew." His brow furrows a little. "Never really thought of it as odd."

My jaw clenches as I realize I'm the minority of people here who believe their businesses are morally wrong. "And you never thought it was wrong?"

He smiles. It's a wicked smile. "Of course, but I was never taught to have a moral code."

I swallow hard. My dad always ensured I knew right from wrong, even if he worked for bad people. On the other hand, Mom didn't care how she got her money as long as there was a lot of it.

"You seem distracted. Is something bothering you?"

"No, I'm just in my head. It's crazy that I will be sold in less than two weeks."

He leans back, scrutinizing me with a seriousness I find unnerving. "I assume you aren't a willing participant of this auction? Your stepdad forced it upon you?"

The mention of Remy makes my heart beat so loud I'm sure he can hear it. "I didn't choose to be sold, if that's what you mean. No. Do any of these girls?" I ask, glancing around the restaurant.

Alex nods. "Most expect it from a young age. I guess you stumbled into this world. How did you adjust?"

I remain silent for a moment, searching for the right words. "I... I don't know. I'm not sure I have adjusted."

He squeezes my hand. "I can help you. If you were my wife, I'd care for you and help you adjust."

I like Alex, and marrying him is my best option. "I hope you do win me, but the amount of money Remy expects for me is ridiculous."

He arches a brow. "Ten million is the reserve. You'll go for far more than that."

I shake my head. "Why pay so much? Surely you can find a wife without an auction?"

He nods. "I could, but she's unlikely to have the connections the girls here have."

"So it's all business?" I don't appreciate that Alex is interested in me solely because I can give him power.

"It was, but then I met you." He smiles, and my stomach flutters. "And you're something special. A beautiful gem."

I give him a skeptical look. "Right, does that line work on all the girls?"

He laughs, shaking his head. "Sorry, I didn't mean to sound cheesy."

"You know, I tried to run away before the first auction dinner."

He looks surprised that I'm telling him this. "What happened?"

"That's why Remy froze my bank account. He knew I'd purchased plane tickets and was intending to run. I had no money to make my escape." I clench my jaw as I remember the way I'd intended to confront him and ended up coming on his face.

"Makes sense now why he froze your account to be fair, but that must have pissed you off."

I nod but the heat at the memories of our time in his office makes me feel like I'm on fire. "Yeah, it's just hard to accept."

"Would being married to me be that bad?"

I tilt my head. "That remains a mystery. Would you control everything I do?"

"No, you'd have as much freedom as you desired. I don't intend to lock my wife up. You'll be my queen, Ella." His ice-blue eyes dazzle with fire, and I wish I felt more excitement about being made a queen by this charming man.

"Then I think I would be lucky to marry you."

He smiles, and while the smile warms me, it does nothing to inspire the desire I wish I felt. We fall into comfortable conversation as if we are old friends. It's a shame friendship is all I feel for the man I will probably spend the rest of my life with.

19

REMY

I pace in front of our most senior men in the famiglia.

Giuseppe, Antoni, Federico and Edoardo.

"What is this about?" Massimo asks.

I halt and look at him. "I asked you to get me answers about Erin's murder, and what do I have?"

When none of them answer me, I continue, "Nothing. Where are we with the investigation?"

They exchange heated glances, and I sense their unease. "We've been working on it, Remy," Giuseppe says.

I narrow my eyes at him. "But what have you come up with? Nothing? How long has it been now? Weeks? Months?"

The men look away from me, not wanting to answer. I know they don't have anything. I'm quickly losing my patience, and just as fast, the room fills with dangerous energy. "Someone needs to talk, or else it'll lose it."

I can feel the tension escalating, and it's clear that they are all scared of me. Finally, Edoardo speaks up.

"Remy, we're doing everything possible to uncover who killed Erin. We need more time and resources. Please don't lose faith in us yet. I swear we won't let you down."

I take a few deep breaths and fill my lungs with air. "Every day that passes without avenging her death makes me look weak." They're trying their best, but it's not good enough. "Get more men on it. I want results soon."

They all nod in agreement and scatter, leaving me alone.

Massimo lingers behind. "Why are you so obsessed with finding the killer? You didn't love Erin."

I glare at him. "It doesn't matter. She was my wife, and someone touched what was mine," I growl, clenching my fists by my sides. "They'll pay."

"I've got a hunch but no evidence," he admits.

I narrow my eyes. "What kind of hunch?"

He looks hesitant about answering that question.

"Tell me, son."

"I think the Vishekov Bratva may have been behind her death."

A pit widens in my stomach as if that were the case, then Ella is in danger. As we speak, she's at a pre-auction lunch with Alex Vishekov, but she has Mia, Luca, and Leo to escort her. I had to stay away after the last time. Watching her with anyone other than me drives me crazy because she's my obsession.

"Dad?"

I shake my head. "What?"

"Did you hear what I said?"

"Yes. What makes you think Vishekov is behind it?"

Massimo grinds his teeth. "As I said, it's a hunch. But the casino Erin had been in before she was murdered on the streets belongs to Vishekov's nephew, Dimity Egorov."

"Vishekov has ties to the Las Vegas Bratva?" I confirm.

He nods. "Yes, it's not something he publicizes, but it's possible he used his family connections to get her murdered. After all, Gregor has been after Chicago territory for years."

"Ella," I breathe.

"What about her?"

"She's at a pre-auction lunch right now with Alex Vishekov. He singled her out the moment we stepped into the first dinner."

Massimo looks concerned. "Do you think she's in danger?"

"I don't know, but I won't take any chances. I'm going straight over there to make sure she's alright."

He nods in agreement before heading out the door. "Let me know what you find out," he says over his shoulder as he leaves.

I grab my coat and car keys before walking out behind him. I have to ensure Ella is safe before it's too late.

My blood boils as I drive, a sense of dread curling in my stomach at the thought of Alex Vishekov hurting her. He may be a smooth talker with money and connections, but he isn't getting away with hurting my family. Not on my watch.

As I navigate through the city's web of roads, the thunderous roar of Metallica's "Enter Sandman" blasts from the car stereo. The aggressive melody somehow mirrors my inner turmoil. I put Ella in harm's way. I'm the reason she's an asset in this auction. It's a grim soundtrack to the gnawing fear in my gut as I near the restaurant.

I park the car outside on double yellows, not giving a shit, and march inside, determined to ensure Ella is safe. I can't raise Vishekov's suspicions until we're sure it was him, but once I am... I'll delight in taking Gregor's and Alex's lives.

The lunch is finished, and some of the attendees are leaving. Luca and Leo are sitting still directly opposite Ella and Alex. Mia is sitting by Ella's side, and instantly, I relax. My family is taking care of her.

Luca spots me first, and his brow furrows as he gets up and comes to greet me. "What are you doing here?"

"Massimo believes the Vishekov Bratva were behind Erin's murder," I say quietly so no one else can hear.

His eyes flash with barely contained rage. My son's leadership skills are wasted in his teaching, but it's like talking to a brick wall. "That's why he's so interested in Ella?"

I clench my jaw. "We don't have any evidence yet other than uncovering family links to the Egorov Bratva."

"We should get Ella away from him now," Luca says, his voice feral.

I shake my head and rest my hand on my son's shoulder. "We're here. She's safe. The last thing we want to do is rouse suspicion. They can't know that we're on to them."

"Fine. You missed the food, though."

I shrug. "I'll survive."

Ella hasn't noticed me yet, and I prefer it that way. She's more at ease than I've ever seen her, and I wonder if that's because she's unaware of my presence.

I want her to see me. I want to see those pretty blue eyes flash with fire.

She doesn't look at Alex the way she looks at me.

"I need a drink." I walk up to the bar and wish I hadn't when I see Gregor fucking Vishekov standing there.

"Scotch on the rocks," I order.

The bartender nods and gets me a drink.

I can see Vishekov looking at me from the corner of my eye, but I try to ignore him.

"Remy. I didn't think you were attending."

I glance at him. "I had a meeting that ran over, so I'm late."

He nods. "Of course, you're a busy man."

The bartender brings me my drink. "It was good speaking with you," I lie, moving away.

He places a hand on my forearm. "Don't you think we should get to know each other better?" His eyes dart toward Ella and Alex. "We're likely to be family soon." His smirk makes me want to punch it from his face. I made up my mind when Massimo told me that the Vishekov family may have been behind Erin's murder.

She's not being sold. I'll pay the fucking reserve on her.

"That remains to be seen."

"Alex and Ella are getting on well. She'll have a good life with him."

I clench my jaw. "Money will talk when it comes to it."

"Don't worry, we have plenty of money to buy your stepdaughter."

I nod my head. "Fine, I'll see you around." I walk away from him before I do something stupid and go to the opposite side of the restaurant, sitting on a plush sofa where I have a good view of Ella.

She's still unaware I'm here, watching her in the shadows like a creep. I am a creep. And now it's come to light that the Vishekov Bratva can't be trusted, I'm no longer going to hold back.

As if she feels my stare, her eyes meet mine. A flash of fire ignites in them as I lift my glass to her.

Her brow furrows, and she turns to Alex, excusing herself.

I shouldn't let her approach, but I do.

She walks over and takes a seat opposite me.

"I thought you were staying away." Her eyes narrow. "Why are you here?"

I sip my scotch before leaning forward with my elbows on my thighs. "Because I am. Is that a problem?"

She tilts her head. "Are you going to be able to control your anger issues? I'm going to continue talking to Alex."

"Is that what you want, Ella? To be married to Alex Vishekov?"

Her jaw clenches. "You know it's not."

Well, she's going to get her wish tonight. Once this stupid fucking lunch ends, I'm taking her away for the weekend. Away from all of this to figure out what the fuck is going on between us.

"When you get home, I want you to pack. Warm clothes. Enough for a weekend."

Her brow furrows. "What for?"

"No questions. Just do it." I walk back to the bar with my empty scotch glass before I change my mind.

Learning Vishekov might be behind her mother's death has made me reevaluate my plan. Who knows who will buy her as a wife or why? I assumed it would keep her safe, but the only way to ensure her safety is to keep her by my side.

20

ELLA

*R*emy grabs my suitcase off me and places it in the back of his SUV alongside one other case. I swallow hard at the look in his eyes. He looks a little insane. If I'm honest, I've never seen him like this.

"Are you going to tell me where we're going?"

His dark eyes find mine. "Get in."

A shudder races down my spine. "Not until you tell me where you're taking me." I raise my chin.

His jaw clenches, and he steps closer to me. "Get in the car before I throw you in, Ella."

I feel particularly brave, taking a step closer to him. "No. You don't get to order me around like that anymore."

His jaw works. "Are you trying to piss me off?"

I cross my arms over my chest. "I'm fed up with this hot and cold treatment. Tell me where you're taking me."

The anger in his eyes intensifies, and he pushes me up against the car, his huge body covering mine.

Heat slams into me as I clench my thighs together.

"You're walking a dangerous line, angel."

I search his dark, intense eyes. "I'm getting whiplash from you, Remy. Make up your mind. Do you want me or not?"

His nostrils flare, and a wicked smirk splits his face. "Careful. It's a bad idea to ask questions you're not ready to hear the answer to."

"I want you." I lift my chin and meet his intense gaze. "That's all I know. What do you want?"

"I want you to get in the fucking car," he growls.

"Then tell me where we're going."

"It's a surprise." He grabs my wrist and yanks me toward the car door. "Get. In. I won't ask again." He releases my wrist, glaring at me as he opens the door.

I don't know why I feel so disobedient, but I run into the wooded area near the driveway instead of getting in.

"Ella!" he growls my name like a feral animal. "Don't make me chase you."

My heart rate kicks up as I sprint through the forest, enjoying the feel of the wind rushing through my hair. I laugh, feeling free.

What's the worst that can happen?

I want him to chase me. I want him to react and stop ordering me about. Spank me. Kiss me. Fuck me. I want everything from him, but I'm unsure how to get it.

The thud of heavy footsteps chasing me makes me sprint harder.

"Stop!" he shouts.

I dodge around a tree and head in a different direction, rushing away from him. "No!"

"Fuck!"

I can hear him getting closer, and fear and excitement heighten at the thought of him catching me. My fantasies have become darker and more perverse the longer we play this game.

Suddenly, his arms wrap around my waist, lifting me off the ground. "Big mistake," he says, his tone dark.

I squeal as he throws me down onto my back in the forest. His huge body covering mine as he pins me to the ground, nostrils flaring and jaw hard set. He's angry and turned on.

"What the fuck do you think you're playing at?" He asks.

I lick my lips as I feel his cock hard and pressed against my center. "I don't like being ordered about."

"Liar," he purrs, lifting the hem of my skirt. "I can see how wet you are through your fucking panties. You love it."

I arch my back at his touch. "Remy," I breathe his name. "I want you."

His jaw clenches. "Come with me in the car, and we'll work this out."

"What is there to work out?" I arch further, grinding myself on him. "We both know what we want." I challenge.

He shakes his head and wraps a palm around my throat, squeezing hard enough to restrict my oxygen. "You're poking a fucking bear, Ella. Careful. I have no intention of taking your virginity out here like a feral animal." He releases my throat.

I lick my lips. "But you intend to take it?"

A muscle contracts in his jaw. "No."

I grunt and push him, but he doesn't budge. "Get off me."

"Not until you promise me that you'll behave."

I sigh, letting my body relax beneath his. "Fine," I grumble. "Just get off me already."

He stands up, looking as angry as ever, extending a hand to help me back to my feet. I take it with reluctance, and we return to the car. Silence falls between us, punctuated by the crunch of leaves beneath our feet.

He opens the car door and helps me in with an almost tender gesture. "Let's get out of here," he says, walking to the driver's side and starting the engine. We pull away from the Morrone mansion.

As we drive, I can feel my heart pounding. I sense that Remy is about to give me something I've been craving since we met: something wild, something wicked. And I'm ready for it.

Once we leave Chicago and head onto country lanes, I place my hand on his thigh.

He growls and looks at me. "Ella."

I tilt my head. "Yes, *Daddy*?"

"What are you doing?" he can barely speak.

I don't reply and unzip his pants, making him tense. "You were very hard back there. I think you need help with that."

"Ella," he growls my name in warning. "If you disobey me, you won't like the consequences."

"What kind of consequences? Are you going to spank me?"

"Fuck," he growls to himself, his cock twitching beneath my hand. He's staring forward, gripping the steering wheel so hard his knuckles are white.

I reach into his pants and pull his cock out, and he groans from my touch. The power trip it gives me is intoxicating, knowing I can affect him from my touch alone.

Leaning down, I drag my tongue around the tip.

"You're going to make me crash the car, baby." His voice is deep and ragged.

I shake my head. "I trust you can drive while I do this." I open my mouth and take his length as deeply as I can in my throat. He leaks precum, making me moan as his masculine taste overwhelms me.

"God damn it." He grabs a fistful of my hair, his other hand gripping the steering wheel hard.

I suck on the head of his cock before taking every inch down my throat, gagging as I do. The need to please him drives me.

He forces me down harder, and I gag so much I think I'll puke. "Good girl," he praises, his dick twitching in my mouth. "Take every inch of me."

I moan as my eyes flutter shut, and I focus on breathing through my nose.

My throat tenses as I take him deeper. I pull back, swirling my tongue around the thick head. He jerks his hips against me, and I know he's close to coming.

The car swerves slightly. His muscles tense as he lets out a low guttural groan, spilling his cum down my throat. I swallow his salty essence as his ragged breathing fills the air. Once I've cleaned him up, I sit back in my chair and gaze at him.

He takes a deep breath and looks over at me with fire in his eyes. "You're a very naughty girl, Ella."

I bite my bottom lip. "Does that mean you're going to punish me?"

"Yes, it does." He doesn't say another word, and a tense silence fills the car.

I clear my throat. "Have you got anything to drink?"

He smirks at me and passes me a bottle of water. "Here."

I'm unsure why he's happy I asked for a drink. My throat hurts from taking him down it, so I down the entire bottle.

I drift off to sleep as I sit in the passenger's seat. Lulled into a sense of security by the car's soft movement and the engine's rumble.

I DON'T KNOW how long I've been sleeping, but suddenly, I feel something inside me.

My whole body feels heavy as I open my eyes.

Remy is between my thighs when I wake. "What the—"

He places a finger against my lips. "Quiet."

I groan as I feel his fingers slipping in and out of my

soaking wet pussy. Neediness sweeps over me as I arch my back, trying to get more from him. "Remy."

"How do you feel?"

I swallow hard. "Weird." I meet his gaze, and his eyes are flashing with dark delight. "What did you do?"

"Drugged you."

My mouth falls open. "What?"

"Don't worry, they were only sleeping pills." He sucks on my clit.

I try to lift my arms and realize they're chained to the bedpost. "Unchain me," I demand.

"Did you forget that you're due a punishment?"

I swallow hard. "No."

"I told you to be careful what you wish for, didn't I?" He slams his fingers back inside of me. "Now there's no going back."

I gaze into his eyes. "I don't want to go back."

His eyes narrow. "Don't be so sure. Once you realize the darkness inside me, you'll probably run in the opposite direction."

"Perhaps there's darkness in me, too."

He chuckles. "You're pure fucking light, Ella." He dips between my thighs, and my hips rise as he licks me. "I'm going to corrupt you."

"Good," I reply. "Then fucking get on with it."

He moves forward and wraps his palm around my throat, squeezing harder than ever. "I don't like disobedient and entitled brats. Now be a good girl for me and stay quiet."

I melt at the dominant tone of his voice, relaxing into the soft mattress. "Yes, *Daddy*."

"That's more like it," he growls before devouring me.

I've got to admit, this is a pretty amazing punishment.

My hips arch toward him as I try to get more friction, wanting him to make me come so bad. He slides two thick fingers inside me, making me moan.

"That's it, baby. Moan for me," he growls, watching me as he feasts on me.

Remy's experienced fingers continue their rhythm, moving in and out of me, hitting the right spot. His tongue lashes against my clit, and a wave of pleasure pierces me. I can feel the heat pooling in my lower belly, the telltale sign of my impending climax. But as I'm about to tip over the edge, he pulls away, leaving me panting and writhing in frustration.

"Don't you dare come yet," he warns gruffly, a devilish grin on his lips. "This is your punishment, remember?" My protests are met with a sharp pinch to my inner thigh before he dives back in, bringing me to the brink again before backing off, the cycle repeating and driving me to insanity. The pleasure is so intense it's almost unbearable. His every touch and stroke designed to tease and torment me, a punishment veiled in pleasure.

"Please..." I whimper, writhing underneath him. My hands yank at the chains, my body trembling from the relentless pleasure he's subjecting me to. "Daddy, please... I need..."

"What do you need?" he taunts, his lips brushing against my thigh, his breath hot against my skin.

"I... I need to..." I stammer, my voice barely more than a whisper as I try to articulate the desperate need building within me. "Please make me come."

"That's right, baby. Beg for it," he growls. But instead of granting my request, he only increases the pace of his fingers, continuing to deny me the release I am craving. "Not yet. Understand?"

His refusal drives me to the edge of sanity, the pleasure too intense, too consuming. I can hardly think, my mind filled with the overwhelming desire for release. But I know better than to disobey him now. "Yes," I gasp, my voice filled with desperation.

And with that, he stops completely.

"What are you doing?" I ask.

"It wouldn't be a punishment if I gave you pleasure, would it?"

I yank at the restraints. "No. You can't leave me like this."

He stands up and adjusts the bulge in his pants. "I can and I will. You have a lot to learn about the man you *believe* you want. I will possess you, dominate you, and completely and utterly ruin you so you'll never want another man."

I pant for oxygen. "You've already done that."

He tilts his head. "What do you mean?"

"I should have wanted Alex—"

He growls. "Don't."

"Let me finish. I should have. He was young, handsome, and charming, but I felt nothing when he touched me."

"I know," he says.

"How?"

"Because you didn't look at him the way you look at me."

I'm not sure what he sees in my eyes, but whatever it is, it makes him step closer to the bed. He leans over, his lips a whisper away from my own. "You know what's coming next?" he asks softly.

I swallow hard. "No."

He leans in until his breath tickles my ear. "This." His lips brush against mine, gentle and teasing at first, then urgent and demanding when I open to him without hesitation. He kisses me with a hunger that takes my breath away, his tongue caressing mine. "You'll wait for release like a good girl, won't you, Ella?"

I swallow hard and nod.

"Rest, angel."

He turns and leaves me chained on the bed, legs spread open and my pussy throbbing. This is what I wanted, but it feels like torture. All I want is to feel my stepdad inside me, tearing away my virginity like the beast I know he is.

21

REMY

*M*y common sense has entirely shattered. The moment I pulled Ella from the auction and paid the organizers her retainer, I knew there was no avoiding this.

I may not have wanted to admit it, but I've never felt this way about a woman before in my life.

Ella is currently chained to the bed, gagging for release. She's been like that for four hours. I haven't told her yet that the auction is off, and I'm not selling her.

I watch her on the camera I installed, my cock hard in my briefs. Despite the fact I've already taken care of myself twice while watching her, not to mention she sucked me off in the car. It's like my dick is demanding I fuck her, and until then, I'll be hard as nails.

I chuck my phone down on the sofa, running a hand through my hair. It took some convincing to get the auctioneer to pull Ella off the auction, but I wasn't taking no for an answer. I had to pay her reserve and then some, but she's worth every fucking penny.

Ella is mine.

She's been mine since the moment we met. It's a fact that I've been trying to ignore and failing miserably. When you ignore something you need for too long, it makes you crazy. Now I've lost it.

Ella might not survive me.

But it's too late. I won't let her go, no matter the cost. She will never leave my side again. I'll make sure of that. She will crave me by the time I'm through with her. Even the darkest depths of my soul.

The line between stepdad and stepdaughter has been obliterated. However, she'll be calling me *Daddy* all night long.

Standing, I walk along the corridor in my cabin to the bedroom where Ella is passed out on the bed. When I woke her earlier, the drugs hadn't fully worn off.

They should have now. The look on my angel's face when I wouldn't allow her to come was priceless. She's used to me being in control, and I plan on keeping it that way.

Opening the door, I see her lying there wearing nothing. Her hair is splayed across the pillow behind her head like a halo as she sleeps peacefully, despite the chains keeping her in an awkward position.

My eyes trace down her body, taking in every curve. She's got a full figure with wide hips and big, firm breasts that I want to spend all night worshipping. I step closer and can feel the heat radiating off her.

My cock twitches in anticipation as I move closer, wanting desperately to ravage her. But not yet. I get onto the bed, the mattress compressing from my weight, and kneel between her thighs. I lean down and suck on her clit while she sleeps, making her make incoherent sounds.

I move my hands up and down her body, exploring every inch of her. Slowly, she wakes.

"Remy?" her voice is sleepy.

"Hey, baby," I breathe, kissing my way up her inner thigh. "How do you feel?"

"Like I need to come."

I chuckle. "Shame you don't get to yet. It's time for dinner."

Her nostrils flare. "Are you serious?"

I wrap my palm around her throat. "Yes, and do you know why?"

Ella shakes her head. "Because if we're going to do this, we're going to do it right."

She raises her brow. "What exactly is right?"

"I've cooked you dinner, and you can dress up for our date."

"Date?" Her throat bobs as she swallows.

"Yes, now I will unlock these restraints, but you must promise me something."

"Anything, Daddy," she replies.

Fuck's sake. I wish Ella calling me *Daddy* didn't drive me to the brink of losing it.

"No touching my cunt, do you understand? It belongs to me now, and I will control all your orgasms from now on."

Her eyes flicker shut, and she moans. "Okay, I promise."

"Good girl," I praise.

I unlock her restraints, and she stretches her arms up with a groan. The movement draws my attention to her hard nipples, which I take into my mouth, sucking on each one.

"Remy," she whines, running her fingers through my hair. "That's not fair."

"Sorry, they were there and begging to be sucked." I spank her ass. "Now go shower and get ready for dinner."

Her jaw clenches. "And I'm not allowed to touch myself in the shower?"

"No," I growl, grabbing her chin. "And I'll know if you do because I've got a camera in there."

"That's a little perverted."

I arch a brow. "I have to keep an eye on you, don't I?"

She releases a long sigh and then jumps out of bed, strutting toward the adjoining bathroom. Before she gets to the door, she looks over her shoulder at me. "Why don't you join me?"

She's a fucking vixen considering she's a virgin.

"While I'd love to, I have dinner to cook."

Ella pouts but then walks into the bathroom, her hips swaying and drawing my eyes to her naked form.

She's the most exquisite thing I've ever seen. Curvy in all the right places.

I shake my head and take a deep breath, forcing myself to turn away. I need to get dinner ready before she comes out. We're in the middle of nowhere, and Ella must be starving.

I call up the video camera in the shower and put my

cell phone propped against a mug by the chopping board. If she even thinks about touching herself, I'll march back in there and tie her up again. My cock throbs as I see her threading her hands through her hair and lathering shampoo.

The cabin is well stocked, and I bought supplies with me, too. I get to work chopping the vegetables for *Melanzane alla parmigiana*. I've not cooked for years. When I was getting to know Giada, my first wife, I used to cook for her. We may have had an arranged marriage, but we became good friends.

While neither of us professed love for each other, we had mutual respect and were attracted to each other. But what I feel for Ella is different. It's profound and impossible to ignore.

Once I've got all the vegetables sauteed, I put together the dish and place it in the oven. Ella is still in the shower. Her hands braced against the wall as the water cascades down her back.

I wonder if she feels as confused as I do. If we do fuck tonight, I know I won't let her go. The problem is that Ella comes across as the kind of girl who longs for a fairytale love. Hell, she told me she believes in it. I don't do love. I'll fuck her. I'll possess her. She'll be mine. But love is not on the cards.

As I lean back against the counter with my phone in my hand, I need to take things into my own hands again. Rubbing my cock through my pants, I shut my eyes. I haven't been this fucking horny since I was a teenager.

The filthy things I want to do to that girl should be

illegal. The problem is Ella is so sweet and innocent, and my tastes are dark. I want to tie her up, choke her while I fuck her, make her almost pass out and see stars so that her orgasm is so explosive she won't know her own fucking name.

A virgin can't handle that shit, so I need to rein it in, at least at first. Before I know what I'm doing, my dick is in my hand, and I'm stroking myself. My balls ache for release as I picture her bent over in the shower, showing me her pretty virgin pussy and asking me to fuck it.

I groan as I imagine how good it will feel to slide myself inside her. It's going to become a reality tonight. Ella will be mine, no matter how twisted up that is.

My sweet little angel is going to be corrupted by darkness.

22

ELLA

I sit opposite Remy as he moves to the stereo in the corner of the room. The soft tune of "Call Out My Name" by the Weeknd adds to the romantic atmosphere as Remy dims the lights, drawing my attention to the lit candles on every surface, creating a soft glow across the wooden walls.

The scent of pine mingles with the tantalizing aroma of dinner, which Remy cooked.

If I thought this man couldn't be any more perfect, he cooks!

The crackling fireplace, the comforting, rustic décor, and the muted sounds of the surrounding woods outside the cabin make this an idyllic, romantic setting. It's our little world, perfectly secluded.

"Did you cook from scratch?" I ask.

He smiles at me, and it's a genuine, beautiful smile. A smile that threatens to make my heart explode. "Yes, I have hidden talents." If he smiled more often, I think I'd die.

I fear his hidden talents will make me want him more. "What's for dinner?"

"*Melanzane alla parmigiana,*" he says in perfect Italian, making my knees weak.

"Sounds sexy."

He tilts his head. "Do you like me speaking Italian?"

"Is the pope catholic?" I nod. "I think I love it."

His eyes flash, and he pulls out my chair. "Siediti, bellissima."

I sit, knowing I won't survive the entire dinner if he keeps talking Italian. "Where did you learn Italian?"

He arches a brow. "Both of my parents were Italian. They emigrated from Bologna."

"Oh, were you born in Italy?"

He shakes his head. "No. Chicago born and bred." He dishes me a helping of the food he cooked, which smells divine. "Now, enough about me, baby. I want to know about you."

"What do you want to know?" It's weird him paying any interest in me, as he's been so cold since the day we met.

"Everything," he answers as he helps himself to some of the food.

I shake my head. "There's not a lot to know." I pick up my fork and taste the food, groaning as it tastes as delicious as it smells. "Damn, this is good."

He smiles at me again, making butterflies erupt in my stomach. "What was your childhood like?"

The question hits me hard, making my stomach churn. "It was okay until my dad died."

Those dark and normally cold eyes soften. "How old were you?"

"Eleven."

His jaw clenches. "That must have been hard. I saw how difficult it was for my children when my first wife was killed."

"She was murdered as well, right?"

There's something dark in his eyes as he nods.

"Did you catch who did it?"

He tilts his head. "Yes and no."

My brow furrows.

"The individual who carried out her murder met a grizzly end. The family who were responsible didn't. Mia married into that family, in fact."

"What?" That is ridiculous. I can hardly imagine Mia would be okay with marrying into a family who were behind her mom's murder, but maybe I don't know her that well.

"There was very bad blood between the Callaghan family and ours. I also ordered the hit on his mom, which made us even."

I stare at Remy and wonder who he truly is, as I hardly know him. He talks of murdering people as if it were nothing but the weather. "Are you serious?"

He sips his wine. "Yes, it's an eye for an eye in our world, Ella."

I shake my head. "How can you be so cold?"

"I thought you knew what kind of man I am."

"I might know it, but I don't like it. What about the trafficking? Are you going to stop that?"

Remy stares at me for a few moments. "What if I don't?"

"Then I don't think I can do this." No matter how badly I want this man, I won't stand by his side while he sells women into slavery. "If you want me, you stop the trafficking."

He doesn't take his eyes off me. "Done."

"And whatever women you have captive, you let them all go home."

A muscle in his jaw flexes. "Deal."

"Just like that?" I ask. Surely, deconstructing an operation like that won't be very easy.

"I want you, Ella. And I'm willing to prove it." He tilts his head. "Just know that I'm still not a good man. I won't be able to stop the crime that the Morrone family is embroiled in, but the trafficking." He swallows hard. "I'll stop it for you."

I know he's not a good man. It's one reason I shouldn't want him.

"Okay," I breathe.

If he's willing to stop the trafficking for me, it proves he's willing to try. "When will it stop?"

He slips a hand into his jacket pocket and dials a number, placing it on the table on loudspeaker.

"Hey, what's up?" Massimo answers.

"Can you talk?" he asks.

"Yeah, what is it?"

I swallow hard as he doesn't take his eyes from me for a second.

"I want you to end the trafficking side of our business immediately."

There's a pause. "Are you being serious?"

"Yes. I want you to let go of the girls in our warehouse and ensure they get home."

Massimo clears his throat. "That's dangerous. What if they rat on us?"

"They won't because they don't know who holds them captive. Get it done. Now."

I clench my thighs together as the way he commands drives me crazy.

"What's with the urgency?" Massimo questions.

"I said get it done."

He exhales. "Sure. I'll let you know once everything is dismantled. It may take a week or two," Massimo replies. "We're going to piss off the Romanians, too."

"Fuck the Romanians. What are they going to do to us over here? Pay them off and tell them the contract is terminated. Simple."

"Sure thing. I've got to go." Massimo ends the call.

Remy takes a sip of his scotch. "The answer to your question is a week or two."

"You want me that badly?" I confirm.

"I want you more than anything I've ever wanted."

Butterflies take flight in my stomach. "What about the auction?"

"I paid your reserve and then some to release you from it."

"So you bought me?" Her eyes flash with rage. "I'm not a possession you can own."

His jaw clenches. "I paid them off, that's all." He tilts his head. "Don't tell me you wanted to spend the rest of your life with Alex Vishekov?" There's a flash of jealousy in his eyes.

I shrug. "I should have. He's my age, handsome, charming—"

Remy's growl cuts me off. "Careful, Ella. I don't want you thinking of any man other than me. Do you understand?"

I smirk at his possessiveness, nodding. "What happens now?"

Remy's brow furrows. "What do you want to happen?"

It's complicated. While I want this man more than anything, I can't see how we have a future.

He's my stepdad. His family won't accept it. I'd hate to think about what Mia would say if I ended up with her dad. *Fuck.*

I'd be her stepmom, and that would be weird.

And yet the answer is that I want him to take me into that bedroom and fuck me.

"I don't know."

His eyes narrow. "Don't lie to me. You know what you want."

"And what do you want?" I ask.

We stare at each other for an eternity until Remy finally breaks the silence. "I want to fuck you."

I stand and walk over to him, touching his shoulder. "I want you to fuck me, too," I breathe.

An animal like growl tears from his lips. "Ella…"

"Yes, Daddy?" I ask.

I see his control snap as he grabs my hips and forces me to straddle him. His eyes darken, and he yanks a fistful of my hair, pulling my lips to his. We kiss as if it's our only way to survive. His hands grip me tight as our tongues fight for dominance.

"I don't just want you. I need you," he continues, peppering kisses across my neck and shoulders. "I need to hear you moan for me. I need to feel your virgin pussy wrapped around my cock. I need everything."

I claw at his hair. "I need it all, too."

The moment is electric, and I feel alive like never before. He stands and lifts me, carrying me down the corridor toward the bedroom. My heart is pounding erratically in my chest.

He drops me onto the bed and climbs between my thighs. His eyes look almost black as he stares down at me. "You've still got a chance to stop this, baby." His fingers move to my hard nipples, and he squeezes. "I'm not a gentle man. I'll devour you. I'll tear you apart."

I shudder as my pussy gets so wet my inner thighs are soaked. "Good," I reply.

"If we do this, there's no going back." He searches my eyes. "I won't let you go."

I hold his gaze as I understand the implications of us crossing the line.

"Remy shut up."

His eyes flash with rage, and I know it's not a good idea to push him.

"And fuck me."

He growls and shifts his weight so that I'm immobilized beneath him. "No one speaks to me like that."

I sink my teeth into my bottom lip. "What are you going to do to me?" I see the doubt rising in his eyes.

"Don't speak. Don't think." I grab his hand and press it to my breasts, forcing him to squeeze. "I need you. Don't spoil it."

"I don't let many people speak to me like that." He wraps his palm around my throat. "But you're the exception to all of my rules. I'm going to fuck you all night. You'll be so sore you'll feel me for days."

I try to swallow, but his grip is too tight, making me lightheaded. Nodding my head, I let him know I won't fight it.

He devours me as he moves down my body, licking and sucking until I'm screaming with pleasure. His mastery of my body is captivating, and when he finally slides his fingers inside me, I'm practically on fire.

This is happening. I'm going to sleep with my step-dad. There's no going back from this. All I can do is hope we're both on the same page.

23

REMY

I tear her panties off her and discard them to the side, parting her thick thighs as I stare at her beautiful virgin cunt.

I've never been so desperate to fuck.

I slide my tongue through her, groaning at how delicious she tastes. I tasted her for the first time only a few hours ago, and I'm addicted. One taste of her is like a hit of the most addicting drug on this planet.

She moans as I work on her clit, sliding my tongue through her center. I watch her as she throws her head back and her lips part. It's been too long since I made her come. Slowly, I build her back toward the edge. Soon enough, she's panting and writhing in the bedsheets.

"Please, Remy," she moans.

I smirk at her as she gazes down at me with those big blue eyes. "Not yet, baby." I let my tongue dip lower and probe her tight little ass.

She tenses and tries to pull away, but I place my hand on her stomach and hold her down. "What are you doing?"

"Exploring your perfect body." I look at her between her thighs. "Or should I say my perfect body, since it belongs to me now?"

She moans and plays with her nipples. The sight makes me crazy. Tightening my grasp on her thighs, I suck her clit into my mouth. Her hips rise off the mattress as she tries to get more from me.

I need her restrained.

"How do you feel about me putting the chains back on?" I ask.

Her cheeks are flushed. "I'd like that."

Fuck.

How is she so perfect?

I stand and fasten the restraints still clipped to the bed around her wrists.

"I've never seen anything more beautiful than you at my mercy."

Her eyes flash with irritation. "You're going to tease me now, aren't you?"

"To fucking tears."

She shudders as I move back to her cunt and slap it.

Her entire body tenses, and she yelps in surprise. "Remy."

I shake my head. "I like it when you call me Daddy."

Her chest rises and falls with heavy breaths. "Please make me come, Daddy."

I climb between her thighs and wrap my palm around her throat. "When you come, I will have my cock deep inside you. And it will be the most mind-blowing orgasm you've ever experienced."

Moving my tongue back to her entrance, I suck on her clit. She moans loudly, every muscle in her body tensing. She's already close again. My girl likes being restrained, which increases my desire for her.

I stop, and she growls. "Why did you stop?"

"I told you that you're not coming until I'm inside you."

Her jaw clenches. "Then fuck me."

"All in good time." I move back between her thighs and push her hips higher to access her asshole.

She doesn't tense when I lick it this time. Instead, a deep, guttural moan tears from her throat.

"You're so fucking wet for me."

She gazes at me. "I've told you before, I'm always wet for you."

"Fuck, angel. You're such a good girl." I delve my tongue inside her and lap her arousal like a man dying of thirst.

She pulls at the restraints as I build her back to the edge with my tongue. And just as I sense she's about to explode, I back off.

"Remy!"

I arch a brow. "I don't know why you expect me to make you come when I've made it clear, no orgasm until I'm inside you."

"You're going to drive me insane."

"Good," I reply, shoving a finger into her tight, wet pussy. "Then you can experience how you've made me feel since I set eyes on you."

Her brow furrows. "You hated me when we first met."

"You've got it all wrong." I shake my head. "I treated you badly because it was the only way to keep you at arm's length. I wanted you from the second our eyes met, despite being married to your mom."

Her lips part. "Then stop messing about and fuck me."

It's a tempting offer, but I want her on the brink of fucking tears.

"Only once you're begging me as though your life depends on it."

"You're sadistic," she murmurs.

"I think you might learn to love that side of me."

I bite her inner thigh, and she groans, her eyes flickering shut. Again I build her toward her climax, my tongue probing her tight little asshole, which drives her wild. Once I'm sure she's close to coming undone, I stop. "This ass is so fucking pretty. I bet it would feel like heaven wrapped around my dick."

She tenses. "I haven't even had regular sex yet. Are you insane?"

I smirk at her. "Don't worry, baby. I'm not going to fuck it… yet."

She shudders as I get off the bed and unbutton my shirt slowly, watching her eyes dilate as they roam over my body. "Are you going to fuck my pussy?"

I tilt my head. "Not yet. I don't think you've begged me hard enough."

Her jaw clenches as I throw my shirt to the side, and her eyes widen. I've got tattoos all over my chest, but I notice her eye dip to the huge scar across my abdomen. I move my hand to my belt and pull it off.

"No more talking." I throw the belt on the floor and remove my pants and boxer briefs.

She moans when she sees my cock, hard as stone and dripping with precum. "Please. I need you inside of me. I want you so bad."

I smile as her attempt to beg is adorable. "Soon, angel." I move between her thighs, rubbing the head of my cock against her clit, making her hips rise off the mattress.

"Oh my God," she breathes.

"Tell me who owns you."

Her eyes are so dilated only a small rim of blue is visible. "You own me. Every part of me."

"That's right." Slowly, I drag the tip of my cock through her soaking wet entrance, coating my dick in her juices. "Are you on birth control?"

She shakes her head. "No, but I don't want you to wear a condom."

My brow raises as I've got no intention of getting her pregnant, even if the primal idea of breeding her is hot as fuck. And the thought of her growing big and round with my baby makes my balls draw up. But I'm too old to have more kids. "I have to, Ella."

She shakes her head. "I can take the morning-after

pill if we get one. I want to feel you inside me with nothing between us, Daddy. Please."

"Fuck, baby." I thrust my cock against her clit, making her moan. "You're so naughty. Do you want me to come in your virgin cunt?"

She moans and arches her back as much as the restraints allow. "Yes, I want to feel it spilling out of me. I want you to pump me so full."

My cock is leaking everywhere. At this point, I'm just torturing myself and her. "Okay, beg me as hard as you can."

Our eyes meet, and hers are full of playful fire. "I'm a dirty virgin who wants her stepdaddy's cock so fucking bad. My cunt is so wet for you. Please fuck it, or I'll lose my mind."

I growl then and position the head of my cock at her entrance. "There's no going back now." I slam into her, making her scream in pain. A scream that is music to my dark soul as her pussy stretches around me.

Mine.

This pretty little angel is all mine, and I don't give a shit anymore about what's wrong or right or why I'm so obsessed with this girl. She kept pushing me, and now she will learn what it means to be owned by a monster.

I struggle to restrain myself as I work inch by inch into her. She's so tight it's unbelievable.

"Fuck, you're tight," I grunt,

The way she squeezes is unlike anything I've ever felt before. The fire coursing through me is only hotter because we've been in a dance of forbidden passion and lust for months, building up to this moment.

I kiss her to swallow her cries of pain. Gentleness is not my forte, even if she's a virgin. And especially after wanting her for this long. It's like I'm trying to claw back a fucking beast from tearing her apart. That's what I am, a feral beast, and this beautiful creature has fallen into my lair.

24

ELLA

*T*he pain is intense as he stretches me for the first time around his thick shaft. Inch by inch, he enters me, and I feel it all.

He's big. Too fucking big.

I have nothing to compare him to other than my dildo, which is considerably smaller. However, I've seen porn movies, and this man is big all over.

Remy grabs my throat. "Relax, angel." He trails his tongue down my face, making me shudder. "It'll feel better once you relax."

It's hard to relax when he's tearing me apart from the inside out. "It hurts," I whine.

"Take it for me. I know you can." He kisses me as he makes soft, shallow movements. I glance between us to see that while about five inches of him has disappeared inside me, there's another five to go.

"It's never going to fit."

He nibbles on my neck, sending little shocks of pleasure through me. "It will fit. You were made to fit me." He sucks on my nipples, making the pleasure heighten as he slips another inch inside and then another.

I gasp when I feel his balls against my ass, looking down to see the entirety of his cock inside me. And I've never seen anything hotter. It stokes the inferno already blazing in my gut.

He licks a path down my neck. "The pain will subside, I promise." He bites my shoulder, holding himself still. "Do you feel how deep I am?"

I swallow hard as I can feel him at the depth of me. "Yes, so deep," I breathe.

"That's right. I'm all the way inside of you."

I moan and shut my eyes as the pleasure and pain are an oddly intoxicating concoction.

His lips find mine, and he kisses me lazily, sliding his tongue into my mouth and tangling it with mine as if he has all the time in the world. It allows me the chance to get used to being stretched wide open.

Finally, he moves. I cry out as the pain and pleasure intensify hand in hand, making me shudder. "Fuck," I breathe, straining against the restraints.

I'd love to slide my nails into his back or pull his dark, thick hair. But I'm immobilized, completely at his mercy, to be used however he sees fit. And it's such a turn-on.

Remy pulls his lip from mine, keeping himself propped on his arms above me. His dark eyes are full of fire that burns my soul. And then he thrusts in and out of me with hard, violent strokes, sending me right to the edge in no time.

"Oh fuck, yes!" I cry, as I can feel myself teetering on the cliff top.

He smirks at me. "This is why I wouldn't let you come. It will feel so good when you come on my cock."

I gasp and pull at the restraints, trying to keep up with his movements. The metal cuts into my skin. Each thrust is like a jolt of electricity coursing through my body, stealing away my breath. That barrier between pain and pleasure blurs until I don't know which is which because it feels so fucking good.

"Fuck, Daddy. I'm going to come!" I tremble violently as the most intense orgasm ricochets through me. It's unlike anything I've felt before. A culmination of all the months of foreplay leading up to this moment. Every muscle tenses, and Remy growls like an animal as he fucks me through it, his jaw tight.

"You feel like heaven, baby, coming on my cock like that." He leans down and sinks his teeth into my shoulder, biting enough to leave a bruise. "I want to feel you come like that on my dick all night. Do you understand?"

I moan at the thought as he pumps in and out at a steady rhythm. "Yes, Daddy," I reply.

"Fuck," he murmurs against my skin. "By the time I'm through with you, you'll be so full of my cum it will be dripping from you for days. And you'll be so sore I'll have to carry you out of this cabin." He licks the side of my neck. "Is that what you want?"

"It's exactly what I want."

Remy slips out of me, and I groan in protest.

"What are you doing?"

He unfastens the restraints without answering me and then flips me onto all fours. "I need to fuck you like this." His finger brushes over my asshole, making me shudder. "I'm going to imagine the moment when I stretch your ass around my cock, too. It's going to be so fucking beautiful."

I shudder while the idea of him stretching such a tight ring of muscles around his cock scares me. It excites me, too. It felt too big in my pussy. What the hell would it feel like stretching my asshole?

He leans over my back and places soft kisses down my spine. And then he grabs a fistful of my hair, pulling me back violently. "Is that what you want? My dick stretching that tight ass of yours?"

I swallow hard. "Yes. I want everything."

Remy thrusts back inside of me roughly. He doesn't have a gentle side, and I don't think I want him to be gentle. Even if it is my first time, I've needed this—him—for too long.

"You feel so good, angel," he murmurs.

My nipples are sharp peaks as he grabs my hips so hard I know he'll leave bruises. I want him to. I want him to brand me as his.

Remy pumps into me with a furious intensity, his hips slamming against my thighs with each movement. He moves so fast and hard that I can barely keep up. He's relentless in his pursuit of pleasure.

"Tell me how it feels, baby. I want you to use your words."

"It feels so good," I cry, clutching the comforter beneath me. "I need to come again," I pant.

He stills inside me and slides his arm around my throat, pulling me unnaturally toward him and cutting my supply of oxygen. "Greedy girl," he breathes, tightening his grasp. "I'm in control, and you get to come only when I say so."

He licks a path up my neck, making me shudder.

"Okay, Daddy," I reply.

"I'm so proud of you, angel."

I don't know what it is about Remy praising me, but it's so hot. He spanks my ass hard enough to sting.

"I'll never get enough of seeing your cunt swallow my cock."

My body turns limp beneath him as he fucks me toward the edge again. This time, as I'm getting close, he slides every inch of his thick cock deep inside me with one thrust.

"Fuck!" My muscles spasm around him, dragging him deeper. My whole body convulses at the intensity of my orgasm. For a moment, it's like my brain stops functioning. The hot, white pleasure takes control of every atom in my body.

"Look at you. Coming on my cock like a good girl." He spanks me again, and the pain intensifies the pleasure. "You're Daddy's good girl, aren't you?"

His praise sends me to heights I never knew existed. "Yes," I gasp.

I can hardly believe it when he fucks me through it, building me toward my third orgasm.

Remy's grip on my hips hurts as he growls like an animal, sinking his teeth into the back of my neck. "I want to watch you ride my cock, baby. Can you do that for me?"

I can't speak, but I nod in response.

"That's my girl," he purrs. And before I can blink, he rolls me on top of him so that my thighs are straddling his. The length of his cock is hot and hard against my center.

His dark eyes are on fire as they drink me in slowly. "Ride my cock like you're made for it," he orders.

I moan, and my body quivers as I reach around and angle his cock upward before sinking onto it and taking every inch inside. Moving my hips, I rest my hands on his tattooed, muscular chest and fuck myself on him as if my life depends on it.

Remy watches me like a predator toying with its prey before going in for the kill. I can sense he won't allow me to be in control for long.

"Do you like watching me ride you?" I play with my hard nipples." It feels so good to be stuffed so full, Daddy."

He growls and grabs my hips so hard I can no longer move. "Tell me, who owns this fucking pussy?"

"You do."

"That's right. Sit still so I can drink you in with my eyes."

I still with his cock deep inside me.

His eyes roam over every inch of me as if he's committing the images to memory.

I try to move, but he won't allow it. "Fuck me," I breathe. "I need you to fuck me."

He tilts his head, smirking wickedly at me. "You've already come twice, baby. What more could you want?"

"A million times coming apart on your cock wouldn't be enough."

He loses it, filliping me over so I'm pinned to the mattress beneath him. "Good thing I intend to make you come more than that. I won't stop until you've come so much you can't keep your eyes open. You'll be exhausted. And even then, I won't stop. I'll fuck you while you sleep because I can't get enough of being inside you."

I groan at the dirty mental image he's putting in my mind. The idea of him fucking me while I sleep is oddly arousing. It sounds so fucking good the idea of being woken up with his cock deep inside me.

"I bet you'd like that, wouldn't you?"

I nod. "Yes, I want you to fuck me while I sleep."

"Fuck, Ella." He sounds completely undone.

He slams into me and slides a hand into my hair. The other wraps around my throat so that he's starving me of oxygen. My release is so close it feels like I'm floating, watching us fuck like animals from above. The pleasure is almost too much.

"I'm coming!" I scream, certain Remy must be ready for release, too.

"Such a good girl he praises."

My body turns limp like a doll as he continues to fuck me through my orgasm, building me toward another before the last wears off. "Please, Remy. I can't give anymore. I need your cum."

His muscles strain as he growls. "I want you to come for me once more."

My jaw drops open because I don't know if I can. I feel drained of everything I have to give. "I don't think I can."

Remy pulls out of me, making me feel empty.

He lifts me off the bed and carries me toward the window, pushing my face against it. And then he's inside me again, fucking me against it as the cold glass presses against my nipples. "You'll come for me once more. And when you do, I'll fill you with my cum."

This position penetrates me differently, hitting a spot inside of me that sets every nerve in my body on fire. "Are you trying to kill me?"

Remy groans and kisses my neck. "No, I'm trying to ensure you never want another man. That you know this pussy is mine only."

I arch my back. "It already belongs to you."

"That's right. Mine." He slams into me with such force I feel like I'm dying. The intensity of this moment is mind blowing.

He spanks my ass hard, and the pain only heightens the impossible pleasure spiking through me.

"Oh God, I'm going to come."

Remy growls behind me, fucking me harder. "Come for me. Let me feel your tight cunt coming on my cock."

His words are all it takes to shatter me.

"Fuck." He slams into me once more, and then I feel his cock swell within me as he climaxes too. We're both panting for oxygen, and my knees are so weak I know I'd be in a heap on the floor without him holding me up.

After a few minutes, he lifts me in his arms and carries me into the bathroom without a word. Gently, he sets me down on the ground and then turns on the shower.

"What are you doing?" I ask.

"Running us a shower. I want to wash you."

Though I'm sore and exhausted, the thought of Remy washing me makes my pussy ache and my clit throb. "That's a bad idea."

He gives me a wicked smile. "I think it's a perfect idea. I told you I want to make you come over and over on my cock."

I groan and shut my eyes, unsure how I can take anymore. And yet, I crave it like an addict looking for their next fix.

I wake up, the morning light jabbing at my eyes like it has a personal vendetta. When they focus and adjust, I turn over to find Ella sleeping peacefully. Her hair is a mess of pretty golden curls across the pillow.

An angel.

That's what she is. And I'm the devil that claimed her. The guilt gnaws at my insides, but that feeling's got a fight on its hands. There's relief, too. Finally, we've given in to the magnetic force pulling us together.

We'd been denying our attraction toward each other since she moved in and trying to ignore it only worsened things. Last night felt like a release—like all the pent-up desires we both had finally found their way out.

The question is, what comes next?

I feel a pang of guilt at the sight of bruises on Ella's neck. She was a porcelain, unmarked virgin when I drove her here, and now I've left bruises on her skin and my mark in her cunt. I couldn't resist coming inside of her as I'd wanted to feel her without anything between us too.

However, It means we'll have to go to the nearest town, about half an hour's drive, to get the morning-after pill from the drugstore and the contraceptive pill.

I climb out of bed and walk toward the window, gazing at the surrounding forest. This cabin has been in my family since I was a kid. My parents used to bring me and my sister, Martina, here for vacations. While darkness surrounded our lives, we felt like normal kids having a vacation with their parents when we were here.

I leave her to sleep and quickly shower in the main family bathroom. Once done, I whip up some waffles and bacon and make coffee, hoping the smell will get her out of bed.

The sun is beginning to rise over the lake, which she wouldn't have seen yesterday in the dark, its orange and pink hues washing over the surface like a magical light show. I want to stay in this cabin with Ella for eternity, as it would make everything easier.

I told Ella I don't believe in love, which hasn't changed. She's my obsession. And I will keep her by my side, but I fear that may not be enough for her.

"Morning," her sweet voice rings through the room.

I turn around to see her in my shirt, two buttons done up and nothing underneath. A rumble vibrates through my chest. "Morning, angel. You should have more on, or I'll end up fucking you before you can eat."

She bites on her bottom lip. "Perhaps I'm hungry for something other than food."

I clench my jaw and shake my head. "No, you

hardly ate any of the dinner last night. You need to eat."
I plate up the bacon and waffles. "Sit down."

An amused smile tugs at her pretty red lips. "Yes,
Daddy." She sits, and those big sapphire blue eyes stare
at me expectantly.

I clench my fists to stop myself from bending her
over the kitchen table.

"Eat," I order, sitting opposite her with my plate.

She picks up her fork and takes a bite of bacon,
moaning. "That's good bacon."

I pour us some coffee. We eat in silence for a few
moments before I finally break it. "We've got to take a
trip to town. It's a thirty-minute drive."

Her throat bobs. "For the morning-after pill?"

I nod in response. "Yes, but you'll probably want to
hold on to it and take it at the end of this weekend."

Her brow raises.

"As I intend to come inside of you a lot," I add.

She moans, and her nipples harden against the
fabric of my shirt. It makes my cock harder than stone
as it tries to punch a hole in my fucking jeans. I rarely
wear jeans, but I always dress more casual here. I
realize my mistake, as the fabric is less forgiving than
my slacks.

I force my eyes away and sip my coffee. "We want to
make it to town early as it gets busier later."

People in the town know me. And I don't want them
asking questions about Ella. Giada and I used to escape
up here regularly, and she loved the small-town life,
getting to know all the locals. While I have no fucking
morals and don't give a shit that Ella is the daughter of

my recently deceased wife, most of society would frown upon it.

"Is it a large town?" Ella asks, sipping her coffee.

I shake my head. "No. Everyone knows everyone."

"Even you?"

I nod. "A lot of them know me, yes."

She sucks on her inner cheek. "And do you think they'll ask questions about us?"

"They'll probably think you're my daughter."

Her nose wrinkles. "How's this going to work?"

"We don't need to think about that right now." I stand and clear our empty plates, dropping them in the sink. "You need to get ready, as there's no way you're going to town like that."

She laughs. "Of course not, but I thought we might have time to have fun first."

I groan and clutch the side of the kitchen counter. "When we get back, I'm going to fuck you for the rest of the weekend, but I want to get to town and back early." I glance at her. "So be a good girl and do as I say. Get ready."

She licks her lips but nods and gets up, her wide hips swaying as she walks past me. And I can't resist.

I grab her, and she squeals.

"One quick taste." I lift her off the floor and place her on the edge of the kitchen table, spreading her thick thighs.

She gasps, and I take my time, tasting every inch of her. Letting my tongue drag down her neck and then between her breasts, lavishing attention on her rock-hard nipples.

When I get to where Ella wants me, she's already a panting, soaking-wet mess.

"You're fucking soaked for me."

Her back arches as I drag my fingers through her pussy, coating them in arousal. "How many times do I have to tell you, I'm always wet for you?"

I don't answer that question. "Open your mouth."

She does instantly, and I slide my wet fingers into it. "Taste how delicious you are. My own personal drug."

Her moan is like a sweet melody as I suck on her clit. There's something so fucking addictive about Ella. I know an eternity of tasting her won't be enough, but will she be satisfied with what I can give her?

A life by my side, but without love. I don't have the capability for it. Hell, I don't even believe in the concept.

She arches her back as I thrust my fingers inside her, drawing her right to the edge so easily. It's like she's an instrument made for me to play.

"Fuck, Daddy," she moans, her tight muscle clamping around my fingers.

"Good girl," I breathe, licking at her clit. "I want you to come." I gaze at her and drag my teeth over her sensitive flesh. "Can you do that for me?"

Her lips part, and she nods.

I keep licking and sucking until she comes hard against my mouth.

"Oh, fuck!" she screams out. Her entire body spasming from the intensity of pleasure. She's only just come apart, and I can't wait to do it again and again.

However, right now, I need to get her washed and dressed.

Lifting her off the counter, I carry her toward the bedroom.

She gazes adoringly at me. "I can walk, you know?"

I kiss her. "I know, but I want to take care of you."

She wraps her arms around my neck in response, snuggling against my chest.

It's as if she fits me perfectly. I carry her into the bathroom and set her down gently on the floor, reaching over to turn the tap and fill the bathtub. Steam rises from the warm water, filling the room with a comforting heat. "Get in," I order.

She watches me, her eyes trusting and filled with an admiration that gets under my skin. I wouldn't say I like it, yet I crave it. I crave her.

I watch as she sinks into the water with a soft sigh. I grab a sponge, lathering it with soap, before running it over her body. I wash her gently, every touch a promise.

She leans into my touch, her eyes fluttering closed as she lets out a soft moan. It's a sound that makes my cock throb painfully.

"You're making me horny again." She looks at me with those beautiful blue eyes and tugs her lip between her teeth. "Do we have to go to town?"

I nod in response. "I want to get you on the contraceptive pill as soon as possible, as it takes a week to work."

Her eyes widen. "Because you want to keep filling me with your cum when we get home?"

"Ella," I growl her name in warning.

She gives me a naughty little smirk. "Yes, Daddy?"

"Stop messing about. You have no idea what you're doing to me."

She giggles. "It's pretty fun seeing you all hot and bothered like this."

I slide a finger inside her, making her groan. "Careful, or I'll get you hot and bothered and leave you needy for release until we return from town."

Her eyes widen, and she instantly sobers because I left her needy yesterday, chained to the bed. "Okay," she breathes.

I don't let her see how satisfied I am that she's so easy to command. Instead, I move behind her and wash her hair, taking the time to massage her scalp.

She groans as I do, forcing me to ignore the constant throbbing in my cock as I finish washing her hair, using the shower head to wash the shampoo away. Once I'm done, I stand.

"Out you get," I order.

She pouts but doesn't question me.

I wrap her in a thick, soft white towel and dry her.

"You know I can dry myself?"

My jaw clenches. "I told you. I'm taking care of you." I kiss below her ear. "Something I think you crave."

Ella nods and doesn't argue, letting me dominate and pamper her.

Once she's dry, I give her a towel to wear around her hair like a turban before ushering her out of the bathroom and back to the bedroom.

"Get dressed," I whisper as I turn away to give her

some privacy, "I want you out in fifteen minutes and ready to leave."

Her lips purse together, but she doesn't argue. I leave her and go outside to get the engine of the SUV running so that the heater warms up. Despite only being September, it's colder than normal here in Minnesota.

I get it running and then move back inside, finding Ella already dressed.

"Ready?" I ask as my eyes roam over her body. She looks good dressed in a pair of tight skinny jeans and a red cami with a thick knitted cardigan over the top. My cock stirs to life again. And even though we fucked last night, and I made her come on the table in the kitchen, I need more.

"Yep," she says, practically skipping toward me.

I grab her hand and lead her to the car, starting the journey toward the nearest town. A tense silence fills the air as if we want to avoid bringing up the glaringly obvious issue of how we explain *us* to anyone back in Chicago. Pushing it from my mind, I intend to enjoy our weekend in paradise.

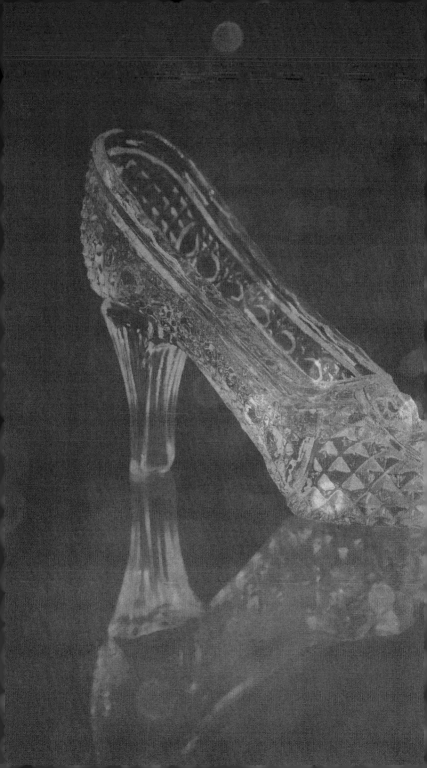

26

ELLA

*T*he town nearby is called *Hartwell*, and it's a proper *small* town.

Remy knows everyone even though he doesn't live here. I feel self-conscious as people ask him who I am, and he tells them my name, avoiding the glaring question.

Who am I to him?

He has to get some groceries, so I walk alone toward the drugstore. His cash is burning a hole in my pocket. Considering what I'll ask for, it makes sense he wouldn't want to go into the store with me.

A middle-aged lady stands behind the counter, and a bell rings as I enter.

"Good morning," she greets, smiling at me.

I smile, but I'm so nervous I can hardly speak. This town strikes me as a place where young women don't go asking for the morning-after pill and the contraceptive pill, which Remy got me a prescription for from his doctor.

"Morning," I manage.

I walk to the counter, licking my lips. "I've got a prescription. But I also need the morning-after pill." I pass the prescription over, and her eyes narrow when she sees it.

"I see." She's no longer friendly as she rings it up.

I tap my foot on the floor as she heads into the back of the store to get the medication. I feel as if she's judging me for what I'm picking up.

I take a deep breath and try to focus on breathing, pretending I don't care what she thinks of me. Last night, I was too caught up in the moment and wanted to feel nothing between us.

The lady returns with the pills and packs them in a bag without a word. I hand her Remy's cash and rush out of the store, not looking back.

As I walk toward the short journey back to Remy's car, my thoughts are all over the place. We crossed an invisible line between us last night, and now there's no going back. I belong to him, that's what he said.

Once I get back to the SUV, I climb into the passenger's side and shut the door.

Someone wraps their knuckles on my window, and I glance up into a pair of ice-blue eyes. It's a young guy, not much older than me. I wind down the window. "Can I help you?"

He smirks. "Hear that you're new here." His eyes drop to the drugstore bag. "How about I take you out tonight?"

I swallow hard as he's attractive, even if knocking on

the car window to ask someone out is creepy. "Sorry, I'm busy."

His brow arches. "Busy doing what?"

"I'm here on a bonding trip with my stepdad to get to know him better," I lie.

He snorts. "Surely you'd rather have fun instead of being stuck inside with some old man."

I shake my head. "I'm sorry, I can't."

A muscle contracts in his jaw, and I see a darkness ignite in his eyes. "Are you rejecting me?"

"No, I'm simply saying I can't tonight."

He clenches his fists, and suddenly, he's pulling open the door to the SUV, yanking me out of it. "Stuck up rich girls like you always think they're better than everyone else." He growls into my face.

I clutch his hand, trying to pull it off my coat. "Let go of me!"

"Perhaps I'll just have a bit of fun with you now. Mom said you just got the morning-after pill. You can take it after." His eyes flash with callous rage. "Has your stepdad been fucking you? Have you got Daddy issues?" His hand moves up my thigh, and I freeze in terror.

Daddy Issues.

Is that why I'm so attracted to Remy?

"Don't," I breathe, hardly able to worry that he suspects me and Remy are fucking. "Please let go of me."

He snarls at me. "Why would I do that?" His hand works at the buttons on my jeans as he tries to get them open.

Suddenly, he's yanked away from me and slammed

into the side of the SUV. Remy growls at him like a beast, and I drop to the floor in shock, my heart hammering uncontrollably in my chest.

"What the fuck do you think you are doing to my stepdaughter, Kevin?"

Kevin, the bastard who thought he could take advantage of me, cowers. "Nothing. I didn't realize she was with you, Remy."

Remy slams his fist into the side of the SUV right by his face. "If you ever look at her the wrong way again, I'll end you."

Kevin is shaking now as he looks up at Remy. "I'm sorry," he exclaims.

Remy looks like he wants to murder him, and considering all I know about him, this Kevin is probably at real risk of getting hurt.

"Sorry for what? Touching a girl when she told you to stop?"

He nods.

"Your lucky I'm not beating the shit out of you out of respect for your parents. Now fuck off." Remy pushes him in the opposite direction. Every muscle in his body is bunched tightly as he watches Kevin sprint away.

I get to my feet, my knees shaking like a leaf. I can't believe Remy stood up for me like that. "Remy," I say his name.

He looks at me, and there's pure rage in his eyes. "Get in the car."

I swallow hard and jump into the passenger seat, buckling myself in. He throws some bags of groceries in the back and then gets in, starting the engine in silence.

A few minutes down the road, he let out a shaky breath. I don't know why that asshole's words have gotten to me.

Daddy Issues.

It wasn't like I never had a dad, but I craved his presence more when he was alive. And when he was dead, it felt like a part of me was missing.

"Are you okay?" Remy asks.

I clear my throat, trying to push that asshole's comment out of my mind. "I think so. That Kevin is a fucking asshole."

He looks at me. "Why did you speak to him?" There's an accusatory tone in his voice.

I arch a brow. "He approached the car and knocked on the window. I wound it down, and he asked me out. I said no, and he lost his shit and dragged me out of the car. How is any of that my fault?"

His jaw clenches. "He's lucky I didn't see him pull you out of the car, or he'd be in the emergency room right now."

My heart is beating erratically in my chest. "Do you think he knows the truth?"

Remy's eyes narrow. "How could he?"

I swallow hard. "I told him I was here to get to know my stepdad. Like a trip to get to know each other better, and that's why I couldn't go out with him."

"That wasn't a good idea."

I bite my lip. "He asked if you were fucking me."

His eyes swirl with a palpable danger I've never seen before. "His mom owns the drugstore. I think they'll put two and two together. What stepdad brings his stepdaughter to the woods, just the two of them? And considering the items you picked up…"

I shrug. "Surely they would know from the news that my mom was killed?"

He shakes his head. "No, they won't. This place is too far removed from everything in Chicago."

We drive on in silence, the tension between us palpable. We both know that what we're doing is dangerous. I can't stop thinking about how Remy stood up for me like that. Seeing him in action makes me long for him more than I did before.

We're silent for the rest of the journey until Remy pulls up in front of the cabin. "Fuck them," he says.

"What?"

"I don't give a shit what they think of me, and neither should you." He leans across the center console and kisses me. "You're mine; the rest of the world will have to get used to it."

I want to ask him what that means.

Am I his girlfriend now? How the hell will that even work?

The thing is, I don't want to ruin this by saying anything. Instead, I nod. "Yours."

His beautiful dark eyes flash with fire. "Time to prove it, baby."

I pull in a sharp breath, knowing he won't rest until I can hardly walk. If he fucks me like he did last night for the rest of the weekend, I'll probably die from too much pleasure. But it'll be worth every second.

"I'm very sore."

He kisses my neck, and I groan. "You'll soon loosen up once I get my mouth on your pretty cunt."

A dark shiver races down my spine. It's unbelievable how this man can ignite my desire with one dirty sentence. One minute, I was too sore now I'm throbbing.

He gets out of the SUV and walks around to open my door. I'm about to jump out when he grabs me and lifts me into his arms.

"What are you doing?"

"I'm looking after my girl," he breathes, carrying me into the cabin.

I'm ready for him to show me exactly what it means to be his all weekend. I hope it doesn't end when this weekend does, as I think I'd never recover from losing Remy after a taste. He's everything my life has been missing. Everything I've craved, even when it was taboo. And I think someone would have to stop my heart from beating to claw my hands off him.

27

REMY

I hate that we're back in Chicago, brought back to reality.

Ella and I have returned to our platonic stepdad and stepdaughter relationship out in the open, but it's a different story at night. I clench my jaw as she has slept in my bed every night since we returned one week ago, and I'm still like a fucking horny teenager.

Thankfully, Luca is back at the academy. And Leo is rarely at the house, so we've not had to sneak around. Not that I think either of them would judge me. I'm pretty sure they both would have taken the chance to have her if she'd been interested.

I sit in the boardroom with my men as they present the evidence they've found against the Vishekov Bratva.

Massimo was right.

They wanted to divide my attention away from the true plan. The bastards are invading my territory, and I will fucking obliterate them for it.

"How did we not notice this?" I ask calmly.

Edoardo shakes his head. "They've been slowly encroaching on the territory, and our men on the ground didn't come to us about it. Instead, they've been trying to deal with it, which hasn't worked."

"Idiots," I reply, running a hand through my hair. "Get it sorted fast. I want all of Vishekov's men out of Chicago before the day is through, got it?"

"Yes, sir," Edoardo confirms.

"I want all four of you on it full-time until it's handled. No other issues matter."

Antoni, Giuseppe, and Frederico all nod in unison.

Edoardo clenches his jaw. "Agreed."

"It makes sense now why the Vishekov Bratva wanted Ella's marriage contract as leverage against us," I add.

"Fucking Russians," Massimo exclaims.

I agree with the sentiment entirely. I can't stand them, and Camilla married one. I shudder at the thought.

"This might warrant a meeting with Spartak. If he knew another Bratva was trying to move into Chicago, he'd probably help squash them," I suggest.

Massimo clears his throat. "Do we want to involve that psychopath?"

I meet his gaze. "You're the one that brokered a deal with him originally. How would this be any different?"

His jaw clenches. "Because I had no choice. We were at war."

Antoni nods. "He's a live wire. It may not be wise to involve him."

"He might be helpful," Frederico intercepts, running

a hand across his jaw. "He knows how the bratva operates, and that could be the difference."

"Exactly," I say.

Edoardo nods in agreement.

"Set up a meeting with him," I demand, running a hand through my hair. "I'll decide whether involving him is worth it or not."

Massimo's eyes flash, and I know he no longer likes me giving orders. He nods. "Fine."

"Good. Is there anything else that needs to be addressed?"

My men are silent.

"Fine, I want an update no later than tomorrow morning on the Vishekov Bratva and where we're at."

As the men stand and leave, Massimo lingers behind. Once we're alone, he crosses his arms over his chest. "What are you doing here?"

"I need to step in since things are going to shit."

Massimo shakes his head. "Nothing is going to shit. I'm the one who suspected the Vishekov Bratva due to their links with Vegas. Let me prove I can handle this."

I realize he sees my stepping in as not trusting him, but it's not that. If I leave it to someone else, I'm gambling with Ella's life. Two wives I've had. My enemies killed both. I won't allow her to meet the same fate.

I place a hand on his shoulder and look into his eyes. "I know you can handle it, Massimo. It's not about whether you can handle it. It's for my peace of mind."

His brow furrows.

"Erin being murdered has put me on edge. They

have it out for me; therefore, I need to bring them to their knees. Do you understand?"

His expression softened. "Yes. I understand that."

"Good. I'm not trying to take over. I'm pissed off and want Vishekov's head on a plate."

"I get it. I'll ensure the men work around the clock to bring the Vishekov Bratva to their knees."

I clap him on the shoulder. "How about the trafficking? Have you ended it?"

His eyes flash with irritation, but he nods. "The Romanians are angry. They say they're going to make us pay."

I wave my hand dismissively. "We'll see about that. If they step foot in our territory, we'll eradicate them."

"Why did you do it?" he asks.

I consider lying to him, but what's the point? Ella is mine. Sooner or later, everyone will find out, and out of all my kids, Massimo is the most mature. He'll take it better than the rest.

"Ella insisted on it."

His brow lifts. "Are you saying what I think you're saying?"

I nod. "She doesn't like it."

"And that's it? Paisley hates it too, but I'm not so much of a pussy—"

I grab the collar of Massimo's jacket. "Careful, son. I would reconsider how you finish that sentence."

His jaw clenches and I release his jacket. "I know we've been considering jacking the trafficking in for a while because it's messy and getting expensive, but because of a girl?" He chuckles. "Maybe this one *will* be different. Do you love her?"

The word love sends a shiver down my spine. And instantly, I feel numb. Love doesn't exist. It's a stupid modern-day construct. "No."

Massimo's brow furrows. "Then what the fuck?"

I shrug. "I want her. It's all it is. I've been hooked on her since the day we met."

Massimo grimaces. "That's fucked up, considering you were married to her mom when you met."

"I know." I run a hand through my hair.

"What are you going to do? Marry her?"

I shake my head. "I'm not planning on getting married a third time."

"She's twenty-one years old with her life ahead of her." Massimo's voice is free of judgment. "Tell me how you'll give her what she most likely wants."

"Such as?" I ask.

"A family of her own."

It has crossed my mind, but Ella and I haven't discussed our future. Our lust blinded us, and nothing else mattered at the time. It wasn't smart, and a part of me wants to continue blindly without getting into that conversation.

Now that I've had Ella, there's no way I'm letting her go. It's selfish, but she is mine.

I shrug. "She'll get over it."

Massimo shakes his head. "I don't think you know what you're talking about. Paisley is a mess because we haven't conceived yet."

I purse my lips together. "Still no luck with IVF?"

Massimo shakes his head. "No, and she said it's breaking her to keep trying. The disappointment each month when she gets her period."

I squeeze my son's shoulder. "Hopefully, this time, it will take."

He looks dejected. "All I'm saying is Ella might be desperate to be a mom. Are you going to take that away from her?"

"Are you suggesting I can't get her pregnant?"

"Can you after the cancer?"

I nod. "I believe so."

"Do you want to at your age?" He asks.

I shake my head. "No. I've done that shit, and I'm not doing it again."

"Good luck telling Ella that. Maybe you'll be lucky, and she won't want kids."

I sense she does want kids. Every Wednesday evening, Ronan comes to the house, and the way she watches me with him, I think she's imagining me being a dad to her kids.

"Fuck." I run a hand through my hair. "Thanks for the reality check."

Massimo raises a brow. "I sense that's sarcastic."

"You could have left me in my bubble longer."

He chuckles. "Sorry about that." He claps me on the shoulder. "I've got to get going."

"Sure. See you later."

Massimo walks out of the room. Our relationship has improved since he stood up and became Don of the famiglia when I was diagnosed. I guess I've changed and taken the time for my children when I rarely did before.

I slump into a chair at the boardroom table and run a hand through my hair.

Despite agreeing with Ella we wouldn't tell anyone about us, I fucked that up almost instantly. Probably because a part of me doesn't want to keep it a secret. A part of me wants to show the world that my pretty little angel belongs to me and me alone.

28

ELLA

I've been so wrapped up in Remy I hardly noticed the date until that morning.

My stomach clenches, and a heavyweight settles on my chest. It's September 19th. My birthday. The anniversary of Dad's death. Tears gather in my eyes, and I draw a deep breath, shaking my head. It doesn't matter anymore as no one even knows or cares when my birthday is.

It used to piss me off that Mom tried harder and harder each year to make my birthday a happy occasion, despite the fact I told her I didn't want to celebrate. She knew why. She didn't care.

And then she started insisting that we celebrate because it was an important day to her too, the day she birthed me. I swallow hard as a lump forms in my throat.

While she was a jerk a lot of the time, I still miss her.

My phone buzzes on the nightstand, and I grab it, checking the messages.

Mia: Don't forget lunch at Vincenzo's. See you later!

I run my fingers through my hair. Things have been so crazy I didn't keep track of the dates and agreed to lunch last week absentmindedly, as she's due to go on vacation this weekend for two weeks. However, I want to curl up and go back to sleep until tomorrow. I throw my cell phone onto the nightstand, deciding I'll reply later.

All I want is to be left alone. I roll over, inhaling deeply, placing the back of my wrist against my head. Remy's scent encompasses me and makes me feel safe, chasing some of the anxiety away.

It's just another day.

Sighing heavily, I force myself to climb out of Remy's bed. It's time to start my day.

I head into the kitchen to make breakfast, wondering if Remy is already at work. It's almost ten in the morning, so he should be. As I get the pans going and start cooking pancakes, I ignore the nagging voice telling me I should be in Washington.

This is the first year since his death that I've not been to visit his grave on the anniversary.

Someone clearing their throat behind me makes me jump, and I turn around to see Remy leaning against the counter, a soft smirk on his lips. "Happy birthday, angel."

I swallow hard, wondering how he knew. "Don't say that," I snap.

He tilts his head, brows pulling together. "Why not? It's your birthday." He holds a small wrapped gift, and my chest tightens. It's the same size as the gift my dad gave me the day before he died. A gift that remains stuffed in the back of my closet unopened. I couldn't open it as it felt like I'd lose the last part of him that I own.

My breathing labors and black dots swim in my vision as I claw onto the counter to stop myself from collapsing.

Remy drops the gift on the side and rushes to me in time, catching me in his arms. "What's wrong, Ella?" His voice sounds far away, and panicked.

I breathe deeply, trying to calm my racing heart as Remy cradles me close. I open my mouth to tell him, but no words come out. All I can do is lean into his embrace and let him anchor me in the present moment, trying to ignore all the pain and fear associated with this day.

"You're okay," he murmurs into my ear. "Come on, let's get you a seat." He leads me to the kitchen table, forces me to sit down, and then gets me a glass of water.

"Thank you," I mumble.

He sits opposite me, quiet and assessing, not yet asking what I know he wants to ask.

"How did you know?" I ask.

"I wasn't going to invite people to live with me that I didn't know everything about, Ella. Dangers follow me everywhere, and both you and your mother were background-checked before you arrived." He shrugs. "I knew it was today and wondered why you hadn't told anyone."

I bite my lip so hard I taste the metallic tang of blood. "Right." I don't meet his gaze.

"Why didn't you?"

I look into his eyes and can feel the floodgates ready to open. "I've never wanted to celebrate my birthday. At least not for the last eleven years."

"Of course…" His jaw clenches. "I should have remembered. He died the same day?"

I nod in response, tears welling in my eyes. "I always visit Dad's grave, and today..." I trail off, unable to get the words out.

"Is that what you want?"

I shake my head. "It doesn't matter."

"It does. I'll fuel the jet if you want to go to Washington."

My head snaps up, and I search his eyes. Remy is deadly serious. "Really?" It would make me feel better to be able to visit his grave today.

"Of course. It's a two-hour flight." He shrugs. "We can spend the night there and return tomorrow."

I swallow hard and then remember Mia. "Shit, I'm meant to be having lunch with Mia."

"Forget Mia. Tell her that it's the anniversary of your dad's death and that you are going to Washington. She'll understand."

I swallow hard and nod. "Okay." I pull my cell out of my jeans pocket and text Mia exactly that.

Remy makes the call to have the jet ready. Once he's off the phone, he walks over to me and kisses my forehead. "Go get ready and don't forget an overnight bag. We'll leave in half an hour." His eyes drop to the gift on the counter. "You don't have to open that."

It was sweet of him to get me anything, and he

didn't realize how hard this day was for me. I shake my head. "I will." I pick it up, my hands trembling.

I take a deep breath and slowly peel away the gift wrap.

Inside the box, nestled on a bed of black satin, lies a delicate necklace. Its slender silver chain glimmers under the light, leading to a pendant that takes my breath away. A perfectly fashioned teardrop-shaped diamond sparkles with an intensity that matches how Remy looks at me.

Tears prickle at the corners of my eyes, not of sadness but of overwhelming emotion. "Remy, it's beautiful," I breathe, more to myself than to him. I look up to see him watching me, a soft smile on his face. I shake my head. "But I can't accept something so expensive."

His jaw clenches. "It wasn't expensive."

I narrow my eyes. "Are you lying to me?"

The corner of his lips moves up. "It depends on your definition of expensive. When you're a billionaire, it's often skewed."

"Anything over a thousand dollars is expensive."

He arches a brow. "Stop overthinking and accept it. I bought it for *you*."

I sigh. "Fine." But I can't help but smile as he takes the necklace out of the box and clasps it around my neck, his fingers brushing against my skin and leaving fire in their wake.

"Thank you," I whisper, my words choked with emotion. It's exquisite, but more than that, it feels personal, intimate even.

He kisses me softly and then pulls back to search my

eyes. "You're welcome. It suits you." He smiles. "I wanted to get you something special after everything you've been through the past few months." He swallows hard, guilt dazzling in his eyes.

I think he blames himself for Mom's death, even though she was the one who ran off without protection.

"It means a lot to me," I breathe as my stomach fills with butterflies. A deep tension falls between us as his eyes darken, and a heaviness settles in the air.

"Good," he murmurs and then glances at his watch. "The jet will be ready for take-off in an hour." He spanks my ass playfully. "Go get ready and pack an overnight bag."

I nod and walk upstairs into our room, feeling lighter than when I woke up and realized the date. My cell buzzes, and Mia's response appears on my screen.

Mia: I'm so sorry. I should have known. Do you want a travel companion? I can get away if you need me.

I can't tell her the truth that her dad is taking me. Instead, I explain it's something I need to do by myself.

Then I head into the walk-in closet, grab an overnight back, pack a few outfits, my toiletries bag, and two pairs of shoes. Once I've got everything I need, I jump in the shower quickly and get dressed in a comfortable pair of jeans and a white tank top.

When I walk back into the bedroom, Remy is waiting for me, casually leaning against the bedroom door. "Ready?"

I shoulder my overnight bag. "Yeah, what about you?"

He shrugs. "I've always got an overnight bag on my jet if I take a sudden, unexpected trip."

That makes sense.

I nod. "Let's go then."

He takes the bag from me, and we walk outside to the limousine waiting for us. The driver opens the door, and we slide in.

All I can think about is how returning to Dad's grave will feel. I used to go every Saturday when we lived in Washington to change the flowers.

Without any money, I couldn't even arrange for a florist to change them regularly until I got my bank account back and arranged for a florist to go every other week and put flowers on his grave.

Since Dad's death, Mom had been to his grave a grand total of three times. My first three birthdays after he died when I insisted I wanted to visit. However, she said I was old enough to make my way there once I was fifteen.

Remy's hand slides onto my thigh. "What are you thinking?" he asks.

I shrug. "Just how it's going to feel returning to his grave."

Remy squeezes. "It's going to be alright."

I know he's right. I take a deep breath and look out the window as we speed down the highway toward the airstrip. Remy's presence makes all of this seem bearable. He's strong and comforting, and I can't help but snuggle against him, placing my head on his chest. "Thank you."

He runs a hand through my hair. "You don't need to thank me, angel."

The car stops at the airstrip within minutes, and we board the plane. Remy ushers me inside, and I sit opposite him in a plush leather seat. He smiles at me. "What are you doing over there?"

I shake my head. "There's no room for me on your chair."

He pats his lap. "There's room here."

I roll my eyes but go to sit on his lap, and he hugs me against him. "It's going to be alright," he whispers.

I take a deep breath, nuzzling closer into his embrace, and close my eyes. Despite the gravity of our destination, Remy's presence is enough to keep me afloat. He's like the anchor keeping me from drowning.

The plane takes off, and soon, we're soaring above the clouds toward Washington. Remy strokes my hair gently, and I shut my eyes, knowing this surpasses any birthday since Dad's death. Because Remy is here, supporting me in whatever I want to do with no questions. It makes a refreshing change.

WE ARRIVE at the cemetery before nightfall, and Remy takes my hand as we approach Dad's grave. I'm surprised at how much the sight of his name engraved in stone stirs up my emotions. It's not like I haven't been here before, but it feels like it's been so long.

"Hey, Dad," I say as I approach.

Remy hangs back, giving me privacy as I crouch down and place the flowers on his grave.

"I'm sorry I haven't been for so long. I moved to Chicago three months ago. It's been crazy." Tears flood my cheeks as I feel thankful I could get here today. "But luckily, I managed to get to you today. I miss you so much."

I stay there for a while, talking to Dad like he is still alive. I tell him everything that's been going on in my life and all the crazy things that have happened, including my relationship with Remy. I don't know what he'd think about our relationship if he were alive. Most people would think it's fucked up, but I guess if he were alive, Mom never would have married Remy.

I realize I can't stay much longer as the darkness presses in.

"Ella," Remy's voice pulls my attention to him.

I nod. "I know, it's getting late."

He nods. "We can return in the morning if you'd like. Before we head back."

I swallow hard. "Yes, I'd like that." I turn back to the grave. "See you tomorrow, Dad."

With one final look, I turn away and lace my fingers with Remy's.

"Seriously, thank you for bringing me here." I gaze at him, feeling my heart swell.

"Of course," he says as we walk away. "Anything for you." He tilts his head to the side. "What would you like to do now? Dinner or straight back to the hotel?"

I don't feel that deep gnawing pit of emptiness for

the first time on my birthday, and going for dinner sounds nice. "I could get some dinner. I know the perfect place."

He nods, returning to the car, where I tell the driver to take us to Giuseppe's restaurant in the center. It's the best Italian in the city.

We sit together in the back of the limousine, and Remy casually rests his hand on my thigh. I lean into him and rest my head on his shoulder. The comfort and support he's shown today resonate in the silence, and I feel a foreign sense of peace. Although I miss Dad, for once, I don't feel alone in this world.

29

ELLA

J sit in the library, my legs curled beneath me, reading a dirty romance novel. Before Remy and I crossed the line, I searched for any romance novels I could get my hands on with a Daddy kink. I would escape into the pages, imagining Remy as the Dom and me as the sub.

We're practically taking on those roles both in the bedroom and out of it. It feels like I'm one of the heroines from the stories.

Granted, I wouldn't mind him being a little rougher in bed and explore more aspects of BDSM.

The door to the library opens, and Remy marches in. "How did I know I'd find you in here?"

I smile. "Because I'm always in here." I put my book down, embarrassed by the cover.

"What are you reading?" he asks.

I shrug. "Nothing much."

He walks over. "Tell me."

I show him the book and the half-naked man on it.

"Erotica?" he asks.

"Kind of. It's got a plot, too." I bite my bottom lip. "I like reading smutty books, especially with a Daddy kink."

He sits beside me and grabs my hand, forcing me into his lap. "Is that right?" He kisses my neck, making me shudder. "How long have you been reading these books?"

"The Daddy ones I started reading shortly after I moved in here." My brow furrows. "But smutty books I've been reading for years."

He smirks. "And do they give you ideas?"

I bite my bottom lip. "A few."

"Tell me what you've read that you'd like to act out in real life?"

I feel the heat rushing through my body at the thought of telling him. "I'm not sure."

He grabs my chin and forces me to look him in the eyes. "Tell me, Ella."

I sigh heavily. "I'd like to be tied up more."

He kisses my neck. "Done, what else?"

I think about some of the hottest scenes I've read. "I'd like you to spank me hard."

"Such a naughty girl," he breathes. "Anything else."

"There's one thing, but..." I trail off as I can't understand why this scene turned me on. It's fucked up.

"What is it, angel? Nothing you can say will be too much for me."

"I'm not so sure," I breathe.

"Tell me," he commands.

"There was this scene in one book where they acted out a break-in and taking the heroine by force and..."

"And that appealed to you?" he asks a touch of surprise in his voice.

"It's sick, isn't it?" I try to fight away from him, but he holds me tighter.

"Not at all. Many women have fantasies about that. It's part of a biological reaction." He bites my collar-bone, and I moan, lacing my fingers in his hair. "You want a man to be so desperate to have you that he takes you even while you scream no, isn't that right?"

I nod. "Yes, I want it so bad."

"Me too. I like the idea of you screaming for me to stop but then taking my dick like a good girl." He kisses me, his tongue thrusting into my mouth. "I'm going to fulfill any fantasy you want."

My eyes widen. "You will?"

He nods. "I'm going to give you an intense experience and make sure you won't ever forget it." He kisses me, and I melt into his arms.

How can this man be so perfect? There has to be a catch.

"When?" I ask.

He chuckles. "You're very eager, aren't you?"

I look into his dark eyes, and my heart swells. This man stole my heart before we even started sleeping together. "Yes," I reply, grinding myself against him.

"I can't tell you when or how. The point is for us to act it out realistically. However, we need to have some ground rules. What goes and what doesn't."

I shift slightly to look at him. "I want anything you'll give me. Nothing is off the table."

He shakes his head. "Anal?"

I clench my thighs together. "Yes."

"Fuck," he grunts, his cock swelling beneath me. "I won't do that for the first time during non-consent role play. However, we'll need a safe word to be sure. A word you can shout out if it gets too much and you need me to stop."

"How about spaghetti?"

He laughs. "Okay, spaghetti it is." His brow furrows. "But if you can't speak at the time and you're tied up, then maybe hum a tune?"

"The national anthem?" I suggest.

He nods. "Okay, that's sorted then."

I kiss him, feeling even more in love with him. It's wild. But I can't help that niggle of doubt at the back of my mind telling me he will never feel it back. And the phrase he said in his office repeats over and over.

Love is a fairy tale, Ella. It doesn't exist in the real world.

I want Remy's love more than anything. And yet, I don't want to bring it up as this is too new, and he already told me he doesn't believe in love.

"Are you okay?" he asks.

I nod. "Yeah, just thinking."

"About?"

I force a smile. "When you're going to break in and tie me up."

He kisses me again and groans as he lifts me off his lap. "Not tonight, as I'm going to take you out."

"Take me out?"

"Yeah, on an actual date to a nice restaurant."

"Isn't that a bit risky? We're supposed to be keeping our relationship a secret."

He chuckles. "It's unlikely that we would run into any of my family, and if we do, I'll say I'm treating my stepdaughter to dinner. Is there anything wrong with that?"

I shake my head. "No, as long as they don't see us kissing."

He grins. "They won't. Now go get ready."

I tilt my head. "Are you coming with me?"

"No chance. Otherwise, we'll never make it to dinner. Plus, I'm already ready." He signals to the tailored suit he's wearing.

"Fine," I say, pouting. "I'll have to get myself off in the shower."

He grabs my wrist. "Don't you dare. Remember who owns this cunt." He cups me between my thighs, making me groan.

I swallow hard. "But—"

"Tell me who's it is."

"Yours," I reply.

"Good girl. And who gets to touch it?"

"Only you," I breathe.

"Exactly." A flicker of amusement enters his eyes. "But I do have an idea. A special treat I think you'll enjoy." He spanks my ass. "Now be a good girl and get ready for me. And then you'll get your surprise."

I purse my lips together. "Fine." I walk out of the room and can feel his gaze on me as I leave.

Heading to our bedroom, I turn on the faucet in the

shower and let it run hot. Slowly, I strip my clothes off, remembering Remy's instructions.

I can't touch myself no matter how badly I want to, as I know he has cameras installed. Instead, I rub my thighs together to stave off the need for friction. And then I walk under the water, running my hands through my hair.

I tease my overly sensitive nipples but don't touch between my thighs. Slowly, I lather myself in soap and allow a few brief seconds to wash between my thighs, biting my lip the moment my finger comes into contact with my clit. I'm like a gun ready to go off. It's been two weeks since we first slept together at the cabin, and I'm getting needier.

I hear Remy enter the bedroom, so I switch off the faucet, wrap a thick white towel around myself, and walk into the bedroom to see what he's doing.

"Are you ready, baby?" He's holding something in his hands.

"What's that?"

"A panty vibrator."

I swallow hard, thinking of him putting it in my panties and using it at dinner. It's like something out of one of the erotic romance novels I've read recently.

"Are you serious?"

He steps closer. "I thought you might like it. Exploring another aspect of the Dom and sub dynamic a little more. One I introduced you to at the cabin. Edging." His eyes are alight with dark desire.

"If you put that in my panties, I'll come instantly."

He smirks, shaking his head. "You won't because I'll be controlling it."

He moves toward me. "What do you say?" He grabs my hips, pulling me close. "Do you want to be dominated tonight? I'll edge you the entire time we're at dinner, so by the time you finally sit on my cock, you'll explode for me."

"Yes," I breathe, the need to please him claws at me.

He yanks my towel away and takes in the sight of me naked for him. I can't deny that how he looks at me makes me feel more wanted than I've ever felt. It makes me feel special.

He grabs a pair of panties that I've never seen before.

"Those aren't mine."

He holds them up. "No, I purchased them for you. Crotchless, so I have access to your cunt easily. However, they will hold this in place." He signals to the little device.

He puts my panties on and slips the device against my clit. Already, I'm overly sensitive. "This is a bad idea."

He laughs and turns the setting on low, making me groan. "It's a good idea. I'll give you just enough to keep you on edge, angel."

I glare daggers at him. "That's torture."

He shakes his head and slips the remote into his pocket. "It depends how you look at it." He laces his fingers with mine and yanks me toward the door. "Come on, we've got a reservation to make."

Remy leads me out the door, his hand firmly

clasping mine. A sleek, black limousine awaits us as we step outside.

He opens the door for me like a gentleman, but we both know he's anything but. "After you," he says, his eyes gleaming with mischief.

I sink into the soft leather seats.

He slides in after me, his presence filling the small space. "How are you feeling?"

I clench my jaw. "Like I need to tear my panties off and finish myself off right now."

He chuckles and rubs his hand gently over my thigh. "Try to think of something else."

I bite my inner cheek. "Distract me then."

"Tell me about your childhood before your dad died."

My brow furrows. "It still wasn't great because Dad was always away working." My face lights up. "However, when he was home it was the best time ever. He used to take me to the movies and we'd eat so much popcorn we were almost sick." I laugh, realizing I've never been able to reminisce about old memories as my mom never wanted to talk about him." I'm so glad that I can talk about him with Remy. "How about you? Tell me about your childhood?"

"Probably as shit as yours most of the time." He clears his throat. "Although my only happy memories were at the cabin we went to for the weekend."

I smile. "You had family vacations there?"

He nods, but doesn't say anything else. We fall into a tense silence as the conversation runs it's course.

It's odd that since Mom died, I feel angrier toward

her. Perhaps because it means I can never get the closure I need. I can't ever call her out on all the shit she put me through over the years. She never considered anyone but herself, and I don't know if I'll be able to forgive her for that.

Suddenly, the vehicle slows to a halt in front of a grand, stately building adorned with antique lights. A sign above the entrance reads '*Le Papillon d'Or*'. It's a fancy restaurant, which makes it even more nerve-wracking wearing this vibrator.

The chauffeur steps out and opens the door, and we climb out, hand in hand, into the cool evening air. The smell of freshly baked bread and simmering garlic wafts from the restaurant, making my mouth water.

Remy leads me up the steps, and as we push open the heavy wooden doors, the warm glow of the restaurant wraps around us like a welcoming blanket.

"This looks expensive," I murmur.

Remy places his hand on the small of my back. "You're worth it." The host guides us to a table near the back which is not too close to other tables.

Butterflies flutter to life in the pit of my stomach. "What do you recommend?" I ask, glancing down at the menu.

"The beef bourguignon is delicious here, and they serve it with dauphinoise potatoes."

My brow furrows. "You'll have to speak English. I don't know what either of those things are."

He chuckles. "Beef bourguignon is a French beef stew made with red wine, mushrooms, onion, and bacon."

My stomach rumbles. "That does sound delicious."

"And the dauphinoise potatoes are sliced potatoes cooked with cream, cheese, and garlic."

"Okay, I'm sold." I slam shut the menu. "What are you having?"

"The same." He smiles at me, making my heart flutter. "I'll order us a bottle of champagne?"

I arch a brow. "What's the occasion?"

"Having you sitting opposite me?"

I heat at his words. "You're being extra cheesy tonight."

The waiter arrives to take our order, and soon afterward, a bottle of champagne is brought to the table, and our glasses are poured.

"To us," Remy says, lifting his glass.

I lift mine and clink it against his. "To us," I murmur, taking a sip.

I'm not sure what that means exactly. Remy told me before we started sleeping together that he didn't believe in love. So I know I'm a fool to think he might start believing in it with me. That somehow he can find a way to love me. Even though I know it's silly, my heart craves it. I'm too much of a coward to broach the subject, though. We've only been intimate for two weeks. It's way too soon to be talking about love.

However, I know deep down that I've loved him long before we slept together. My heart was his from the moment our eyes met.

"What are you thinking?" he asks.

I take a sip of my champagne. "Nothing much. Just trying to bear this damn vibrator."

He smirks. "It's only on the lowest setting."

I almost spit out my champagne as it doesn't feel like it's on low.

He slips his hand into his pocket, watching me as he pulls out the remote control and turns it up, making me jolt in shock.

"Remy," I breathe, clutching the table. "That's not fair."

His eyes darken with desire, the intensity shattering down my spine. "*Fair?*" He chuckles, mischief sparkling in his eyes. "I warned you tonight was going to be unforgettable."

Suddenly, the champagne isn't the only thing making me feel intoxicated. His teasing, wicked gaze and the relentless vibration of the device turn my body into a live wire. I can barely think straight.

"Well," I manage to say, my voice trembling. "You're doing an excellent job at it."

Remy grins, turning up the vibration again.

I clench my thighs together and bite my lip to stifle the moan trying to tear from me. My fingers grip the edges of the table so hard they're turning white.

His grin turns predatory, basking in the way he's affecting me. The restaurant buzzes around us, oblivious to the torrid game we are playing under their noses. "Angel," Remy murmurs, his voice gravelly. "Are you enjoying your... appetizer?"

I glare at him, but it's weak and doesn't have the desired effect. "You're being cruel," I say.

"Cruel?" He chuckles, arching an eyebrow, his gaze never leaving mine. "No. This isn't me being cruel.

You'd soon know it if I were." He turns the device up again, and I'm sure I will come right here in my seat in the middle of this fancy restaurant.

I can barely breathe, my chest heaving as I struggle to maintain control. The air between us crackles with electricity, so intense it's almost tangible. "I need you," I breathe, unable to stop myself from begging for something we can't do here. "Please."

His jaw clenches, eyes darkening. "What are you asking me to do?"

I swallow hard. "Anything. Everything."

He growls softly, and the tension is broken when our entrées arrive. Even so, that dark glint remains in his eyes. We eat our food, but as soon as we've both finished, Remy stands. He walks over to my side and leans down. "Meet me in the restroom in two minutes," he whispers in my ear, his voice husky before disappearing.

My heart hammers against my rib cage as I stand up, leaving our half-finished champagne behind. I'm not sure what will happen next, but as I push open the restroom door, I know it will be unforgettable.

I step inside, taking in the stark contrast between the bustling restaurant outside and the tranquility of the restroom. The tiled walls echo with silence, broken only by the soft hum of the air conditioning. Moments later, the door creaks open, and Remy strides in with a predatory glint in his eyes. He swiftly locks the door behind him, and he's on me in an instant.

His hands are everywhere— exploring, caressing, claiming. His mouth presses against mine in a heated kiss that leaves me breathless, his tongue exploring with an urgency that matches the throbbing between my legs.

He slides his fingers into my panties and pulls out the device which has been torturing me all evening. "I think you've had enough of this," he murmurs into my ear, his voice a delicious rumble that sends a shiver down my spine. "You need my cock, don't you?"

I swallow hard. "Yes, Daddy."

He lifts me effortlessly, setting me down on the counter, stepping between my legs, his fingers working quickly to unfasten his trousers. My core throbs as he releases his huge cock, hard and dripping with precum.

"I thought you said I had to wait. What happened to edg—"

He wraps his hand around my throat. "I can't wait to have you. Watching you across the table and begging me to fuck you." He bites on my bottom lip. "It's torture." And then he slams into me through the hole in my crotchless panties, filling me with his size. With every thrust, he drives me closer to the edge, the restroom echoing with our heavy breaths and moans.

His thrusts become erratic and forceful. The sound of our bodies colliding echoes in the room. "You like that, don't you?" he growls, a glint of satisfaction in his eyes. "You like being fucked hard in this restroom while everyone outside has no idea?"

I moan in response, knowing I've never been so turned on.

He leans in, his lips brushing against my ear as he whispers, "You're so fucking wet for me, angel. I love how you're clenching around me, your pussy squeezing my cock so tight. You were made for this, made for me to fuck."

"Oh God, yes," I moan, arching my back as he sinks deeper. "Please."

He stops, making me whimper. "Please, what? I need to hear you say it."

"Please make me come," I beg.

He releases a low, satisfied growl, his grip on my hips tightening as he complies, driving into me with an intensity that threatens to shatter me.

A flood of pleasure crashes over me, making my body convulse around him as I come undone. "Remy!" I cry out, my voice echoing off the restroom walls. His name is a prayer, a plea, a proclamation. My fingers dig into his shoulders, clinging onto him like he's the only solid thing in the world.

His pace quickens, his breath ragged and hot against my ear. "Fuck, Ella, so damn perfect," he grunts. I feel his cock swell, each stroke sending aftershocks of pleasure coursing through me.

A low growl rumbles in his chest as he comes, buried deep inside me. His grip on my hips is bruising, a testament to the intensity of his climax. His forehead drops to my shoulder, his hot breath fanning over my skin as we ride out our orgasms together.

The world outside the restroom door continues, oblivious, while within these four walls, we've created a universe of our own.

30

REMY

"*I*'m surprised you're here tonight, Dad." Leo looks at me over the rim of his whiskey glass.

"Why?"

He shrugs. "You haven't been here since you married Erin."

It's true. This is the first time I've been to Secret Obsession, mainly because I've been obsessed with my secret. Ella. However, I needed somewhere to kill time tonight until Ella went to bed. She believes I'm out of town tonight on business in New York. I'm here in Chicago, planning to act out her roleplaying fantasy.

She's been on tenterhooks since we discussed it, desperate for me to do it already. And tonight, I intend to.

"You know I've never been a lover of this place, but I fancied a change tonight."

Luca is back for the weekend from Maine. "How is Ella?"

I look at Luca. "Fine, why?"

He shakes his head. "Just surprised you pulled her from the auction."

"Massimo found evidence that Alex Vishekov was trying to move in on our territory. I couldn't let her marry him and give him a claim over Chicago."

Luca nods. "Fair enough, but who's she going to marry then?"

I clench my fists. "I'm still working on that." The best way to deal with the question is to be brief.

"I'll take her if you can't find anyone," Leo says, smirking. "You've told me I need a wife. And she's a fine piece of—"

"Don't fucking finish that sentence," I growl.

His eyes widen. "Woah, calm down." He holds his hands up. "Since when did you become defensive of Ella? You've often joked about fucking her even when she's in the room?"

Luca nods. "Yeah, what's changed?"

Fuck.

My possessive streak will reveal our relationship to the rest of my family if I'm not careful. I'm not ready for my two youngest sons to know. "Nothing, it's just sick the way you talk about fucking your stepsister."

"Don't tell me you haven't thought about fucking her, Dad? We've all got eyes. She's beautiful," Leo says.

I have to shove down the beast that wants to tear free and pummel my son into the ground. "She is," I say, clutching my whiskey glass tightly. "But that's not the point." I pull my cell phone out to check the camera I installed in my bedroom, where Ella always sleeps.

Thankfully, the lights are off, and she's in bed, which means I can get the fuck out of here.

I knock back the rest of my whiskey and put my cell back into my pocket. "As fun as this has been. I'm going home."

"Pussy," Luca says, shaking his head. "You don't have it in you anymore, Grandpa?"

I glare at him but don't stoop to his level. "See you later." I turn, walking out of the VIP section of my club and down the stairs onto the street, where the valet has my car ready.

"Here you go, Mr. Morrone."

I take the keys. "Thanks." And get in behind the wheel of my Ferrari. It's not often I drive myself, but on this occasion, it works best, as I intend to park at the end of the driveway. I can't let Ella hear me coming.

I race home on the highway, my heart pounding and adrenaline pumping through my veins.

When Ella told me about her fantasy, I could hardly believe it. Consensual nonconsent is something I have always wanted to try, but I've never been with someone who's up for it. It proves how perfect my angel is for me.

Once I reach the gates, I press the button to open them and drive the car inside, shutting them again. If I want Ella to be surprised, she can't hear me. I text my driver to collect the car and drive it to the garage in half an hour, by which time I'll be in the bedroom.

It feels odd sneaking into my home as I climb out of the car and open the trunk. I pull on a pair of leather gloves and then pick up my bag of supplies, including a mask with an in-built voice distorter, ropes and bindings to tie her up. I'll ensure she knows it's me, but I want her to get the full experience she craves.

I want to give that girl everything, which is new for me. All my life, I've been selfish.

The front door is locked, so I slide my key in and enter quietly, knowing Ella won't hear because the house is too big.

Silently, I ascend the staircase with my heart pounding in my chest. Pausing outside our bedroom door, I open the gym bag, pull out the mask, place it over my face, and switch on the voice distorter.

My cock is rock solid. It has been since I got in the car. I turn the handle and enter our moonlit bedroom. Adrenaline rushes through me at the sight of her sleeping beneath the covers.

I move silently toward the bed and place the gym bag on the floor. Once I'm within reach, I peel back the covers so that Ella's bare body is visible. She's only wearing a lacy thong and a sheer nightgown I picked out for her.

I shake her awake. The moment Ella's eyes flutter open and she sees me looming over her, her body jolts, and a piercing scream fills the room. I'm prepared for it, though, and in an instant, my gloved hand clamps firmly over her mouth, muffling her cries.

Her eyes are wide, filled with the perfect mix of surprise and fear. We had planned this, but it still feels so thrillingly real.

"No one is going to save you, angel."

Her throat bobs and her eyes dilate as she searches mine, realizing what's happening.

She shakes her head and begins fighting against me, making me harder. I remove my hand from her mouth and grab her wrist.

"No! Please don't do this!" she cries, wriggling beneath me.

"Shut it," I snap, tearing her nightgown off her body. The sound of fabric ripping echoes through the room. I pull her panties down her legs and ball them up. "Open your mouth."

She shakes her head, clamping her lips shut.

I growl and force them open, pushing the panties inside. "That will keep you quiet."

She kicks out, trying to get away.

I roughly grab her tits and squeeze them, making her gasp.

She tries to run for the door as I reach down into the gym bag and pull out the thick coil of rope, but I'm too fast. Before she's taken two steps, I've got my hand around the back of her neck. There's a palpable tension between us as I force her to face me and bind her hands together, the rope tight and rough against her soft skin.

She squirms and struggles, so I tighten the knots further, ensuring she won't be able to escape.

Next, I move to her legs, binding them to her arms so she's completely immobilized.

The sight of her, bound and helpless, is intoxicating. Pulling my cock from my pants, I force her back onto the bed and drag her to the edge roughly so her head is over it and pull the balled-up fabric from her mouth, slamming my cock deep into her throat.

"Your throat is perfect for fucking," I growl,

thrusting to the back and making her gag. "Such a good little slut." Saliva spills down my cock as tears spring to her eyes.

She gags violently at the intrusion, tightening her throat around my dick.

"I bet your cunt is soaking wet right now. Desperate to be fucked while you tell me to stop, isn't it?"

She tries to shake her head but can't. Tears spill from her eyes as she gags again as my size hits the back of her throat.

"Such a dirty little bitch getting wet while she's getting raped," I grab a fistful of her hair, pulling her mouth off my cock.

"Tell me how much you don't want it," I demand.

"Fuck you!" she spits, making my cock harder.

"Wrong answer." I grab the panties and stuff them back in her mouth before lifting her with her bindings and placing her on the floor. I step back to admire her bound and spread open for me.

"You're soaking wet," I say, kneeling before her and running my fingers through her cunt. "Desperate for cock."

She shakes her head and mumbles something behind the makeshift gag.

I smirk and fist my cock, watching her back arch out of instinct. "It looks like you're a dirty little slut who likes being raped." I slam into her wet pussy viciously.

Ella cries out, biting her bottom lip. It's a beautiful sight to behold. The power flooding through my veins is intoxicating as I watch her act like she doesn't want it.

Thrashing against the restraints and glaring at me with a fire of angry desire.

"There's no use fighting. You might as well enjoy it."

As if she can't deny me anything, her body goes limp. Her expression full of desire but also unshed tears as I watch her through the peepholes of my mask, wishing I could kiss her.

I love her perverse kink, as this is one of the hottest things I've ever done. "You'll take it. You'll take that cock like a good girl." I fuck her hard and deep, enjoying every sound that comes from behind her panties.

Her eyes roll in her head as she nears her climax, forcing me to stop. I pull myself out of her, and she whimpers, and then I lift her with the rope and force her onto her front so her face is pressed into the ground.

She groans as I slam back inside her, every inch buried deep. In this position with her bound, she's spread open for me, her beautiful asshole on display. I spit on it and then rub my finger over the puckered ring of muscles. "A beautiful ass. I bet you'd love my dick in it."

Her body tenses, but she doesn't hum the tune for me to stop, so I push my finger inside, using her soaking wet arousal as lube.

She moans behind the gag, her body relaxing.

I don't stop there, pushing in two fingers and then three. Ella cries out as I move my fingers in and out of her tight hole, my cock slamming deep inside her cunt as I push her closer to the edge.

"Do you like it?" I ask, my voice sharp and demanding, "Do you like being taken against your will and fucked like a little toy?"

She moans behind the gag, unable to answer me. Her body shakes suddenly, and her muscles tighten around my cock and my fingers as she reaches the peak. I hear her scream behind the gag, and then she squirts liquid all over my cock.

"Fuck!" I shake my head, struggling to hold on as my cock swells. "You squirted on my cock. That's so fucking hot."

I sink deep into her in one final thrust and then come, my release spilling at her depth. I groan as I fill her with cum.

Standing, I admire the view of her still tied up as my cum dribbles out of her tight little cunt. Her ass looks stretched and perfect from my fingers sliding inside.

"So fucking sexy. You look so good with my cum dripping out of your pussy." I clench my jaw. "You'd look even hotter if it was dripping out of your ass, too."

I notice the way she tenses, her body starting to shake. And I realize that perhaps the adrenaline and shock of being woken by me for the roleplay was more than she could handle. She did think I was out of town.

Quickly, I yank off my gloves and mask before untying her wrists and then her ankles. "It's okay, baby," I lift her into my arms, kissing her forehead as I carry her toward the bathroom. "It's me, angel. You didn't say the safe word. Was it too much?"

Tears flood down her cheeks, but she shakes her head. "No, it's just... I don't..."

"Ssh," I press my lips to hers and kiss her. "It's okay.

Daddy's here." I place her down on the mat in the bathroom and go to run her a bath. "I'm sorry if I went too far."

"You didn't."

My brow furrows. I know I did from the state she's in, so fragile and breakable, and I can't believe how guilty that makes me feel. "I did."

She shakes her head.

I pull my clothes off so that I'm as naked as her. Once her bath is run, I lift her again and climb into the huge tub with her in my arms. After she relaxes more against me, sighing as the water soothes her tension, I gently wash her hair.

"I'm an idiot. I should have known to be softer for your first time."

Ella glances at me over her shoulder and shakes her head. "You don't understand. I loved it. It was the best sex I've ever experienced."

"Then why were you crying?"

"Because it means I'm as fucked up as I always thought." She shakes her head. "You roleplayed breaking in here in a fucking mask and raping me, and I've never come that hard before. It's sick."

I kiss her neck. "I've told you, there's nothing wrong with it. I loved it too, if that's any consolation."

"You did?" she asks, her voice achingly innocent.

I grab the shampoo and work it through her golden strands, massaging her scalp. "Yes. It made me so fucking hard."

She moans, arching against me. "It was overwhelming, is all."

"An adrenaline rush?" I confirm, washing the shampoo out. And then I grab her sweet strawberry conditioner, spreading it through her hair.

She nods. "Yes, the adrenaline is like nothing I've felt before."

Relief coils through me as I realize it was the shock and adrenaline, not what I did to her. "I'm glad it wasn't what I did. I wanted to make it good for you, baby."

"It was far better than good."

I smile as I grab the hose, turn it on, and wash the conditioner out. "You were perfect. We can do it again if you liked it that much, but maybe I'll give you a little forewarning next time."

"No, I don't want any warning. What you did tonight was perfect. Thank you, Remy." She turns and straddles me, kissing my lips. The look she gives me is one of pure adoration, and I don't think anyone has ever looked at me that way.

I swallow hard and nod. "You're welcome."

She presses her head against my chest, and I hold her, knowing I'm getting in too deep with her. The problem is I couldn't stop if I wanted to.

31

ELLA

*M*ia sits opposite me at the cafe near Ronan's preschool. We've made it a regular thing to meet on Wednesday afternoons here, but she has been on vacation for two weeks with Ronan and Killian in Mexico, so I haven't seen her since I started sleeping with Remy.

There's a tension in the air that's not normally there. "I've missed having our coffee mornings. How was Mexico?"

She shrugs. "It was good." Her jaw clenches. "How have you been?"

I bite my inner cheek as heat coils through me. I feel bad sitting opposite her and saying I've been fine when I've been fucking her dad. "I've been good."

Her eyes narrow, and she sips her macchiato, seeming far less chatty than normal.

"What did you get up to in Mexico?"

She sighs heavily. "Not a lot. Just relaxing."

My brow furrows as she's acting off. "Is there something wrong?"

She nods. "When you went to Washington alone, how come you took Dad's jet?"

My stomach churns. "What?"

She drums her fingers on the table. "I took Dad's jet to Mexico as the Callaghan's was in use, and the staff let it slip." Her eyes narrow. "You weren't *alone*, either."

Panic hit me as I didn't expect her to find out. "Your dad tried to wish me happy birthday, but I broke down and admitted that I hadn't told anyone about it because it's the same day my dad died."

Her expression softens. "Oh, that sucks," she breathes, her brow furrowing. "But why did Dad go with you?"

I swallow hard at the mention of Remy. It just makes me feel way more guilty. Mia doesn't deserve to be lied to, but how can I tell her he came with me because I've been fucking him. "He offered to escort me, and I agreed." I shrug. "I didn't want to be alone, but I'd already accepted his offer before you text me back."

She draws in a deep breath. "And Dad pulled you out of the auction, too?"

I hadn't thought about how I'd explain why he'd pulled me from it.

"Yeah." I laugh and hate how nervous it sounds. "I guess he listened to me telling him I don't want to get married." I shrug and take a sip of my coffee.

A muscle in her jaw tenses, and she shakes her head. "Unusual for Dad to change his mind." She clears her throat. "Why don't you stop bullshitting me, Ella?"

I draw in a deep breath. "What do you—"

"No!" she snaps, shaking her head. "I'm not an idiot. I can put two and two together. My dad would only escort you to Washington if he were fucking you."

Heat slams through me at her brazen accusation. "I-I... I don't know what to say."

She shakes her head. "Nothing. Don't say a thing." Her jaw clenches. "I just don't like being lied to."

"I'm sorry... It just—"

"Don't apologize. I'm not angry at you." She waves her hand dismissively.

"You're not?" I ask.

She shakes her head. "I'm fucking pissed at Dad."

I swallow hard, as I'm not sure she'd say that if she knew how I begged him to take my virginity.

"He's fifty years old. He should know better." She shakes. "You're only twenty-one, Ella. You have your life ahead of you. What are you thinking?"

I don't know how to explain it to Mia. I've had this impossible-to-ignore connection with her dad since I set eyes on him. "It's hard to explain. I've never felt so drawn to a man before."

Mia downs the last of her coffee. "It doesn't make it right." She stands. "I need to use the restroom."

I watch as she walks away; so much for keeping our relationship a secret. Mia put two and two together far too easily.

I sigh. It's not like I'm scared of the judgment. I've never cared what others think about me, but I'm not sure what will come from our relationship.

Remy doesn't believe in love, and something tells me I

won't change his mind. And I want kids at some point, something I'm sure he won't want at his age. He's done the whole kid thing five times. I know pursuing him will hurt me, but I can't stop. Maybe I'm a glutton for punishment.

He's like a drug, and I'm addicted. Mia is right. Our relationship isn't right in society's eyes, but nothing else in my life has ever felt this good or real. He makes me feel safe and protected. I know it's not something most people would understand, but I've craved stability for so long, and despite what Remy does for a living and the danger surrounding him, he gives it to me.

Mia returns and sinks into her seat, eyes narrowing. "What's the end game for you two?"

It's a good question. One I can't answer.

"Honestly, I have no idea. We haven't talked about—"

"Of course you haven't. Typical Dad. He isn't the kind of man you deserve, Ella. Even if he's my dad, he's a fucking asshole."

I'm surprised to hear that from his daughter.

"He's always been a womanizer. Where do you think Luca and Leo get it from?" Her jaw clenches. "Massimo was as bad until he met Paisley."

I shake my head. "Can I be honest with you?"

"Always." She grabs my hand and squeezes. "That's all I want."

"I think I love him."

Mia's eyes soften to pitiful. "Oh no."

"What's wrong?"

"I don't think you realize the monster you've fallen

296

for. Dad doesn't love. He's toxic and always has been." She clears her throat. "I mean, he married your mom. He didn't love her."

"No, but my mom didn't love him either. She loved money. That's all she ever loved." It was a marriage of convenience for her.

Mia smiles sadly. "All I'm saying is to be careful and not give your love so freely. I'm not sure my dad can reciprocate."

"Why is he so closed off?" I ask.

Mia's brow furrows. "I think it stems back to his childhood. My grandparents never showed him any love before they died."

"And he showed you love?"

Her expression turns wistful. "In some ways, but Dad's always been quite detached. My brothers and sisters were my source of love."

"Does he have any siblings?" I ask, realizing I hardly know anything about him.

"Yes, he has a sister. She lives in San Diego. They were never close."

I nod in response, silence falling between us.

She looks at her watch. "It's time to get Ronan. You still want to come?"

I bite my bottom lip as I stand. "I'd love to if I'm welcome?"

She walks over to my side and places an arm around my shoulder, squeezing. "Of course. I'm not going to be mad that you like my dad. As I said, I'm more angry with him."

I feel a rush of relief that she doesn't hate me. "Okay, I'd love to then." I stand. "Let's go."

We walk out of the cafe arm in arm, but I hate that my conversation with Mia has given me doubts. I've been flying as high as a kite, and she's brought me back down to reality. Remy and I haven't discussed what happens next or our feelings.

We get to the preschool, and Ronan runs out. "Aunty Ella!" He runs into my arms, and my chest aches.

I'd never given too much thought to becoming a mom until I met Remy. Seeing Ronan and how adorable he is makes me want children with Remy. Something we also haven't discussed. "Hey, sweetheart. How was preschool?"

"It was fun. We drew pictures." He's holding one in his hand. "This is for you."

I smile. It's a stick figure with blonde hair, which I believe is supposed to be me. "I love it. Thank you so much."

He smiles widely, so proud of himself that it warms my heart.

Mia takes his hand. "How about we go for some burgers and shakes?" She looks at me.

I smile and nod.

Ronan practically jumps a mile high. "Yay!"

I'm thankful my secret with Remy hasn't destroyed my friendship with Mia, but am I heading straight toward heartbreak?

Deep down, I know the answer.

Remy isn't going to give me everything I crave in life. Until I hear it from him, I'll never know. I feel a little sick and reluctant to return to the house, as I know I will have to ask him sooner rather than later.

Can a man like Remy love a girl like me?

REMY

*I*nstantly, the smell from the kitchen catches my attention as I enter the house. It smells like a rich homemade ragu sauce, just like my mom used to make, which my chef would never cook because he's always making fancy dishes rather than sticking with the classics. My stomach rumbles as I walk in that direction.

When I get to the door, I pause and admire the view. Ella is cooking. Even though she doesn't need to, considering I hire a full-time chef. She's prancing around the kitchen in an apron and a beautiful blue dress as she prepares dinner.

I clear my throat, and she almost jumps a mile high. "What are you doing?" I ask.

A mischievous smirk appears on her face as she turns to me. "I'm cooking dinner for us, of course. What does it look like?"

I take a few steps closer and wrap my arms around her waist. I can feel her heart beating against my chest as I pull her close. "It looks like you're up to something naughty," I whisper in her ear.

Ella giggles and breaks away from me. She turns back toward the stove and continues stirring the sauce before pausing to look at me again. "Tell me about your day."

I clench my jaw as my day was shit. The Vishekov Bratva is becoming a more formidable opponent than I'd anticipated. Massimo has finally set up a meeting with Spartak for tomorrow so he can help us. "Same shit as always," I reply.

Her brow furrows. "You seem tense."

I let out a deep sigh, shaking my head. "Just business stuff."

Ella moves closer. Her sweet strawberry scent engulfs me, making my cock throb in my briefs. She grabs my hands and looks at me with those beautiful blue eyes. "You can talk to me about it, you know?" Her jaw clenches. "I may not like what you do, but it doesn't mean you have to shield me from that side of your life."

I take a step closer so that our bodies are flush together. I can't believe such a sweet and pure angel is willing to stand by a man as dark and corrupt as I am. "I know." I press my lips to hers in a gentle kiss. "Thank you," I breathe.

She groans and pushes closer, sliding her tongue against my lips as she begs for more.

I chuckle and pull away. "Now, what's for dinner?" I ask, leaning against the counter and ignoring my hard cock.

"Lasagna." She smiles. "It's almost ready."

"Shame I won't have time to eat you first, isn't it?"

"Gross." Leo's voice startles both of us apart. "What the fuck is going on here?"

I swallow hard as I face my son. There's no point beating around the bush. "Ella and I are dating."

Leo's expression is furious. "Oh right, it's okay for Ella to fuck her stepdad, but not me or Luca?" He clenches his fists by his sides. "You've been telling us to stop being disgusting about being with her, and that's because you wanted Ella."

Ella grabs my hand and squeezes. "The difference is, I didn't want to sleep with you, Leo. Not ever."

His eyes narrow. "You two are fucking sick." His gaze pauses on me. "She's younger than Mia, for fuck's sake. What's wrong with you?"

I cross my arms over my chest. "Let's be honest here. You don't give a shit about that. You're pissed that Ella wanted me instead. And why?" I shake my head. "So she could just be another notch on your bedpost? You have a problem, Leo."

Leo growls and then turns around, storming out of the kitchen without another word.

"Oh dear," Ella murmurs, shaking her head. "Our secret is definitely no longer a secret."

Does she know that Massimo is aware? I didn't tell her, knowing it would make her tense.

She notices my confused stare and elaborates. "Mia figured it out. She took your jet to Mexico, and apparently, one of the staff mentioned we'd been to Washington together."

I purse my lips together. "Sounds like I need to fire my staff."

Her eyes widen. "For gossiping?"

I don't particularly appreciate that my staff aren't loyal to me when I'm the one who pays them. "Perhaps. How did she take it?" I change the subject, wondering if the bridges with my daughter are well and truly burned. We're still trying to repair things since she married Killian.

"Better than I expected, although she said she was angry at you because you should know better."

I clench my jaw and nod. "I should know better." I grab her hips, pulling her toward me. "I do know better." I breathe into her ear. "But did you tell her what a naughty little tease you've been, tempting me?"

Her throat bobs as she swallows. "No."

"I didn't think so." I kiss a path down her neck. "Let her think I'm the villain. I don't give a shit. All I care about is you." I kiss her then, and she wraps her arms around my neck, moaning into my mouth. Our need for each other is palpable as our tongues tangle together. When she pulls away from my lips, I growl.

"I don't want the food to burn," she protests, trying to break free.

"Turn off the stove, then," I whisper. "I'm hungry for you."

Her eyes darken with desire, and her breathing shallows. "At least have a small taste. I spent all afternoon preparing *lasagne al forno* for you."

I smirk. "Okay, but a quick taste, and then I'm having dessert."

Her thighs clench as I let her go, and she retrieves the dish, placing it on a heatproof mat on the countertop. "I guess we won't be eating in the dining room?"

I shake my head. "What's wrong with here?"

She pouts. "I made an effort if you hadn't noticed." She pulls her apron off to reveal her stunning dress in its full glory.

My already hard cock becomes uncomfortable as it's the sexiest dress I've ever seen, hugging her body like a second skin and accentuating every one of her curves. The neckline plunges daringly low, leaving much of her chest bare and exposed. And she's not wearing a bra, so her nipples are visible through the fabric. "Fuck," I growl. "If you wanted me to sit and eat, you wouldn't have worn that dress." I stalk toward her, making her eyes widen like saucers. "I will have you for an appetizer, entrée, and dessert."

I grab her throat and yank her toward me, teasing my tongue along the seam of her lips. "Open your mouth, baby."

She does, and I spit into it, making her moan.

"Good girl." I move my hand up her thigh and then part her legs, finding she's not wearing any panties. "I love it when you're so wet and ready for me. I'm so proud of you."

She moans louder, arching her back to feel my fingers where she needs them, but I stop.

"How about that taste of lasagne, then?"

She glares at me. "That's not fair."

"Neither is that." I signal to the hard nipples poking

through her dress, "The quicker we eat, the quicker I get inside of you."

"Fine." She returns her attention to the kitchen, grabbing two plates while I fetch the silverware.

"It smells amazing," I tell her as she places a plate before me.

"Hopefully, it tastes as good." She watches me, biting her bottom lip as I take a bite.

It is amazing. As good as my mom used to make, and my mom was an amazing cook. "Wow," I say, unsure what else to say. "Where did you get the recipe?"

She pulls out my mom's old handwritten cookbook. "I hope you don't mind. I found it and wanted to try cooking for you."

"Definitely not. I've missed my mamma's *lasagne al forno*. It's the best." I smile. "And you've done an amazing job with the recipe. I love it."

Her smile lights up the room and makes my heart soar. "I'm glad you like it."

We continue eating in comfortable silence, and when we're done, she brings out some *cannoli* for us to share. She looks so adorable as she places the plate on the table between us with a shy smile.

"Cannoli is my favorite." I bite one of the little pastries before giving her one. "These are good. Is it your first time making them?"

She takes it from me and nods. "Yes. I'm glad they turned out well."

Once we've eaten a couple, my mind moves to the gutter. "Come here," I demand.

Her eyes flash, and she walks toward me, her hips swaying temptingly.

"Sit on my lap," I order.

She straddles me, her sweet strawberry scent invading my senses and driving me feral with need.

Our kiss is passionate and consuming as I slide my hands up her curves, committing them to memory as her warm, soft body presses against mine.

I break the kiss and look into her eyes. "You are perfect," I whisper, pressing my lips to her neck.

"Remy," she moans, lacing her fingers in my hair and tugging.

"Tell me what I want to hear." I yank her head back and look into her stunning sapphire eyes.

She licks her lips, making my cock pulse. "Fuck me, Daddy."

"Good girl," I murmur, releasing her hair and lifting her in my arms. She wraps her legs tightly around my waist as I carry her to our bedroom.

I place her on the bed and kneel between her thighs. The hem of her skirt rides up to her hips, showing off her glistening wet cunt. "I want to claim every one of your holes tonight."

She tenses, and her eyes widen. "It'll hurt too much."

I kiss her inner thigh softly. "I've got a lot of lube. You'll love it, I promise."

She shudders, eyes clamping shut as I kiss a path to her center.

I spread her legs wider, groaning as her cunt practically begs to be fucked with how wet it is. I take a moment to memorize her like this, loving how her body quivers in anticipation. Leaning in, I tease her with the tip of my tongue, tracing a circle around her clit before delving lower to taste her sweetness. I hear her sharp intake of breath and feel her body arch in response.

"Remy," she moans, her hands tangling in my hair.

I nip her clit. "Wrong name."

Her lips fall open, and she groans. "Sorry, Daddy."

"Fuck," I growl, increasing my exploration as I delve between her legs.

I feel her body tremble, her breaths coming in short gasps. She's so close to falling, and I've only just started. A good start considering I need to have her mindless with need if she's going to take my cock in her virgin ass. I don't let up, continuing to taste and tease her.

"Oh, fuck, yes, Daddy!" Her entire body tenses as she writhes beneath me.

One final, well-aimed stroke of my tongue shatters her.

"Yes, yes!" she screams.

I keep my hands tight around her hips and hold her against the bed, tasting her. She's panting when she comes down from it, but I don't intend to stop.

"Remy, I need you—"

I spank her pussy, and she gasps.

"I'm in control. You will get my cock when you're good and ready." My voice is rough with lust.

She jumps as I trail my finger over her clit and down her slit, making her moan.

"I'm going to make you come so many times, angel."

"I don't think I can take it. I need your cock—"

I silence her with a deep kiss. "You can. And you will," I tell her, slipping a finger inside. She's so wet and tight. The sensation makes my cock throb. I pump in and out slowly, my thumb brushing over her clit.

"Remy…" she whimpers, her body writhing beneath me.

"Relax," I murmur, adding another finger. Her body arches toward me as I stretch her pussy. Seeing her like this, so needy for me, is more than I can bear.

"Please…" she begs, her voice barely a whisper.

I curl my fingers inside, hitting that sweet spot that makes her scream. Her walls clench around me, her entire body shaking as she climaxes again.

"Good girl," I praise, pushing her through her second orgasm with my fingers still deep inside her. She's panting, her body limp beneath me, but I know she's ready for more. And I can't wait to give it to her.

With a swift movement, I flip her onto her hands and knees. Her breath hitches as her arms brace against the soft sheets, her ass in the air. I take a moment to appreciate the sight while my cock leaks into my briefs. I reach over to the nightstand, rummaging in the drawer until my fingers close around a bottle of lube and a vaginal vibrator that will sit perfectly inside her cunt and against her clit, giving her double the pleasure.

I press the button on the vibrator, and it buzzes to life in my hand.

Ella glances over her shoulder. "What are you going to do with that?"

I spank her ass hard enough to warn. "No questions."

She bites her lip, and if it isn't the sexiest fucking thing I've ever seen with her ass in the air and her innocent blue eyes staring back at me.

I press the vibrating toy against her slit, coating it in her wetness. She moans at the contact, her thighs twitching. I slide it up and down her folds, teasing her, making her whimper and buck against me. And then I slowly push it inside her.

She gasps, her body tensing as the vibrator fills her and the other part rests against her clit. I can't help but groan, my cock aching with need as she gets even wetter. I adjust the speed of the vibrator, watching as her body reacts, her moans getting louder with each increase. "That's it, baby," I whisper, "Such a good girl, aren't you?"

She nods, gazing at me over her shoulder.

"Stay still," I command, popping the cap of the lube. I squeeze a generous amount onto my fingers.

Her body tenses, and a shiver runs through her as I trail my slick fingers slowly down her back, over the curve of her ass, and toward her tight hole. I circle it gently, one finger rubbing the slick lube around her entrance.

"Daddy.." she whimpers.

I don't rush, taking the time to relax her. I press one finger inside her tight hole, and she gasps, her knuckles whitening as they grip the sheets. I add another finger, slowly stretching her, preparing her for my dick. Her moans fill the room, the sound driving me wild. It's taking all my willpower not to shove my cock in her ass and be done with it.

I slide a third finger into her, groaning at how tight she is.

There's tension in her muscles, but she doesn't fight it. Her breathing is heavy as her back rises and falls with each breath. I move my three fingers in and out of her, letting her get used to the stretch. Once she's ready, I slowly slide a fourth finger inside.

Ella cries out, her entire body shuddering as I stretch her ass.

"Relax, angel," I whisper, my voice husky. "You're doing so well."

I fuck her ass with my fingers, stretching her and preparing her. Her moans fill the room, sending jolts of pleasure down my spine. I can feel her body relaxing and her muscles loosening around my fingers.

Suddenly, her body convulses, a strangled cry escaping her lips as she climaxes with the hands-free vibrator deep in her cunt. It's the third time she's come tonight in a short time. A testament to how much she's enjoying having her ass explored.

Her body thrashes on the bed, moaning and whimpering. Seeing her, lost in her pleasure, makes me ache with need. I ignore my cock and move my fingers in a steady rhythm in her ass, keeping her pleasure going for as long as possible. I can't wait to be inside her and feel that tight ass around me.

But first, I intend to fuck her cunt and make her come for the fourth time before her ass gets my dick. I reach into the nightstand and grab a thick, vibrating butt plug, spreading lube onto it.

"I'm going to put this plug in your ass, okay?" I ask, my voice straining with need.

She nods, her eyes heavy with lust as she glances back at me. I slide the plug inside her, pushing it in until she's filled with the toy. She cries out as I turn it on, the vibrations sending shockwaves through her body coupled with the vibrator in her cunt.

"Oh my God, it feels amazing," she groans, her hips moving of their own accord as she seeks more pleasure. I've never seen anything so beautiful.

"Such a greedy girl." I press kisses over her back, and suddenly, she's coming apart, her cries filling the air.

"Oh fuck, yes!"

I smirk against her spine. "Do you want my cock in your pussy now?"

She can't speak, gasping for oxygen as she nods.

I pull out the vibrator in her pussy, and she whimpers in protest. Before she can say anything, I slam my aching and leaking cock into her dripping pussy.

She cries out with pleasure as I fill her up, the plug pushing against me as I stretch her to her limits. I give her a few moments to adjust to my size in addition to the vibrator in her ass before slowly moving in and out.

I fuck her. My thrusts are deep and powerful. The sound of our wet bodies slapping together fills the room. I angle my hips, hitting that sweet spot inside her that makes her gasp and twitch. The vibrations from the plug in her ass make her writhe beneath me.

Her inner walls twitch around me, a sure sign that she's close to climaxing *again*. I increase my pace, fingers bruising her hips as I pound into her. "That's it. Come for me," I growl, a command more than a request.

With a loud cry, she climaxes hard, her pussy clenching and pulsating around my dick. It's a battle of willpower to hold back my orgasm, especially with her tightness milking my cock.

But I won't come. Not yet. Not until I'm balls-deep in her ass. I slow down to give her time to descend from the heights of pleasure, my breathing ragged as I struggle to maintain control. This is just the beginning.

ELLA

*M*y breaths are short gasps as he fills me. His cock is buried deep inside my pussy, and the vibrating plug is lodged in my ass, driving me crazy with pleasure I've never experienced.

But Remy hasn't come.

He's pushing me further than I ever thought possible. He's brought me to orgasm *five* times but hasn't fucked my ass yet.

"Remy," I murmur his name while arching my back. "This is crazy."

He responds by wrapping his huge hand around my neck and pulling me up so I'm bent at an unusual angle. "No." His voice rumbles against my ear. "This is perfect. You're wetter than you've ever been. So fucking wet, we'll need to change the sheets." His fingers gently stroke the curve of my spine as he continues. "Your ass is almost ready."

"Almost?" I squeak.

He doesn't respond, his fingers gently tracing the

curve of my spine. Anticipation thrums through me like electricity. My heart beats erratically as he reaches into the nightstand drawer and pulls out a dildo smaller than his cock.

I feel him slowly pull the vibrator out of my ass, making me cry out in protest as I suddenly feel empty. The sound of the lube squirting and then the head of the dildo against my stretched entrance makes me tense. The thought of being stuffed with both the dildo and his cock instills both fear and desire.

He puts more pressure slowly, and I open up to the invasion. The dual stimulation of his cock in my pussy and the dildo in my ass sends jolts of pleasure and pain through me.

How will it fit with Remy's cock still in my pussy?

Each pulse of his hardness is a reminder of his unspent desire.

I glance back at him to see his gaze locked onto my ass, his eyes dark with the same want coursing through my veins. "Breathe, Ella," he murmurs, his voice a gravelly echo. "Trust me."

I nod, a hushed whisper of consent escaping my lips. I shut my eyes and take a deep breath, releasing it with a quiet exhale. I feel the subtle shift in pressure, the slow but persistent intrusion of the dildo against my ass.

The moment it slides through my sphincter and deep, I moan. It's a raw sound, a sound I've never made before. The sensation is overwhelming, the combination of Remy's cock and the dildo filling me in a way I never thought possible.

The pleasure is coupled with the right amount of discomfort.

Remy growls like an animal. "Fuck."

I glance over my shoulder to see his jaw clenched hard as he tries to hold on to a semblance of control.

"So damn tight. You're such a good girl taking my cock and this dildo at the same time."

I moan, craving his praise. "I love it," I breathe.

A muscle flexes in his jaw. "It's so fucking tight."

My body is on fire, a deep, throbbing pleasure I can't escape. I'm filled to the brim as Remy fucks me with slow thrusts at first. He's too far gone to hold himself back as the thrusts turn relentless.

His fingers wrap around my throat and squeeze, blocking my airways. Stars appear in my field of vision, and I moan, knowing I've never felt like this before.

"I want you to come for me again before I take that ass. Do you understand?"

I nod my head as best as I can.

"Good girl," he breathes, reaching around and brushing his thumb over my clit as he continues to restrict my airways.

I scream, but it's muffled by his hand around my throat. My orgasm tears a black hole through me, engulfing me in a wave of pleasure that almost makes me pass out.

"That's my good girl. Come on my cock. I knew you could take it." He releases my throat, and I take a gasp of oxygen into my lungs. "I think you're ready to take my cock in your ass."

I arch my back. While my mind believes it's impossible, my body begs for it. "Yes, Daddy. I want it."

"Tell me how much you want it. I want you to persuade me." His voice has a teasing lilt, and I'm in awe that he's so in control while I'm a needy mess.

A guttural moan slips past my lips, carrying a need so immense it almost shatters me. "I want it, Remy. I need it. Please fuck my ass." I look at him over my shoulder, begging him with my eyes. "Fill me up and own me completely. Make me yours in every way."

He groans, and his cock slips from my pussy. I whimper in protest at the loss of him inside of me. "You're such a good girl. How could I refuse?" I feel him pull the dildo out next and grab the pussy vibrator again, sliding it into my pussy and switching it on.

The vibrations make me jolt forward in shock. "Oh God."

"I'm going to make you come so many times tonight you'll pass out from pleasure."

I shudder as he's already made me come so many times I've lost count. The tip of his cock presses against my stretched hole, and I glance over my shoulder to see him pouring lube over my ass and his cock.

"Are you ready?" he asks, meeting my gaze.

I nod. "So ready."

He pushes inside me, and it's an overwhelming stretch that feels both painful and pleasurable. I gasp, my fingers clutching the sheets so hard my knuckles are white. He's so large, so thick. I can't imagine it fitting.

My body tenses. An instinctive reaction to the invasion.

"Relax, angel," he whispers, gently massaging my hips. His voice is like a salve, soothing me. "Take my cock, baby. I know you can do it."

He's patient, easing in slowly, inch by inch. His praises wash over me, encouraging me. "That's it, Ella. You're doing so well. So fucking tight and perfect."

I close my eyes and breathe deeply, feeling him fill and stretch me in the most impossible way. It's a mix of pleasure and pain, intensity and intimacy, and a sense of being truly claimed beneath it all. Claimed by my *stepdaddy*.

Once he's almost all the way, he shoves the last couple of inches inside, splintering my flesh and sending jolts of pleasure through me. I thought I'd reached my limit, but he proves me wrong. He's all in, and I feel so full, so owned and utterly taken by him.

He's still for a short while, clawing at my hips hard. And then he moves, pulling out slightly, only to push back in. Each thrust is slow and measured at first, a teasing rhythm that has me biting my lip. The vibrations from the device in my pussy add another layer of pleasure, making me squirm and building an electrical storm inside me.

The slow rhythm becomes faster and more urgent.

I moan, my body rocking with him, meeting him thrust for thrust. He's driving me to heaven with each movement. I feel my body clench around him. God knows what number climax is building to a crescendo.

"You like that, don't you, Ella? Taking my cock in that ass like a good girl," Remy growls, spanking my ass cheek hard enough to add another dimension to the pleasure. He pulls out and slams back into me repeatedly, and each thrust hits a sweet spot inside me.

I can't speak. The pleasure is overwhelming; my mind is a blank canvas of nothing.

"Fuck, Ella, your ass was made for my cock," he grunts. "So fucking tight. You're squeezing me so good."

His praises are all for me, feeding my desire and pushing me closer to oblivion. I can tell he's close, too. His movements are more erratic, his breathing labored. We're spiraling, spiraling toward that inevitable, explosive climax.

"Oh fuck, Daddy," I gasp, my world narrowing to him and the overwhelming pleasure.

He growls. "That's right, baby. Take my cock in that tight little ass. I want to feel you come while I'm deep inside you." The sensation builds until I can't hold it in any longer. My orgasm rips through me, a tidal wave of ecstasy that leaves me shaking and moaning.

"Daddy!" I cry out.

"That's it, Angel," Remy growls. "So fucking beautiful. You're milking my cock with your ass. It feels so good." He grabs my throat and squeezes, leaning to whisper in my ear. "I'm going to come in your ass now." His voice is a low growl. "I'm going to fill you up so that you've got my cum deep inside you, and then I'm going to put the plug back in so you're sleeping with my cum inside you all night." He presses his lips to my shoulder. "And you are going to take it, aren't you? You're going to take my cum like a good girl."

"Yes," I moan.

His cock throbs, a sign of his impending release. "Fuuuck," he groans, his voice guttural. I can feel his cock pulse, his hot cum spilling deep.

The thought of being filled with his cum and wearing the plug all night sends another wave of ecstasy rippling through me. I squirm against him, my walls clenching around him as another orgasm tears through me, milking every last drop of his release.

"Fuck, you came again for me." He spanks my ass softly. "Perfect. You are fucking perfect." He pulls his cock out of my ass, and quickly I feel the plug replace it.

And then he flips me over and forces me to lie down against his chest. My eyes flutter shut from exhaustion as I press my face against his chest. And fall fast asleep within seconds, wrapped in the safety of his arms.

MY EYES FLICKER OPEN, and I find Remy's side of the bed empty. Glancing at the clock on the nightstand, it's only two in the morning.

Pushing the covers away, I get up and pad over to the bathroom. Remy is leaning over the bathroom counter with his eyes shut.

"Are you okay?" I ask.

"I couldn't sleep." He straightens and clears his throat. "I'm sorry if I woke you."

I shake my head. "You didn't."

He has an odd expression on his face, inscrutable and distant. As I gaze at him, I can't stop Mia's words from repeating like a broken record. I've been too much of a coward to bring it up even though I intended to over dinner—a dinner which ended up being rushed because Remy couldn't wait to get me into bed. I had no complaints.

I lean against the doorway, biting my bottom lip. "Remy," I start, my voice a mere whisper in the silence of the bathroom. I pause, indecision gripping me.

He steps toward me. "Something on your mind?"

Stop being a coward.

"What... what happens next for us?"

His eyes meet mine, clouded with emotions I can't quite decipher. "What do you mean?"

I sense he's putting off answering, as it's a pretty simple question. "What is the endgame? How does this work with us?"

His jaw clenches, and his eyes flash with an undetectable emotion. "I don't know."

I draw a deep breath. "I know how I feel about you, but I don't know if you feel the same."

His eyes narrow, and I notice him shuffle on his feet. "What do you feel, Ella?"

I feel nervous about saying those three words. It's not something I've said much in my life. Mom rarely said them to me. "I love you," I breathe, my chest aching.

The panic etched across his beautiful face is palpable. "I told you well before this started that I don't believe in love."

My stomach churns. "But—"

"There are no buts. I don't love. I'll protect and provide for you, but that's all." His jaw is tight, and the seriousness in his expression makes me sick. "Love isn't an option."

I could have accepted that he wasn't quite there yet. But he is saying it's never going to happen. Tears fill my eyes, but I don't allow them to fall, drawing a deep breath.

"And you expect me to be with a man who doesn't love me?"

His nostrils flare. "I told you I didn't believe in love before anything happened between us. Did you think I was joking?"

I walk back into the bedroom and sit on the edge of the bed and grab my shirt, pulling it over my head. "I don't know what I thought."

"What are you doing?" he asks, grabbing my wrist as I stand.

I glare at him. "I can't be with a man who doesn't love me."

He searches my eyes. "What are you saying?"

I yank my arm from his grasp and step back, rubbing my face in my hands. "I can't be with you if you don't love me and never will." My stomach is a mess of nerves. "We have to stop this. I need to leave."

Remy blocks my path with possessive rage in his eyes, stopping me. "I think you forgot something, Ella."

"What?" I ask, my voice small.

"I told you before we fucked in the cabin that if we crossed that line, there was no going back."

Shit.

I remember him saying it, but I didn't think he was serious.

"I have no intention of ever letting you go," he adds.

"And no intention of ever giving me the love I crave?" I confirm.

"I don't have it in me to give you that." He shakes his head. "I don't even fucking believe in love."

I hug my arms around myself, feeling wounded by his statement. "And what about my future? I want to get married."

He shrugs. "If that's what you want, we'll get married."

My heart skips as I can't understand why he'd marry me if he doesn't love me. "You want to marry me?"

He shrugs. "It doesn't bother me either way. We can be married, or we can be together. Whatever you want."

I hate that he doesn't want to marry me. It hurts.

"I want kids," I say.

His expression darkens, and he shakes his head. "I can't give you that."

I feared this would be an issue. He's fifty and has five children already.

"I can't give up my dream of being a Mom."

His eyes narrow. "Perhaps you should have brought this up before we crossed the line." His voice is cold and detached. "You're mine. It's that simple. So you'll have to get used to our life together."

I shake my head and move away from him. "I don't want to get used to it. I want you, but not if I must sacrifice everything I wanted from life." I move around him quickly, and he doesn't stop me this time as I march for the door.

"Where are you going?" he asks.

I don't look back at him. "I need some time alone. I'll sleep in my room tonight."

He doesn't argue. Instead, he lets me go. Tears fall the moment the door is shut, and I realize how much of an idiot I've been. Of course, Remy doesn't want kids. Deep down, I knew that would be his answer, but I'd held onto this hope that maybe I'd be the one to change his mind about love.

Pathetic.

I rush into my bedroom and shut the door behind me, breathing deeply. If I'm going to have the life I want, then it won't be here with Remy.

The problem is he made it clear he has no intention of letting me go, which means I need an escape plan. There's only one person in Chicago I trust. And she's the daughter of the man I'm trying to get away from.

*I*t's four o'clock in the morning, and I've packed all my belongings into a heavy suitcase. I don't know how I feel, other than numb.

The happiness of being with Remy doesn't overcome the obstacles in our way. A deep sadness sinks into my bones and makes me feel heavy. I thought he was the one. So convinced that he would change his mind about love and fall for me.

Remy is never going to love me. He won't let me go, either.

It means I've got one choice.

Run.

I'm going to Texas, and I hope he never finds me. As I've lost who I am here. I've got a few friends who moved to Texas, and I can try to get a part-time job at the pizza chain where I used to pick up shifts in Washington.

Mia booked me a ticket on a flight leaving at eight

this morning, and she's picking me up to take me to the airport at any moment.

She was sad when I told her I had to leave as we've grown close since I arrived. However, she understood completely. Her dad won't let me go willingly but won't give me the life I want.

It hurts like hell.

I can't believe I fell head over heels for a man who will never be on the same page as me. It was stupid because I just ignored the warning bells going off in my head because of the draw he had on me.

Remy may be wickedly handsome and capable of making me feel things I never knew existed, but it was all a lie. My heart aches as I take one last look around the bedroom. I've spent many nights here since I arrived, but this room never felt like mine. This place only felt like a home once I started sleeping in Remy's room.

There's an odd sense of grief as I'm leaving Mom here. She's buried in the cemetery nearby, and Mia said she'll take me to visit one last time. I won't be able to return, at least not for a while.

Once things die down and Remy forgets about my existence, perhaps it won't be such a big deal.

My cell rings, and I see Mia's name on the front.

"Hey."

"Hey, I'm out front. Are you ready?" she asks, whispering.

We both know we'll be screwed if we get caught. "Yeah, I'll be out in a minute."

"Great, see you soon." She ends the call.

I swallow hard and grab my suitcase, dragging it out

the door. Being quiet with your life packed in a suitcase is difficult, but I do my best. My eyes linger on Remy's bedroom door. The ache intensifies as I realize this is it. There's no going back.

I get to the front door, and Mia is waiting there, looking nervous.

She rushes toward me. "I'll help with that."

"Thank you so much for helping me," I say.

She smiles at me. "Of course! What are sisters for?"

It's wild that she's going against her dad like this, but I'm so thankful, as I had nowhere else to turn.

"I got Killian to get you that bank account," she says as we drag my heavy suitcase to the trunk.

"Thank you! I can change the payee account now for my book." I feel a flood of relief as Remy thinks he controls my money, but I won't let him from now on.

"You're welcome." She passes me a folder. "The details and cards are in there." She purses her lips. "I did put a little in to see you through."

I narrow my eyes. "What's a little?" I ask.

She shrugs. "Twenty grand."

I shake my head. "I can't accept that, Mia."

She crosses her arms over her chest. "You can and you will. You'll need somewhere to stay and a deposit on a place. Think of it as giving you back your money for the account my dad stole."

"I didn't have twenty grand."

"With interest," she says.

I laugh. "I'm going to pay you it all back."

"You better not."

I glance at my watch. "We need to get going before we get caught."

"Okay, let's go." She jumps into the driver's side of her Mercedes soft top, and I get in on the other side.

A tense silence fills the air before she clears her throat. "I can't believe I'll never see you again."

My stomach churns as she drives away from the house. "Me neither, but surely, after a few years, it'll all be forgotten, and I can return, right?"

Mia's brow furrows. "Unlikely. Dad doesn't forget easily."

I swallow hard. "Not even for me to visit my mom's grave?"

She taps her fingers on the steering wheel. "If you had a quick, fleeting visit, you might be alright, but it's a risk." Mia glances at me. "I got the flowers you wanted. Lillies, right?"

I glance in the back and nod. "Yeah, thank you."

Mom's favorite flowers were lilies, and while we never had the best relationship, I miss her. She's been there all my life.

Mia turns the radio up, and I lean my head against the window, watching as she drives me down the ridiculously long driveway. And turns left toward the cemetery where Mom was buried.

The car stops before the cemetery gates, and Mia turns off the engine. "Are you ready?"

I draw in a deep breath. "Yeah, it just feels so final leaving her here."

Mia squeezes my shoulder. "Do you want me to come in or stay here?"

"I'd like to go on my own."

"Of course. I'll wait here for you."

I get out of the car, realizing it's been almost four months since Mom died, and I've not returned since we buried her. A part of me felt too guilty to face her grave because all I'd been doing was lusting after her husband. It felt wrong. Another part of me felt guilty for being relieved that I was finally free from her holding me back, withholding my bank account, and controlling my life.

I take a deep breath and reach Mom's grave, laying the lilies before her headstone.

"Hi, Mom." I swallow the lump in my throat. "Sorry that I haven't visited since you died." I clench my jaw. "And I won't be able to visit for a while. I'm running away."

I shake my head. "Funny thing, I think you'd tell me I was being an idiot for running from Remy since he's rich and can provide for me." I exhale a deep breath, slumping to the ground. "But I want more than money in my life. I always have. I want to love and be loved."

Tears start to fill my eyes, and I can feel the heavy weight of sadness in my chest. "I guess I just hope you understand why I'm leaving."

I lean forward and kiss her headstone, a knife twisting in my gut. "Goodbye, Mom," I whisper before standing and walking away from her grave for what might be the last time.

My heart aches as I turn to walk back to the car.

I look back at the grave before getting into the car with Mia. She looks at me with sadness, as if she understands everything. I guess she does, as she's lost her mom, too.

"Ready?" she asks.

I nod. "Let's do this."

She smiles and then reverses the car, turning around to head back toward the highway. Freedom is within my grasp. It feels like a weight has been lifted from my shoulders, knowing that I'll be in Texas and starting a new chapter today. One where no one controls what I do with my life or where I go.

The mix of grief and hope are odd as while it kills me leaving Remy, I've got a future ahead of me. Even so I feel the depression that's settled over me is going to be tough to kick. For a while it felt like I was made for him and vice versa. I just wish he knew how to love.

In time I'll learn to overcome it and find someone who wants the same things and who can love me. I deserve that as the bare minimum.

The journey to the airport feels like it takes forever, but Mia parks once we finally get there.

"You don't have to come in with me."

She shakes her head. "I'm seeing you off safely. There's no changing my mind."

I sigh and grab my suitcase, wheeling it by my side as we enter Chicago O'Hare airport. I find the desk, check my bag, and then turn to Mia. "Thank you so much for doing this. I hope your dad doesn't kill you."

She chuckles. "I'm hoping Dad never finds out I helped you."

I find that difficult to believe, considering Remy has

security cameras. He will check the cameras and find her picking me up.

"Ella?"

I turn and see Alex Vishekov standing behind me.

"I thought that was you." He beams at me. "What are you doing here?"

I bite my inner cheek, wondering if he would betray me to Remy. "Going home for a visit."

Mia's brow furrows. "Alex, what are you doing here?"

"I have some family I'm going to visit in Nevada."

I smile. "Oh, we can keep each other company then. What time is your flight?"

Alex glances at his watch. "Just over two hours."

I turn to Mia and hug her. "I'll message you later."

"Okay, have a good flight." She gives Alex an odd look, leaning toward me to whisper, "Be careful around him."

I nod in agreement and then give her one last tight hug. "Bye, Mia. Thanks for everything." Tears collect in my eyes but I don't let them fall.

She smiles and nods. "Of course. Take care of yourself."

Alex and I head toward security.

"I'm surprised Remy is allowing you to go home to visit. And that he pulled you from the auction."

I shrug. "He listened to what I wanted. I didn't want to be sold."

Alex looks a little offended, holding a hand against his chest. "I was looking forward to marrying you. That was obviously one-sided."

I feel guilty, as Alex was kind to me, but I never felt that spark with him. "You were kind, and I enjoyed getting to know you, but I want to marry someone I love."

We're about to head into security when Alex forcefully grabs my wrist. "There's no such thing as love, Ella." He yanks me forward, and I feel something sharp stab into my neck.

"What are you doing?"

"Claiming what's mine."

I try to open my mouth to scream, but whatever he's injected into my bloodstream makes it difficult to move.

Alex drags me toward the airport exit, and it's like I'm trapped in my body, watching what's happening but unable to fight or speak.

Once we get outside, a black van pulls up in front of us, and he shoves me inside roughly, my head bouncing off the floor and making my vision swim.

As Alex gets into the back of the van with me, everything goes hazy. And everything fades to black.

35

REMY

*M*y heart slams against my rib cage as I search the house for the second time.

Ella's gone.

All her stuff is gone, and no one knows where she is.

This can't be happening.

I can't protect her if she's not here. God knows where she's gone. It feels like Erin all over again, but this time, I'm more scared than ever of losing someone. While I didn't want any harm to come to Erin, I didn't feel like this, as if my world would end if anything happened to her.

I call Massimo.

"What's up?" he answers after the second dial tone.

"Ella. She's gone." I can hardly believe how panicked my voice sounds.

"What do you mean?"

"All her stuff is gone, and no one knows where she is." I tap my foot on the ground. "What if Vishekov got his hands on her?"

Massimo clears his throat. "If he has, he'll use her as a bargaining chip."

My grip tightens around my phone. "I need to find her."

"Why would Ella leave?" Massimo pushes.

"We fought," I admit.

"About?"

I clench my jaw. "Our future together."

"Shit. Why would you bring that up?"

I grind my teeth. "I didn't. She did."

Massimo clears his throat. "In that case, she left of her own will. Unhappy that you can't give her what she wants."

I growl. "Erin left for a vacation, and look what happened to her?"

Massimo exhales. "True. You want me to send a team to look for her?"

"Yes, but I want you and I to head up the team. Get our best men to our headquarters as soon as possible."

"I'm waiting for an appointment at the fertility clinic. I'll make the call, but I'm unsure how long I'll be."

Fuck.

I can't wait.

"Okay, we'll get a head start, and I'm going to drag Leo out of that fucking club. He needs to pull his weight on this."

"Good call. See you later." Massimo ends the call, and I try Leo's cell, knowing he won't pick up. It goes to messaging almost immediately.

"Fuck."

I dial Secret Obsession, my club, and the manager, Kai, picks up. "Hello, Secret Obsession. How can I help you?"

"Kai, it's Remy. Is Leo there?"

He chuckles. "Is the sky blue? One moment, I'll pass you to him."

"What?" Leo snaps.

"I need your help. Ella is missing."

He sighs heavily. "I'm still pissed at you for fucking her."

"Leo," I growl his name in warning. "She could be in danger."

"Are you sure she hasn't just run away?"

I clench my jaw as it's possible, but we have to find her either way. "With the Vishekov Bratva out for blood, I don't want to take any chances. We need to find her."

"Fine. Shall I come to the house?"

"No, meet me at our headquarters. I'm assembling a team."

"See you soon." He ends the call, and I march out of the front door to the town car waiting for me.

The privacy screen winds down. "Where are we going, boss?" Vincenzo asks.

"Morrone Headquarters. As fast as possible."

"Got it." The privacy screen returns, and I loosen my tie, knowing I've never felt this out of control.

Ella could be in the hands of my enemy all because I was a fucking idiot and wouldn't at least tell her I'd think about what she wants from life. I'm not sure I can give her the things she craves, but the idea of losing her strikes fear into my heart so intense I know I won't survive.

The car stops in front of our headquarters in downtown Chicago, and I jump out, heading inside.

"Good afternoon, Mr. Morrone," the lady at the front desk says.

I nod at her and rush for the elevator, pressing the button for the top floor where the boardroom is located. I haven't stepped foot in the offices of our legitimate holdings since I had cancer. As I leave the elevator, Elaine, my secretary, rushes over with wide eyes. No doubt the lady on the desk gave her a heads-up.

"Mr. Morrone. I wasn't expecting you."

"No, I've called an urgent meeting with some of my men. They'll be arriving soon. Send them in."

She nods and goes to sit back down behind her desk.

I walk into the boardroom and loosen my tie as it's suffocating me. Or perhaps that's the situation and panic. Ella left because I was an asshole.

My cell rings, and I see it's Mia. Sighing, I pick it up. "Dad, Ella isn't in danger."

I tense, wondering if she's with Mia. After all, they've become good friends. "Is she with you?"

"No, she's on a plane out of here. I dropped her at the airport this morning."

I clench my jaw. "Where's she going?"

"I promised not to tell you, but Leo called me and said you were going fucking mental about Ella. So, I said I'd put you straight."

"Mia," I growl her name. "Do you realize the danger she is in?"

"What danger?" she asks.

"Ella is a target, like her mother was. The Vishekov Bratva are targeting us."

"Shit," she breathes.

"What?"

"Alex was at the airport, too. He saw Ella and said he'd keep her company. She seemed happy to see him, so I thought nothing of it..." She trails off.

"Alex Vishekov?" I confirm.

"Yes."

"Fuck!" I end the call and throw my cell across the room, smashing it against the wall. The empty room before me feels too small as if the walls are closing in on me. My men can't arrive quickly enough, but it'll be at least half an hour until they get here.

Leo walks through the doors, surprising me as I was sure he'd be last here. "Mia says she's not in danger. She ran away to Texas."

I want to punch my son. "I've just spoken to her and she said Alex Vishekov was there at the airport. He escorted her through security."

Leo's jaw clenches. "Shit."

"Yeah, exactly."

He runs a hand across the back of his neck. "I'm not okay with you fucking her, by the way."

"You're an adult and need to get over it."

His eyes narrow. "You're such a hypocrite. Luca tried, and you told him not to be disgusting. At least he wasn't married to her mom."

I start toward him, fists clenched. "She told him *no*, and Luca kept pushing," I growl. "None of this matters because she's in Vishekov's hands right now. The same fuckers who murdered her mother."

Leo takes a step back. "Do you think Ella is alive?"

The question pierces through my soul as if she's not; they might as well end me now. I won't be able to live with her death on my hands. "She's better be, or I'll kill every fucking Vishekov I can get my hands on until their blood paints the streets red."

Leo nods in agreement. "Okay. What's the plan?"

I lean over the table, bracing my hands on it. "I don't know. Where the fuck are we going to start? They could have taken her anywhere."

I feel like I'm spiraling out of control. Panic is something I've never really felt before.

Leo lays a reassuring hand on my shoulder. "We'll find her," he assures me.

I close my eyes and take a deep breath. He's right. We have to figure this out fast. I'm not letting Ella die, no matter what the cost is. If she's in Vishekov's hands, then they're sure as hell in for a fight. I will sacrifice my life to get her back.

36

ELLA

he hard surface beneath me doesn't give way as I roll over, groaning.

What the hell happened?

My head is pounding as I open my eyes and shut them instantly. The light assaults my irises, making me squint a little to adjust.

"Get the boss. She's waking," a voice says from nearby.

I swallow hard and try to focus on the people, but they're just fuzzy figures. Trying to bring a hand to my head, I realize they're tied together.

"What the fuck?" I murmur.

The door opens, and I blink a few times as a figure approaches me.

"Wake up, princess."

"Alex?"

My vision clears and I see him smirking at me. "I've been waiting for a chance to take you since Remy pulled you out of the auction."

And then I remember what happened. Alex took me from O'Hare airport. I'm his prisoner.

"Why?" I ask.

He tilts his head. "Needs must. Remy pulled you out of the auction, but I wasn't going to let that ruin our plan."

"Your plan?"

His eyes flash with enjoyment. "Yes, my plan. To bring down the Morrone family. And once they're gone, I'll be married to the sole heir of Remy Morrone —you."

I clench my jaw. "I won't marry you."

He ignores me. "Once I take over the Morrone mafia territory, a war will erupt again. The Chicago criminal groups' alliance will collapse, and chaos will ensue."

I have no idea what he's talking about. Whatever alliance the families of Chicago have, I'm completely in the dark. "And you're going to do that? How exactly?"

"With Remy and his outfit out of the picture, the other criminal factions will argue over the territory belonging to me. Once they try to take it, my family will squash them and claim the entirety of the city."

I shake. "I'm unsure how you intend to kill the Morrone family."

"Remy cares about you, which means you're the perfect bait. Cut the head off the snake, and the rest will follow to their demise." He paces in front of me. "The Morrone family is particularly ruthless regarding those who harm their own, but that's also a weakness. As they rush into situations too quickly."

"You're wrong. Remy doesn't care about me." I laugh. "Why do you think I was running away?"

His eyes narrow. "We'll see. I never took you as a girl with daddy issues."

I glare at him. "Fuck you."

Alex steps closer. "You remind me of your mom."

My brow furrows. "How did you know my mom?"

"She was an obstacle that needed removing. Unfortunately, I underestimated how much she meant to Remy."

I can't breathe for a moment, his words hitting me like a punch to the gut. He murdered Mom.

"You?" I snarl, trying to stand in rage but being held back by the bindings. "You killed my mom?"

His admission is as chilling as the smile on his face.

"You fucking bastard!" I growl, not needing the answer.

Alex moves forward and strikes my cheek with force, silencing me. The taste of blood fills my mouth as I bite my lip from the impact, and my eyes sting with unshed tears.

"Shut up, Ella," he hisses. "Your little outbursts are irritating. You're a pawn in a much larger game."

I pull at my bindings, my heart pounding as I spit the blood from my mouth. "You won't get away with this."

He laughs. "I believe I already have." His gaze drops to my lips, his smile fading into a sneer. "Fucking your stepdaddy, Remy, wasn't your smartest move. Was it? My men followed you to the cabin in Minnesota..."

Heat and shame merge together at his words. "I won't ever marry you."

"You will." His cold, emotionless eyes never leave mine. "And once I get what I want, you won't go to waste," he continues, his voice a menacing whisper. "Once you've played your part, served as the bait, and married me to give me the claim to power, you'll make a nice little fuck toy for the Bratva."

"You're a monster," I reply, the thought making fear strike deep into my bones.

He senses my fear, continuing. "Any of my brothers who need a fuck can use you." His words trail off into a sadistic chuckle. "It's funny that you thought I was interested in having *you* as my wife because I liked you. You're no one."

I clench my fists by the sides, wishing I could slam them into his face. Acrid hate coils through me. I've never felt so much dislike for someone before. Alex is a very good actor.

"Good thing I never fucking wanted you, anyway."

He steps forward and wraps his palm around my throat. "No, I'm too young for you, aren't I? You've got issues spreading your legs for a man old enough to be your dad. It's sick," he spits.

His grip tightens as he glares into my eyes, his face contorting with rage. But I refuse to break under his gaze. Instead, I shake my head and draw in a shaky breath, the words spilling out in a defiant whisper.

"I wanted a real man, Alex," I say, trembling but firm. "That's why I chose Remy. Because, unlike you, he's not a fucking pussy."

"You stupid little slut," he seethes. "Do you know what I'm going to do to you? I'll ensure you end up in the whore house after the Bratva has ruined you." A cruel smirk crosses his lips. "You'll be a sex slave and won't get out of this alive." With that, he releases me and takes a step back, leaving me to contemplate the fate I've been sentenced to.

I take a deep breath, trying not to let the fear consume me—trying not to give Alex the satisfaction of seeing me cower. Instead, I hold his gaze despite every hope inside of my crumbling to ashes.

"Enjoy rotting here while we draw your stepdaddy out to kill him." His smirk is wicked. "I'm going to enjoy murdering him in front of you."

"Remy will kill you," I snarl.

"We'll see." He turns his back on me and nods at the two men in the room.

They approach me, and suddenly, one of them slams his gun into my head. Pain filters through my whole body, and my vision blurs as I pass out. As everything goes black, I see Remy's dark brown eyes and beautiful smile.

A smile I'll probably never see in person again.

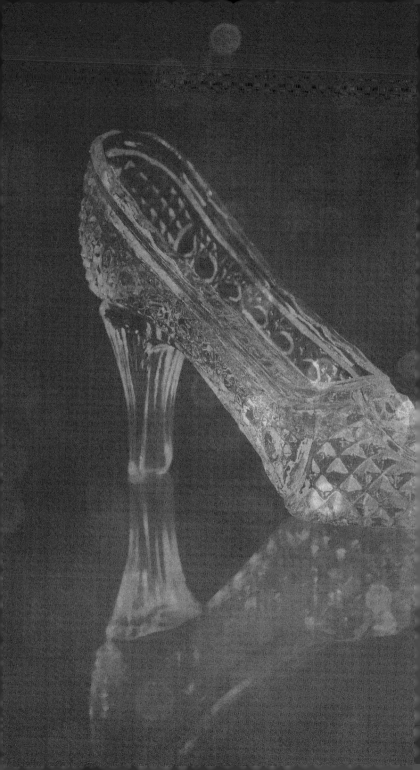

$\mathcal{M}$y head pounds with agony as my eyes flick open.

There's a droning in my ears, and when I open my eyes, it's no longer light like before. I'm in the back of a dark van, being transported somewhere. God knows where.

As I sit there, an overwhelming fear takes over. I'm going to die. It would fit my family's pattern of being murdered by mobsters. First, my dad, then my mom, and now me.

My heart is pounding like a jackhammer. My vision narrows, and my mind reels.

I clench my jaw and focus on breathing to prevent the oncoming panic attack. It's been years since I've had one, but I can feel the tightness in my chest increasing.

Fuck.

My hands are shaking, sweat coating my palms while my mind screams for me to escape, to do something.

The back of the van spins, and my breaths come in rapid, shallow gasps.

I feel like I'm going to pass out. The feeling of terror is all-consuming. A tidal wave sweeping over me, pulling me under.

And then I think of Remy, picturing his face in my mind calms me a little. The van jerks to a sudden stop, making me jolt forward. I hear the engine turn off and feel that panic return.

I pant for air, knowing I'll pass out if I'm not careful. Alex opens the door to the back of the van, glaring at me with those ice-blue, emotionless eyes. "No need to look so worried, Ella."

I shake my head. "What do you expect? You told me you are turning me into a sex slave."

He smirks at me. "I may have been a bit over the top. I was angry." He shrugs and yanks me out of the back of the van. "We need to have a chat about your boyfriend."

I squint to adjust to the light, and after a moment, I realize we're at an airstrip where a jet is waiting to take off. "Where the fuck are you taking me?" I try to fight away from him. "Let go of me."

"I'm taking you to Las Vegas for safekeeping."

The panic tightens its grasp on me as that's where Mom was murdered. "Why Las Vegas?"

"Because I have family there."

It makes sense now why she was murdered there. I clench my jaw and let him guide me toward the jet. "Why are you doing this?"

"It's nothing personal, Ella. It's business." Alex's eyes

darken. "And I think once you hear what I say, you may want to switch sides, anyway."

My eyes narrow. "Unlikely."

He smirks. "We'll see."

Alex drags me toward the jet and I struggle against him. But it's no use. His strength is a steel vice around my wrist, unyielding, and I realize with a sickening twist in my gut that I can't fight him.

As the doors of the jet close behind us with a thud, I feel my hope disappearing. Remy won't bother to look for me after our fight. It'll probably suit him not having to deal with me whining about love and kids.

"Sit," Alex commands.

I comply, shooting him a hateful glare as I sink into the plush leather seat. The aircraft lurches forward, gathering speed; before I know it, we lift away from the ground.

As the landscape below morphs into a blurry tapestry of greens and blues, the cabin falls into an uncomfortable silence. It's deafening, punctuated by the engine's hum and the occasional turbulence that makes me grip the armrests like my life depends on it.

"Look, Ella," Alex breaks the silence. "I can see you're scared, and I'm sorry I was an ass before." He shrugs. "The pressure gets to me sometimes."

He wasn't just an ass. He was a sadistic monster, and I don't believe a word he's saying now."

I arch a brow. "Why the niceties now?"

"You should be thankful that I saved you from that monster, Remy." He grimaces. "Am I right that you were fucking him?"

I heat at the question. "It's none of your business."

He shakes his head. "Whatever." He pulls an envelope out and passes it to me.

"What's this?"

"Evidence," he states.

"Evidence of what?"

He nods at the envelope. "Take a look."

I don't trust him, but I pull up the flap and pull out some old photos. My stomach dips when I instantly recognize the two men in the photo.

Dad and Remy.

"What is this?"

"Your father was his employee. The man who ordered the hit on him was Remy Morrone."

Numbness snakes through my veins like liquid ice. I shake my head, knowing it can't be true. "You're lying." I can't believe Mom would marry the man involved in my dad's murder. Although if what he's saying is true, she may not have known.

"I wish I were," Alex says. "But it's true. The man you have been fucking is indirectly responsible for your dad's death."

The information hits me like a ton of bricks. I don't want to believe it. Tears sting my eyes as I try to stop them from falling.

He tilts his head. "I'm not a bad man, Ella. I'm trying to help my Bratva." Alex reaches for me, but I shrug him away. His words before ringing in my ears. I don't believe a word he's saying.

Once you've played your part, served as the bait, and married me to give me the claim to power, you'll make a nice little fuck toy for the Bratva

"How do you know my dad worked for Remy besides finding these photos?"

Dad traveled a lot and met with his employer's clients. Remy could have been a client he visited.

He's trying to get into my head and while a part of me fears he might be telling the truth, the other part reasons that I need to keep a level head.

He leans forward, his hands clasped in front of him. "I have my ways." He takes a breath. "You can do whatever you want with the information, but I thought it was important for you to know."

I try to return the photos to him, but he shakes his head. "Keep them."

I stuff them into the back pocket of my jeans.

"What's the point of telling me this when you're holding me hostage, anyway?"

Alex smirks. "You may not be a virgin anymore, but I still want to marry you." He taps his chin. "Although I won't be paying a dime."

I shake my head. "I told you already, I'm not going to marry you."

"Maybe not willingly, but I'll soon have a ring on that finger. Even if it's by force."

His words hang in the air like a thick cloud of smoke and the glimpse of that dark, twisted monster from before comes to light. I glare at him, my heart pounding against my ribcage as I struggle to steady my voice. "Over my dead body."

Alex grins at me coldly, the warmth that was once in

his eyes now replaced by an icy chill. "You say that now, Ella. But you're mine now. You'll be Mrs. Vishekov before the week is through."

"I'll fight you every step of the way. I'm not a possession. I'm a person."

"Don't be so dramatic, Ella. You might as well get used to the idea as it's happening."

I take a shaky breath, forcing myself to meet his gaze. "There's no way in hell it's happening. I escaped the Morrone family and will escape from you, too." I stand.

Alex grabs my wrist forcefully and stands, too. "You will do as you're told and stop acting like a fucking brat."

I yank my wrist free. "Never. You make me sick."

And then his hand connects with my face as he hits me again, stunning me into silence. I press a hand over my stinging face, feeling the tears wanting to come but not allowing them to fall. "You're a fucking asshole."

He slaps me again. "This is how our marriage will be if you continue acting like a bitch." He turns away, walking toward the back of the plane. "I'll leave you to cool off and think about how you want the rest of your life to pan out."

I'm left alone in the vast space, the only sound is the hum of the engines. The tears I've held back fall, tracing hot paths down my stinging cheeks.

A storm of emotions whirls within me. Fear, disgust, defiance. But above all, a shattering sense of betrayal. I find myself torn. The seeds of doubt sown by Alex take root.

Could Remy be responsible for the tragedy that ripped my life apart over eleven years ago?

The thought is unbearable. It makes my chest ache, and for once in my life, I don't know where I want to be. Most kidnapped people would long to go home, but I don't have a home anymore.

I've never felt more lost in all my life.

"*A*ny news?" I ask as Massimo barges into the boardroom with a grave expression.

"A source confirmed he left on his private jet with a woman heading for Las Vegas."

"Fuck. How long ago?"

"About three hours now."

I run a hand through my hair, knowing they're trying to draw me into their territory. And then I'm at their mercy. "Those fucking Russian cunts."

Someone clears their throat behind me. "I hope you're not talking about me, Remy."

Shit.

I forgot that Spartak had been invited to the meeting. Turning around, I shake my head. "Of course not. I'm talking about Alex and Gregor Vishekov."

Spartak grins. "I quite agree. They are fucking Russian cunts." From the few occasions I've met Spartak Volkov, it's clear he's not sound of mind. He has this look in his eyes and a way of talking that warns people.

It's the main reason I was so shocked that my niece fell in love with him.

"How is Imalia?" I ask.

His expression softens. "She's doing amazing. And she is the best mom ever to our two kids, Anastasia and Ivan." There's a long pause before he continues, and I can tell there's something else he wants to say. "I know she'd love for you to meet them, Remy."

I clench my jaw at the idea. While I accepted my daughters' rebellious streaks, Imalia went too far. She inflamed the tension between our families and made the war ten times worse. "I'll think about it."

He smiles, but there's that insane look in his eyes. "Perfect. So it sounds like you are in a pickle with the Vishekov Bratva. Am I right?"

I run my hands through my hair. "Yes."

He nods his head and takes a deep breath. "Let me guess, you want me to help you out?"

There's no other way around it. I need him if I'm going to get Ella back safe and sound, as he knows his way around the world of the Bratva. "He's taken her to Las Vegas."

He laughs. "That's not good."

"Why?" I ask.

"Because that means she's in Egorov Bratva territory."

"They aren't an ally of yours?" I confirm.

He shakes his head. "They're not an ally of anyone other than the Vishekov Bratva, since Damien Egorov is Gregor Vishekov's brother-in-law."

I nod. "We know they have ties with the bratva there."

Spartak taps a finger on his chin. "Are you asking me to overstep my mark and help you retrieve a girl I don't fucking know or care about in another Bratva's territory?"

I nod.

He laughs, and it's a laugh that only adds to the psycho vibes he emits. "I love it. It's going to get bloody. But those fuckers think they can take a piece of Chicago, and they'll be met with backlash from the Volkov Bratva."

Massimo clears his throat. "So we can count on your help?"

Spartak nods. "Not myself, personally. I don't have a death wish, but I'll send a few of my best men with you."

I exhale a sigh of relief. Spartak may be crazy, but he wants to protect his territory, so he's willing to help and stray onto another's turf. "Thank you." I hold out my hand to him.

He takes it and yanks me close. "I think this deserves at least a dinner to hear your niece's side of the story, don't you?" His voice gives away his true motive, that he is only doing this to help mend bridges with me and Imalia.

"Sure. Whatever you want. When it's over, I'll hear Imalia out."

He smirks. "Perfect." He claps Massimo on the shoulder. "My men are already on the way here. I assumed you'd want to move quickly and arranged their arrival before I left. If you are three hours behind Vishekov, time is of the essence." He winks and then strides out.

The motherfucker knew I'd agree to his deal. The clock is ticking, and we've got to get Ella back before Vishekov hurts her.

Massimo stands, his hands resting on the back of a chair. "We should take our jet and our best men to Las Vegas." He throws a glance my way, his expression full of determination. "We have an Italian contact there, an ally who's well connected. He'll help us remain as covert as possible." His voice is steady, a comforting sound amid chaos. "We can use this to our advantage. Stay under the radar, move swiftly, and strike when the time is right."

"Do we know where in Las Vegas they're keeping Ella?" Leo asks.

Edoardo stands from the worn leather couch holding a document, his eyes hard and focused. "We have a list," he states. "All the places run by the Egorov Bratva in Las Vegas. It's an extensive list of forty establishments, homes, and hidden compounds. They will move hostages often to ensure they can't be rescued easily."

I take the document and growl. "How do we narrow forty down to one?"

Giuseppe clears his throat. "We start from the top and work our way down. We've got enough men to cover all bases."

I shake my head. "We can't go charging into Las Vegas with an army. And with just a few men it will take too long."

Antoni nods. "I've got to say I agree. We need a better plan of attack."

I meet Massimo's gaze. "Is our contact in Los Angeles looking for Vishekov?"

Massimo nods. "We have them monitoring some of the private airstrips. So hopefully when he lands they'll find him. But there are not enough men to monitor all of them."

"Fuck!" I slam my hand into the boardroom table hard.

My secretary, Elaine, opens the door and clears her throat.

"What is it?" I snap.

"Three Russian gentlemen are here to see you. They said their boss sent them."

"Spartak's men," Leo confirms, nodding at the glass window where three of his men are standing.

"Send them in."

The men enter the room and bow their heads. "We are here to help." A red-haired man speaks first with a scar through his right eyebrow. "I'm Akim."

"I'm Oleg," a dark-haired and muscle-bound man says, bowing his head.

"And I'm Viktor." The last one, tall but not quite as tall as me with dirty blonde hair, introduces himself.

"Perhaps you three could be of more use than my men. We have a list of Egorov Bratva establishments, but no idea where they'll be keeping Ella. There's about forty possible places."

The three of them chuckle, which only sets the rest of us on edge. We're not used to working with Russians.

"There's only one place they keep the hostages," Oleg says.

Viktor nods. "The Rainbow Lounge."

I clench my jaw. "Is that a strip club?"

They all nod. "They like to play with their prisoners."

My fists clench, and I'm about ready to slam all three of their faces into the table despite it not being their fault. They had nothing to do with it.

"Massimo. Is the jet fueled and ready?"

He nods. "Of course. I instructed Francesco to have the jet on the runway for take off as soon as I heard Alex took her to Las Vegas."

"Okay, we're all leaving for Las Vegas right now."

Massimo stands, but I place a hand on his shoulder. "Except for you. You stay here and keep an eye on everything on the ground. I can't risk you coming to harm if this goes wrong."

His jaw clenches. "I want to help."

I shake my head. "You're Don of the Morrone Mafia. Your place is here in Chicago."

He bows his head, and the rest of us march out of the building to face the wrath of the Egorov Bratva. I don't care if I have to burn down the entire fucking city of Las Vegas. I will ensure I get Ella out in one piece, alive and well, even if I die. She's in this mess because of me; I'll do anything to save her.

39

REMY

*T*he jet lands at the private airstrip on the outskirts of Vegas.

Leo appears from the back of the plane, his hair a little disheveled and his eyes red from sleep.

"Any news from the contact?"

He nods. "They were spotted heading to the Egorov Mansion in Spanish Hills."

"Fuck." I run a hand through my hair. "That's going to be complicated."

While I'm thankful that they haven't thrown her to the wolves at a fucking strip club, getting to her at a highly guarded mansion in Spanish Hills is going to be near on impossible.

"Any smart ideas?" I glance at the three men Spartak spared us.

Oleg nods. "I've got one, but it's fucking crazy."

"I'm all ears."

"Any of you Italians skydived before?" He asks.

Akim and Viktor grin like idiots.

Frederico and Edoardo nod.

I shake my head. "I haven't. Why?"

He shrugs. "The only way to get onto that property without being seen is from above. Skydiving is the only way in. Simple."

I'm not scared of heights, but I don't fancy throwing myself out of a moving plane. "How do you sky dive and make sure you land on the property?"

"You will have GPS, but the Egorov Mansion is a one-hundred-acre property. If you miss it, you have a serious fucking problem," Akim says.

I don't like these Russians. They're cocky and irritating. However, I can't deny their wealth of information on the Egorov Bratva is invaluable. "Fine. Skydiving it is." I glance at Leo, who looks shocked at my agreement. "Call our contact and get him to arrange it for tonight."

Leo goes to grab his cell phone.

"Are you sure you want to act that soon?" Viktor questions.

"The sooner, the better," I say.

He shakes his head. "The mansion is huge. We all need to understand the building well and its layout."

"We also need to work out the most likely places they are keeping her," Akim says.

Oleg nods. "Going in there blind is a suicide mission."

"Fuck." I clench my jaw. "How long to prepare?"

"With a lot of effort, we can be ready for tomorrow night," Viktor suggests.

Edoardo clears his throat. "I have to agree with the Russians. Going in blind is a very bad idea."

I take in a deep breath. "Tomorrow then."

Leo's about to make the call when Edoardo stops him. "I know a guy who can get us the equipment and a plane for tomorrow night."

"You trust him?" I confirm.

Edoardo nods. "With my life."

"Fine. Make the call."

Leo puts his phone away, clapping me on the shoulder. "Let's get to the hotel and get a drink."

I nod in response, as whiskey is needed right now. We walk off the plane and toward the two limousines on the tarmac. My men join us in one, and the Russians go in the other.

"Anyone else hate working with the Russians?" Giuseppe asks once we're away from them.

Federico shrugs. "They know what they're talking about, at least."

"True, but they're too cocky for their own good," I say.

Leo shrugs. "I don't think they're that bad."

The rest of us look at him like he's crazy.

"What?" he says defensively.

It's odd for Leo to be with the men. He's often at the bottom of a bottle or too busy fucking strippers to bother with work. It drives me crazy. I'm unsure where I went wrong with him, but he reminds me a little of myself before my father straightened me out. My attempts to straighten him out have not worked.

"Can we trust them is the question?" I ask.

Federico nods. "I think so. Spartak has no reason to betray us."

He's right. Getting rid of the Vishekov Bratva from his territory only benefits him. Silence falls between us, and all I can think about is Ella. I hate that I failed to protect her.

The limousine eventually comes to a stop in front of the hotel. We all get out and walk into the lobby, where our contact, Aldo, is waiting with our key cards.

"Good to see you, Aldo."

He bows his head. "And you, Remy."

Aldo is an old contact of my parents, whom we have trusted for many years.

"I'm going to get a drink," Leo says, eyeing up the bar and a young blonde sitting at it.

Aldo shakes his head. "Bad idea. You can use room service or the minibar in the rooms, but we can't risk any of you being seen."

Leo clenches his fists and shakes his head but doesn't say anything.

"Okay, let's go up to my suite and start on the plan for tomorrow night."

We all head up to the penthouse suite, getting to work assessing the blueprints of the mansion, which is bigger than I expected. It has to be double the size of our house in Chicago. We'll need to be careful, as the chances of getting caught are high. And if we get caught, Ella has no chance.

The weight of our task weighs heavily on me. One mistake and Ella could be dead or worse. I clench my jaw as flashbacks of how Alex looked at her at those events drive me crazy. If he touches her, I'll ensure his death is slow, painful, and bloody.

"This is by far the best drop site," Viktor argues with Giuseppe.

"Why?" Giuseppe asks, shaking his head. "If we drop here, we have better access to the back of the property. The back of the property is always the least guarded."

"That's a stupid fucking assumption," Viktor says. "The back of the property is always the most heavily guarded, because that's where they assume an attack will come from."

"How about we cover all bases?" Leo suggests.

Everyone looks at him, most of them surprised to hear him speak. He's mainly been silent since we entered the penthouse suite.

"Explain," I demand.

"We split into two teams. One team aims for the front of the property and the other at the back. We have more chance of success if we split up."

It makes sense that if one team were to get caught, we would still have a chance of all of us getting out alive. "I agree." My brow furrows. "Although it gives me an even better idea."

Everyone looks at me. "If we split into two teams and the one that drops at the front of the property is caught on purpose, it will make it easier for the other to slip in undetected. And perhaps when they take the first team into holding, it will bring us to Ella."

Viktor nods. "It's crazy, but not a bad plan." His jaw works. "I think it will have to be us as the decoy team. We're Russian, and we know how Russians work."

My cell rings, and it's an undisclosed number.

371

I pick it up. "Hello?"

"I have your stepdaughter."

My stomach drops, and I glare at my phone. "Alex," I growl.

All my men stiffen, watching me.

"Where is she?"

He chuckles on the other end, and I put it on speaker so we can hear him. "She's safe with me. I will marry her like I planned, even if you took her virginity."

"If you touch a hair on her head, I swear to God—"

"What are you going to do? You have no idea where she is."

I bite my inner cheek to stop the retort that wants to escape from my lips. We know exactly where he has her, but it's good that he thinks we're clueless. "What do you want?"

"I want you to give us Chicago territory."

"Over my dead body!" I growl.

Who the fuck does this kid think he is?

I knew I should have dealt with Gregor Vishekov years ago when he and his men were nothing but a little gang. And Alex was in fucking diapers. Now they're becoming a royal pain in my backside.

"Then your precious Ella will be fucked by every member of the Bratva before being sold into slavery for the rest of her pathetic life."

Leo snatches the phone and shakes his head, knowing I don't have a level enough head to respond. "We can arrange a meeting to discuss." I want to tear the boy's throat out for suggesting anyone other than me touch her.

"Which Morrone am I speaking to now?" he asks.

"Leo."

"The black sheep of the family."

Leo's jaw clenches, but he doesn't comment. "A meeting. Do you agree?"

"Yes, tomorrow evening in Seattle."

I smirk, as this idiot has no idea we're on to him. If he goes to Seattle tomorrow evening, we will break into his uncle's home and steal Ella back.

"Done. Text a time and place, and we'll be there," I reply.

Alex chuckles. "I'm going to enjoy this."

He ends the call, and all of us exchange glances.

"Is it a coincidence that he calls when we arrive in town?" Oleg questions, a skeptical look on his face.

"It's a fucking blessing is what it is," Frederico says, shaking his head. "It means he'll be out of town while we break in."

"I gotta admit, it's convenient," I say, drumming my fingers restlessly against the tabletop. However, it feels a little too easy to be honest.

Leo's eyes are clouded with suspicion. "It seems a little too easy."

Antoni clears his throat. "It's still going to be difficult. The Egorov Mansion will be heavily guarded, and the absence of one man won't make it that much easier."

He's right.

"Exactly. It changes nothing. We go on as planned." I lean over the blueprints. "We split into two teams. One drops at the property's front, the other at the back. And we go in and steal back what's rightfully ours."

Edoardo brings a bottle of whiskey over. "I'll drink to that, sir."

I nod in response, and he pours us all a large glass. It reminds me of how I used to criticize Ella for pouring me such a large drink at the start. She was always so compliant though, never talking back. It's clear she's a people pleaser, perhaps to her detriment.

We all raise our glasses, clinking them with a hollow, melancholy sound that echoes throughout the room. As one, we down our drinks. The burn of whiskey is hardly noticeable in the rush of anticipation coursing through my veins.

Each of us is lost in our thoughts, sitting in silence and contemplating the enormity of the task ahead. The quiet in the room hums with determination and the shared understanding that tomorrow could end in victory or disaster.

40

ELLA

The door to the room I've been locked in swings open, and Alex marches in.

I can't believe I thought he was charming. He's a fucking abusive asshole. He hit me so hard in the face that I've got a bruise on my right cheek. And then he thought I'd fall for him acting like the nice guy on the jet afterward.

"Morning, princess."

I glare at him. "Don't call me that. What do you want?"

His smirk widens. "Oh, just to check on my future wife."

"Never in a million years will I be your wife," I retort.

He strides over to me and grabs my arm, his fingers digging hard into my flesh. "You don't have a say in it." He moves his hand onto my thigh, and I'm thankful I'm wearing jeans when he moves it upward, making my skin crawl. "I bet you're gagging for it." When he's almost between my thighs, I bring my knee up and slam it into his balls.

"Fuck!" he cries out in pain, letting me go as I scramble away from him desperately.

"I will never be your wife. You're nothing but a monster."

Alex recovers quickly and charges at me with a feral look. But I'm ready for him. As he reaches for me, I lash out, striking him with my only weapon. My hand.

The diamond ring on my finger slices across his face. It's the ring Dad gave my mom when they got engaged. She hadn't worn it for years before she died, so I began wearing it as a memento to remember him by and to stop her from pawning it.

Alex's expression turns dangerous as he clutches his bleeding cheek. "You bitch. I'll enjoy breaking you and whoring you out to the Bratva." He bares his teeth. "It will be fun watching my brothers tear you apart at the same time while you scream for mercy."

A cold shiver skates down my spine at the thought. This man isn't just a monster. He has no heart. "I thought you said you only said that because you were angry."

He advances toward me slowly, and there's nowhere for me to escape. "I lied. I would enjoy nothing more than watching you become a plaything for the Bratva. In time, all you'll crave is cock and drugs. You'll be nothing more than a toy."

It's a stark promise of a future filled with terror. The words hang heavy in the air, tainting the atmosphere with a poisonous dread that I can almost taste.

His eyes gleam with savage satisfaction as he continues. "I'll find immense pleasure in witnessing your transformation." He is so close now, making me shake in fear.

Alex strikes me hard across the face with a swift, brutal movement. The impact is so forceful that it sends me to the floor, my cheek ablaze with pain. For a moment, everything spins, and I can taste the metallic tang of blood in my mouth. His fury is palpable, a dark energy that fills the room, making the air heavy with fear.

Alex grabs my arm so tight I know he'll leave more bruises, yanking me up. And then he pulls me out of the bedroom I'd been locked in.

The mansion is like a freaking maze, with all these identical hallways. He drags me through corridors, past rooms filled with fancy furniture.

A sick sense of dread creeps over me as he stops in front of a door that opens to a dark set of steps descending below ground level. I almost trip over the first step.

"Pick up your feet!" He snaps.

I shiver as we go deeper and the air grows colder and damper. Every step feels like I'm moving away from any hope of escape.

The basement is a grim, dank place with the smell of decay hanging heavy in the air.

Alex pushes me further into a room at the bottom of the stairs.

The walls are bare, the light from a single bulb swinging overhead casting deep shadows. It's colder here, and the silence is oppressive. I stumble on the uneven floor, shuddering as I catch sight of the chains attached to the wall.

"Strip," he commands. The word hangs in the air, ice-cold and venomous.

I shake my head, backing away until the cold, rough stone wall stops my retreat. "I won't." My voice barely more than a whisper.

His grin turns sadistic. "You will," he says, his voice chillingly calm, "Or I'll make you." The threat in his words is clear, and my heart pounds in response.

I swallow hard, knowing I don't want him to touch me. My only choice is to do as I'm told.

Reluctantly, I comply, stripping down to my underwear. The cold air wraps around me, each goosebump a cruel reminder of my situation. Alex eyes me, and a cruel smile crosses his face.

"Underwear, too."

I feel a fresh wave of humiliation wash over me, but I know I have no choice. So I remove my bra and panties, crossing my arms over my chest to hide my breasts. My nipples are hard because of the cold, and it's embarrassing.

"My brothers will enjoy fucking you. You're very pretty and have a lovely body." His eyes roam down to my pussy, and I wish I could hide myself, but I'm bare to him.

I want Remy to find me, but he won't even be looking for me. Tears well in my eyes, and for once, I can't stop them from falling in front of my captor.

He steps forward, the smell of his cologne overpowering and nauseating. His hands reach for me, and I flinch, unable to stop the instinctive reaction. He forces my arms down and cups my breasts roughly.

Bile rises in my throat. I want to fight, claw, bite, and kick, but I've learned that resistance only leads to more pain.

"Stay still," he growls, his fingers digging into my flesh.

I grit my teeth, forcing myself to remain motionless. And then he spins me around and claps my wrists into the chains affixed to the wall, forcing my stomach hard against the rough stone.

He yanks the chain without warning, and I'm pulled tighter against the wall. The chain is wrapped around my wrist, the metallic links biting my skin.

Before I can process what's happening, I hear the snap of something behind me. Apprehension settling like a stone in my stomach. And then I feel the slice of a whip against my back, making me scream in agony.

This basement is a place of nightmares where hope comes to die. And I'm trapped here with no hope of escape. I keep my eyes tightly shut and accept my punishment. I wish I didn't see Remy's face every time behind my shut eyelids, as I know I'll never touch or kiss him again, and it hurts more than anything Alex can do to me.

41

REMY

*T*he plane cruises at ten thousand feet as we get our equipment on.

Edoardo's contact, Jimmy, explains the GPS we will use to land correctly. We're diving in tandem since there's less chance of going off course, as one can focus on the GPS.

Leo looks about ready to shit himself.

"Are you going to be alright?" I ask.

He nods. "Yeah, I'm just not a fan of heights."

I clap him on the shoulder. "Man up."

His jaw clenches, and he nods.

Frederico clears his throat. "We've got this."

"Alex won't know what's hit him," Edoardo says.

Antoni laughs. "The fucking idiot is on his way to Seattle to meet us."

His call came at the perfect time. The opportunity to arrange a meeting at the same time we intend to strike was what we needed.

We were sure he wouldn't take Ella, and a contact at

the airstrip he took off from confirmed that she wasn't with him, even though I insisted that he bring her as proof of life.

Oleg clears his throat. "Don't get so cocky. Alex may not be there, but the mansion will be guarded to the fucking hilt."

It takes the Russian voice of reason to bring us down to earth. While I don't like the Russians, I can't deny that they're a valuable asset. They're better thinkers than my men, and I'm glad Spartak sent them.

Jimmy clears his throat. "Two minutes until you guys need to go. Are you ready?"

"Of course," the three Russians say in unison. They're all fucking fearless.

This isn't Edoardo's first jump, and Federico has done a couple before, but the rest of us are newbies. Besides the practice dive we did with an instructor this afternoon, we haven't dived alone.

"As ready as I'll ever be," Leo says, looking a little pale as he glances out of the plane's open door. "Fuck."

"We'll be fine," I say, forcing my son to look me in the eye. I'm not scared of jumping out of a plane. The only thing that scares me is not saving Ella from a life of torture. I need to get her back.

"It's time," Jimmy announces.

The Russians go first, fearless. One of them is diving solo since there's an odd number. I watch as they take their leap into the unknown. Frederico and Giuseppe go next. And then Edoardo and Antoni.

Leo takes a deep breath and stands up, ready to jump with me attached behind him. We both take the plunge, and my stomach flips as the air whooshes past us. The wind is loud in my ears, and I can't feel anything.

An alarm signals we're at the point of opening the parachute, and I pull it, the force of the wind jerking us aggressively.

As we soar through the air, it feels like time slows down. I reflect on life and what is important and realize how much of an idiot I've been with Ella. Telling her I don't believe in love is complete and utter bullshit, as I didn't want to cross the line with her because I knew she was different all along. That our relationship would be different.

I do love her. If we get out alive, I will tell her daily how much I love her. And while I'm not ready to contemplate kids yet, I'll keep an open mind for her.

The parachute swings us down gently into the clearing at the back of the property under the cover of darkness. According to the GPS, the Russians are approaching the front of the house, with the intention of getting caught.

Gunfire ignites, and we tense as I unclip myself from Leo's harness.

"Fuck," Leo says, running a hand through his hair as he pulls his skydiving equipment off and shoves it into the nearby bushes. "Are they going to survive this?"

I honestly don't know, but I'm not sure Spartak will be happy if we get his men killed. "I hope so."

Frederico and Giuseppe landed closest to us, a few feet away. "It doesn't sound good," Frederico says, pulling his gun from his belt.

Giuseppe and Leo help me shift our parachutes out of sight.

"Come on. We stick to the plan." I glance at the GPS watch on my wrist. "They're still moving, so they can't be dead."

We hustle off into the darkness, making our way around the house to sneak in through a side door on the blueprints. This place was built fifty years ago, so we have to hope nothing has changed since then.

Adrenaline courses through my veins as I lead us closer and closer to the entrance, my heart pounding against my chest. Edoardo and Antoni are close behind.

We get close enough that we can hear the voices of the Russians inside the mansion walls, and my fingers slowly curl tighter around my gun handle.

"Be alert," I whisper as Frederico steps forward and breaks the locks on the door, swinging it open.

We all hesitate, looking at each other.

"Remember the plan, split up, and keep on comms. If you find Ella, get her out quick."

My men nod, and we walk inside, splitting into pairs. Leo remains with me. We're checking the second floor for her.

We step through a small hallway, brushing past the old paintings that adorn the walls. We reach an intersection, and I motion for Leo to take the east side.

I take the west, and soon enough, I find myself standing outside a bedroom door, hearing commotion inside.

"Leo, I've found something," I say over the comms.

Within a minute, he's by my side.

"What is it?"

"There's someone in here."

His jaw works. "What makes you think it's Ella?"

"The door is locked."

"And if it's not her?"

It's a good question, as barging into the room and not finding her could be a big mistake. I press my ear against the door, listening for a voice on the other side.

My heart stops when I hear her muffled voice on the other side.

"It's Ella," I say, standing back and glancing at Leo. "You got the lock pick?"

He nods and works on the lock. After a few moments, it opens, and we both burst into the room.

She's bound to a chair with bruises on her face and arms. Rage slams into me, hot and heavy, making me want to rip apart whoever did this to her.

"Ella," I growl her name, and she looks up at me, eyes wide as she shakes her head.

"No, it's a trap!"

Before I realize what she means, Alex appears from the adjoining bathroom, pointing a gun at me.

"You left for Seattle," I say.

He smirks. "That's what I wanted you fucking imbeciles to believe. A contact of mine knew you were in town, and that's when I rang you to arrange the meeting, knowing you'd strike while I was supposedly *out of town*. So I had my jet take off as if leaving for Seattle. We circled back and landed at another airstrip."

I grind my teeth, realizing how gullible I was, believing he'd call the night we arrived in town.

"What the fuck do you want?" I growl.

Three men holding rifles exit the bathroom, aiming them at Leo and me.

"I wanted you here."

I swallow hard. He's using Ella as the bait to lure me to my death. "I'm not sure what your endgame is, but you won't win, Vishekov."

Alex laughs. "I already have." He glances at his guys. "Tie them up and take them down to the basement with the girl. I'm going to enjoy this."

His men nod in agreement before grabbing us and our guns, tying our wrists together. Thankfully, none of them notice the GPS watches on our wrists, so we still have a chance that our guys can find us and break us out.

I know they'll have heard everything over the comms. Now, we must sit, wait, and hope they don't get caught. Otherwise, it's game over.

42

ELLA

The guard throws me into a cell, and I land on my knees, scraping them on the hard concrete.

Leo is thrown in next, followed by Remy.

Remy.

I can't believe he's here.

Why is he?

He made it pretty clear I don't mean much to him.

"The boss will deal with you all soon." The guard slams the door shut and locks it.

Remy crawls over to me and grabs my shoulder. "Ella, are you okay?"

I sob at his touch and the sound of his voice.

He lifts me in his arms and then cradles me on the bed in the corner of the cell. "It's okay, angel. I'm here now." He strokes my hair from my face. "I'm trying to save you."

I shake my head. "Why?"

His jaw clenches, and I see a hardness in his eyes. He doesn't want to answer. "Because I care about you."

"It didn't seem like it the other day when we argued." I hate that I can only think of one thing as I gaze up at him. Alex's possible lies about Remy killing my dad, but I don't want to ask him now.

Remy's jaw clenches, and he glances over at Leo, clearly not wanting to have this conversation with an audience.

Leo holds his hands up. "Don't mind me."

His eyes narrow. "I don't want to have this conversation here and now," he murmurs.

"We probably won't make it out alive, so why not have it?"

He cups my cheeks and kisses me softly, making my chest ache. "We're going to make it out. Four of my men are still in the house and undetected." He glances at an odd-looking watch on his wrist. "They're heading this way as we speak."

"To rescue us?"

He nods.

I sob harder, struggling to believe there's a way out.

"Who did this to you?" he asks, his fingers tracing the bruise on my face and then lower to the bruises on my arms and chest.

I swallow the pain. "Alex."

Remy's fist clenches. "I'll kill him."

"How are you going to do that locked in here?"

His eyes narrow. "I will. I'm going to make him pay for touching you." He presses his forehead against mine, and my chest aches harder. "I promise."

I swallow hard as while I don't condone violence, the way Alex has treated me since he captured me makes me sure he doesn't deserve to live. All he will do is hurt another unsuspecting victim. "Thank you," I murmur.

If Remy knew everything he said he would put me through, I know his rage would be untamable.

"So, what now?" I ask.

Leo clears his throat. "Now we wait and hope."

Remy nods. "I have faith in my men. They will find us."

I wish I had as much faith. This place is like Fort Knox, and four men trying to go undetected here will be difficult. It's guarded heavily.

"You don't have anything to pick the lock?" I ask.

Leo stands straighter, brow furrowing. "Possibly." He steps toward the lock and inspects it. "It's quite an advanced lock, though. It may take a while."

Remy nods. "Try. It's worth a go and will speed up the escape if the guys find us." His arms tighten around me as he holds me in his lap. "You can sleep, baby. I'll hold you."

I have hardly slept since being captured, except when I was knocked unconscious. My eyelids feel heavy while I'm wrapped in Remy's arms because he makes me feel safe, even while his enemy holds us in a cell.

Before I know it, I'm drifting off into a deep sleep.

My eyes fly open as a shout startles me.

I bolt upright and then realize I'm still in Remy's arms. He's cradling me to his chest, and instantly I relax.

"Calm down, baby."

I glance at him, and my heart squeezes in my chest. "What was that?"

He gives me a beautiful smile. "Leo cracked the lock."

I jump to my feet and see Leo smirking as he holds open the cell door. "Wow. How long was I asleep?"

"Half an hour," Remy says, standing up and cracking his neck. "Where the fuck are the guys?" he asks.

Leo stares down at his GPS watch. "Same place. Do you think they've been caught?"

Remy shrugs. "And the Russians?"

His brow furrows. "I think they're somewhere down here in a cell."

Remy clenches his jaw. "I guess we better rescue them."

"Russians?" I question.

Remy meets my gaze. "Spartak's men. He is helping us with this mission."

I have no idea who Spartak is, but I nod. "Okay, let's get out of here."

Remy nods, and Leo leads us down the corridor, searching for the Russians. Suddenly, we hear a cheer to the right.

"Knew you fuckers would save us," a man says with a thick Russian accent and red hair says.

Leo snorts. "Didn't think you'd have much faith in Italians."

The tallest of the three with dark blond hair stands. "Never doubted you for a second."

The other I notice has dark hair as he steps forward from the shadows, staring at me. "You found her, too. Good work."

I'm not too fond of the way he looks at me. It's almost predatory, and I sense Remy doesn't either as he pulls me closer. "Stop staring and back up," he barks.

Leo doesn't bother to pick this lock as he grabs a huge sledgehammer propped against the wall and slams it into the lock.

"Fuck, what about the noise?" The dark-haired guy says.

The red-haired one squeezes his shoulder. "We're below ground, Oleg. They won't hear."

Leo takes a second swing at the lock, and metal cracks as the door falls open.

"Well done, kid," Oleg says, clapping him on the shoulder.

"I'm Oleg, by the way," the dark-haired man says as he exits the cell. "Akim." He points to the red-haired man.

"Viktor." The last man holds his hand up.

Remy clears his throat. "Now the introductions are over, let's get the fuck out of here." He takes my hand. "We're in the heart of the wolf's den, and getting out isn't going to be easy."

I nod, squeezing his hand. "Let's go."

We hurry out of the basement and split up to search

the rooms near the GPS signal showing Remy's four men. Remy keeps his hand tight around mine as we go from room to room in the area but don't find them.

"Fuck," he breathes. "The longer we're here, the more likely we'll get caught." He runs his hands through his hair. "I need to get you out of here." His eyes look panicked.

His brow furrows, and the panic eases. "They've found them." His hand tightens around mine as he leads me toward the room where his men have been found. As he turns the corner, he freezes.

One of the men is dead, blood pooling beneath him. Two of them are slumped against the wall, holding bloodied hands against their wounds. And another looks relatively unscathed.

"Shit. What happened?" Remy asks.

"Ambushed," one of them says, standing. "Antoni took a bullet to the chest. There was no saving him."

I see a flicker of anguish in Remy's eyes before it turns to pure rage. "Motherfuckers." His fists clench by his sides. "I'm going to murder Alex Vishekov if it's the last thing I do."

One of the injured men gets to his feet, shaking his head. "First, let's ensure we get out of here alive."

Remy takes a deep breath and nods. He turns to me, his face unreadable. "This could get dangerous. I want you to do as I say and run if things go to shit."

"But I—"

"Promise me, Ella. I need to know that you will run if you can."

I shake my head, tears gathering in my eyes. "I could never leave you."

He cups my face in my hands. "You must. What good would it be if we both got caught? Promise me now."

I clench my jaw and then nod. "Fine, I promise."

"Good girl." He kisses my forehead before turning to his men. "Let's get the fuck out of here. We have a plan. We need to stick to it."

We all make our way safely down the hall without being seen and out into the night. The spotlights illuminate us on this side of the property, and instantly, I hear dogs bark.

"Shit! Run!" Remy shouts.

We take off, our feet pounding on the pathway as we head toward a forest. The trees will at least provide us cover from being shot, but I have no idea what the plan after that is. I sprint by Remy's side, sensing he's holding back as he practically jogs at my speed.

I fear I'm not quick enough to outrun our pursuers, and I'll get the man I love caught or worse. Alex wants Remy dead. That much is crystal clear. I'll do anything to ensure that doesn't happen.

43

REMY

I know it will be difficult for my injured men to keep up.

Ella runs by my side, but she's not fast enough as I lead her toward where the getaway vehicle is parked. Shouting goes off in the distance, followed by wayward gunshots, as the guards aren't in range.

"They're going to catch us!" Ella shouts.

I shake my head. "Just keep running."

She nods and moves faster, forcing herself to push through the pain written on her face. We make it to the forest, which gives us some cover, but Ella slows down even more on the uneven terrain.

I grind my teeth, knowing we won't make it at this rate.

"Ahh!" Ella screams as she trips over a rock.

I turn back and rush toward her with our enemy hot on our trail. She clutches her ankle and gazes up at me with those big blue eyes full of fear and pain. "It's twisted."

Fuck.

The dogs barking in the distance, are closing in on us every second.

I stoop down and lift her over my shoulder. "This is going to be bumpy." I run toward the van, trailing behind the rest of my men.

The shadows of my men are faint outlines in the distance, too far ahead to make out clearly. The two injured ones are dragging themselves along, but they're still moving faster than us.

Over the headset, Frederico's voice rings out, as clear as the danger snapping at our heels, "I'm at the van. Going to drive into the forest to pick up the stragglers."

My heart pounds less wildly at the news, but I know we're not out of the woods yet. We keep moving. The only option we have. Every labored breath, every jolt of pain in my muscles is a prayer—a desperate plea to whoever or whatever might be listening—that Frederico and the van will reach us before Vishekov catches us and hauls us back to that basement.

I clench my jaw as I push harder, but the sound of dogs is so close now. They're feet away.

One of them manages to nip my heel, and I tumble to the ground with Ella. The leaves and twigs scraping my skin as I go.

She cries out in pain, and I look up to see she's face first on the ground. Quickly, I stand despite the pain of the dog bite and help her to her feet. And that's when I realize the snarling dogs have surrounded us.

"Shit," I murmur, running a hand through my hair.

"Where are you, Remy?" Frederico asks.

"Surrounded by a pack of dogs. We're caught. Get out while you still can."

"No chance," Frederico says. "We're coming for you."

I feel relieved that my men are that loyal to me. On the other hand, the Russians probably couldn't give a shit and want to get out of here. I have to hope Frederico holds them back and retains control.

The crunch of leaves underfoot draws my attention to the left, where Alex approaches, holding a shotgun.

"I do like hunting," he says, a sadistic smirk on his lips. "Especially when the prey is my enemy." He casually holds it under his arm, not pointing it at us.

"Call your dogs off," I demand.

He tilts his head. "Why would I do that? It's rather fun watching you sweat."

"I'm going to enjoy putting you in your place," I say, stepping forward despite the dogs circling us. "This is far from over, Alex."

His eyes narrow. "I'm not sure what upper hand you think you have, but you don't. You have a pack of hungry dogs circling you, and I've got a shotgun."

Alex stands between us and our freedom. However, Frederico is on his way.

"It was so easy to break out of your prison. I hardly feel like you tried."

Alex bares his teeth. "Don't think that you're getting away. No one gets away from me." His cockiness is gently easing. He lifts his shotgun and points it at Ella.

"She must have one hell of a cunt for you to risk your life to save her."

I clench my fists by my sides. "Shut up, or I'll—"

"You'll what?" He laughs. "You can't do fuck all with my dogs keeping you back." He cocks his gun, the sound echoing off the surrounding trees.

My men will be driving in our direction. I just have to hold this son of a bitch off long enough for them to return.

"How do you think you will take down the rest of the families in Chicago, even with my territory?"

I need to keep him talking.

Ella's hand clutches mine so hard as she remains behind me. I know she's scared, but I'm not letting anything happen to her. I'd die before she comes to any harm.

Alex gives me a smug smirk. "You think I'm going to tell you my plan?" He laughs again and shakes his head. "I'm not that stupid."

The roar of an engine tells me that the van is close.

Alex's eyes narrow when he hears it.

And then it speeds into the clearing where we're standing. The only issue is the dogs, but as the van approaches, they run away out of fear.

Frederico slides open the side of the van. "Get in!"

Alex shoots at the van, trying to take out the tires, but he's a terrible shot.

I help Ella inside and then jump up myself, glaring back at Alex. "You are going to regret this, Vishekov."

He shoots at me, and I dodge out of the way, the bullet embedding itself in the metal carcass of the van.

"Drive!" I growl.

Frederico slams his foot on the accelerator, and I have to hold on not to fall out of the van. Once I can't see Alex anymore, I slam the door shut.

"The bastard will be after us. We need to get out of the city fast."

Oleg nods. "Already on it. Jet is fueled and ready to take off when we get to the airstrip."

"Good." I nod in response. "But we need a nurse onboard."

Viktor clears his throat. "I can pull a favor and get one to the airstrip."

"Do it," I reply, feeling oddly thankful that Spartak's men are here. Two of my men are badly injured, and I can't help but feel the guilt build that we had to leave Antoni back there.

It wasn't my fault, but I still can't shake the feeling. Antoni won't get a proper burial. He's been a loyal follower for twenty years and deserved better.

"Shit," Frederico says.

I stand and lean over the driver's seat. "What's wrong?"

"A car is tailing us."

The rearview mirror shows a sleek, black sedan closing in on us fast. Its headlights are a pair of fierce, predatory eyes in the dark - unblinking, unyielding. Frederico's knuckles turn white on the steering wheel, but he doesn't say a thing. He doesn't need to. The tension in the van is a living, breathing entity, wrapping itself around us.

"Remy," Ella's voice is barely a whisper. "They're catching up."

"I see it," I growl, my gaze not leaving the mirror. The sedan's bumper is almost kissing our rear bumper now. It swerves left, then right, trying to find an opening. A weakness. A moment of hesitation.

But Frederico is on fire tonight. He's driving like a man possessed, swerving and accelerating, braking and accelerating again. I can feel the engine's vibrations under my feet, each pulse a testament to our struggle for survival.

"Remy, do something!" Ella's voice startles me out of my trance, her fear starkly contrasting the adrenaline surging through me.

"Frederico," I say, my voice steady. "Push it harder."

He doesn't hesitate. He nods, and I see him brace himself against the steering wheel. The van surges forward, and I hear the engine screaming in protest. But Frederico pushes it harder until we're hurtling down the road like a bullet, dodging obstacles.

And then, at the last possible moment, he swerves. The van's tires shriek in protest. The sedan never stands a chance. It tries to swerve out of the way, but it's too late. There's a sickening crunch of metal on metal, and then the sedan is spinning out of control.

"We did it," Frederico breathes, the tension ebbing away. "We got rid of them."

We all collectively breathe with relief washing over us, like a wave breaking on the shore. But then Frederico hammers the accelerator again.

"Now, let's get to that airstrip," he says with a new

determination. "Let's hope that's the last of Vishekov's men we see tonight."

A silence falls upon the van, tension still hanging in the air like the remnants of a storm. No one dares speak, as if our voices might bring back the danger. The only sounds are the low growl of the engine and the soft hum of the road beneath us.

We pull into the airstrip. My jet is bathed in the moonlight. Every muscle in my body uncoils as Frederico pulls the van to a stop a couple of yards from the jet and kills the engine. A sigh of relief escapes from everyone, a stark admission of the fear we had all held. There's no sign of Alex's men, and I see a way out for the first time tonight.

As we jump out of the van, a recognizable droning draws our attention to the sky.

"No fucking way!" I shout.

A helicopter hovers above us, looking to land.

Alex.

"Get on the plane now, Ella!" I yell, pushing her toward the plane.

She hesitates, gazing at me.

"Now!" I growl.

She hobbles away on her swollen ankle and up the stairs as I help Giuseppe out of the van. His injury has taken a toll on him, especially after running, and the blood is staining his shirt.

The helicopter lands, and I know we don't have much time.

The jet's engine is already firing as I help Giuseppe up the steps and into the jet. When I turn back, Alex and his men are sprinting across the tarmac, holding machine guns.

"Get this shut!" I growl. "Now!"

The hostess rushes forward and pulls the door across, locking it.

"We need to take off now."

Bullets ricochet off the bulletproof body of my jet, and I'm thankful that I paid an extra two million for it, as a hole in the plane would mean game over.

Ella cowers on a chair, her eyes screwed shut.

"The pilot is working as fast as he can," the hostess says.

"Well, if he doesn't want a bullet in his fucking brain, tell him to work faster!"

She rushes to the cockpit, and within a few moments, the jet taxis down the runway. I wait with bated breath, expecting a rocket to come flying through the windows at any moment.

But it doesn't come. Instead, we are airborne and out of harm's way. The tension slowly recedes from my body. We made it out alive. I pause, as not all of us did. Antoni is still lying dead in a room in the Egorov mansion.

The hostess brings us glasses of whiskey, but none of us says a toast. We're all too mentally exhausted and emotionally drained. I move toward Ella and squeeze her hand. "There are a few bedrooms in the back. Go and have a rest. Get some sleep."

Her brow furrows, as I know we have much to discuss, but I can't have that conversation now. She needs to rest and get her ankle looked at.

"I'll send the nurse back with some ice for your ankle."

Instead of arguing, she presses her lips together and nods, walking back to one of the bedrooms.

I watch her go, knowing that I love her. No matter how badly I didn't want to believe it. The fear I felt when I saw her tied up, bruised, and scared in that room was untenable. She's my reason for living, and I won't ever let her get away again.

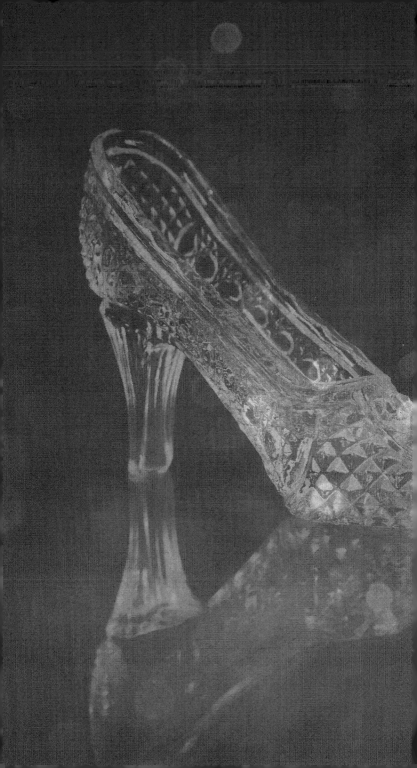

44

ELLA

*A*s the jet flies us away from danger, I lie on the bed and stare at the ceiling. I could have died or worse, all because I ran away from my problems, but what Alex told me on his jet was impossible to shake from my mind.

Your father was his employee. The man who ordered the hit on him was Remy Morrone.

I swallow hard, knowing that while I have ignored much of what he does, I can't ignore that if it's true. I must confront him. The question is, will he even remember?

There are a few bedrooms in the jet. The injured guys are being tended to in one of the others, and the nurse gave me an ice pack for my ankle.

The door slides open. Remy's huge form takes up the entire doorway as he enters. "How are you feeling?"

I sit up and look at him. "Like an idiot. One of your men died because of me." I swallow hard, unable to overcome the guilt, but in the back of my mind, I'm trying to work out how to bring up my dad. It feels like the photo Alex gave me is burning a hole in my pocket.

He shakes his head. "Running away may have made it easier for Alex, but he would have struck at some point, no matter what."

I clench my jaw and nod. "Alex told me something. Something I hope isn't true."

Remy tilts his head. "What is it?"

I draw in a deep breath and pull out the photos. "Alex said you employed my dad and ordered the hit on him."

Remy takes the photos and looks over them, his expression not revealing the truth. "I didn't kill this man."

Relief coils through me; I know he could have easily ordered Dad's murder. I hate to think how many men Remy is responsible for killing or ordering their demise. "You promise?" I ask, knowing it would kill me if he lied.

There's no hesitation as he nods. "I promise. He was a contact for the Navarro cartel in Mexico. I met with him about a drug deal." His jaw clenches. "It didn't go too well, and we didn't agree to a deal, but I didn't order a hit on him." He runs a hand across the back of his neck. "I'm not stupid enough to cross Ileana Navarro."

My brow furrows. "Who is she?"

"A ruthless woman. One I'm thankful I've never met in person."

I nod, and a resigned silence falls between us. Remy sits at the end of the bed and stares at me, eyes full of an undetectable emotion. "I've never been so scared as when I realized you were gone the morning after our argument."

"Scared?" I ask, wondering why. "Surely you knew I was angry and took off."

He nods. "Yes, but look what happened to your mother—"

"Alex admitted he killed her," I say, a sob breaking out. "He was the monster all along."

He clenches his jaw. "I know. We found out a while back that Vishekov was behind her death."

I sit up straighter. "And you didn't think to tell me about it? At least then, I would have known I wasn't safe when I bumped into him at the airport."

Remy's eyes flash. "I didn't know I needed to warn you, as I didn't expect you to take off in the middle of the night after one little argument."

My shoulders slump. "I've never been good with confrontation."

Remy clears his throat. "Do you know why I was so scared, angel?"

I look him in the eye and shake my head.

"Because despite insisting I don't believe in love, the truth is I've fallen in love with you."

My breath hitches, and I feel my chest soar. Is it possible? Could the man I've fallen for really love me?

"Are you just saying that?"

He cups my face in his huge hands and looks into my eyes intently. "No. Do you think I'd come all this way and risk my life if I didn't love you?"

She shrugs. "I assumed it was important you make

Alex pay. After all, you've got to keep up appearances as the big bad leader of the Morrone Mafia."

"Massimo is the leader, and while that's true, it's not why I came for you. It's because I love you."

Tears well in my eyes, hearing him say those three words to me. "I love you, too," I murmur, shaking my head. "So damn much."

He kisses me then with hungry passion, his tongue thrusting into my mouth forcefully. I whimper at his touch, unable to believe he came for me. He saved me.

Back in Alex's capture, I had lost hope, longing to see Remy again but knowing I never would.

"I'm going to make him pay for touching you," he murmurs, pressing soft kisses down my neck. "He will die a painful death."

"Good," I say, shocking myself with how easily I say that about a man's murder, but I guess Remy has changed me. Before, I would balk at the idea of a man being murdered, but the way Alex spoke to me and what he did to me... I can't find any reason why Remy shouldn't end him.

"Did he touch you?"

I knew this would crop up in conversation. "In what sense?"

Remy's jaw clenches. "Sexually or violently. I need to know."

I purse my lips. "Sexually, not really. Other than forcing me to strip."

Remy stills. "Why did he force you to strip?"

I swallow hard, tears prickling my eyes. "It might be easier to show you?"

The rage in Remy's eyes deepens as I pull off my dirty, ripped tank top and jeans. And then I turn so he can see my back, showing him the proof of Alex's punishment.

A growl echoes through the small bedroom. "If I knew about those while we were down in that forest with his dogs, I wouldn't have left until the bastard's blood painted my skin."

I turn to face him and squeeze his hand. "I'm glad you didn't, as you'd probably be dead, and so would I."

He knows I'm right because his shoulders dip. "That stupid bastard will wish he was never born when I get my hands on him."

Without another word, I hoist myself up and straddle Remy, a grunt escaping him as I settle onto his lap. His hands instinctively find my hips, thumbs tracing circles into the bare skin. I cradle his face in my hands and kiss him.

Pulling away slightly, I look into his dark chocolate eyes. "I don't want to talk about Alex anymore," I say, my voice steady and sure. "In fact... I don't want to talk at all right now." I press my lips against his lips, allowing my body to speak louder than any words could.

His jaw clenches. "Are you sure? You've been through a shitty experience."

"I want you," I breathe against his ear, kissing just below it. "No, scratch that. I need you."

Remy's eyes never leave mine as he lifts me from his lap and lowers me to the bed. His hands are tender on my body, careful not to awaken any lingering pain. Once I'm settled, he stands and begins to strip.

He's torturously slow as each piece of clothing falls to the floor, revealing his body's hard planes and muscles covered in dark ink. The room fills with a thick, tangible tension but a current of pure, raw tenderness beneath it. It's a moment you wish to capture, hold on to, and relive repeatedly.

As he finally drops his briefs, the sight of his cock rock hard and jutting toward me makes me heat. I'll never get tired of seeing him like this.

He climbs onto the bed. "Tell me what you want," he demands, but there's a gentleness in his voice.

"I want you," I breathe, moving my fingers over his chest. His body is a canvas of scars and tattoos, each telling a story.

"Be more specific. Use your words for me."

I swallow hard. "I want your cock deep inside of me."

He groans, fisting the length between his powerful thighs. "Is that right?" He rubs the head through my soaking wet entrance. "You are soaked. Is this all for me?"

I nod, my eyes fluttering shut as this man can undo me with his dirty talk. "Yes. All for you."

His response is immediate. Remy slams into me smoothly, filling me with his thick cock.

My fingers curl around the sheets beneath us. I bite my lip so hard I taste the metallic tang of blood, trying not to be loud as we're not the only ones on this plane. "Oh God," I breathe.

He kisses me, tongue thrusting into my mouth with as much force as his dick.

Each thrust is forceful but slow.

His taste is intoxicating, a heady mix of desire and love that I can't get enough of. His tongue explores my mouth, his kisses growing more desperate as he shifts his rhythm, the slow, steady thrusts replaced by a faster, frantic pace.

His hands trace down my body, each touch leaving a trail of fire in its wake. His eyes never leave mine as he pulls out and slams back into me. Each thrust of his cock slams against the sweet spot inside me.

"Fuck, angel," he groans, the words barely a whisper against the shell of my ear. "You feel so good clamped around me."

My heart hammers in my chest as I clutch onto him, my nails digging into his back. My body tenses, the pleasure building inside me as his pace becomes relentless.

Remy growls, the vibrations rolling through me. "You're so tight, squeezing me just right." He pushes deeper, pausing momentarily, fully seated within me and gazing where our bodies join. "Look at you, taking all of me so beautifully."

My back arches off the bed, my body moving toward him. "Fuck, Daddy... more," I whimper, unable to form coherent sentences as his cock stretches me.

There's a dark promise in his eyes. "More? Such a greedy girl," he teases while his hips move again, sliding in and out of me slowly, torturously. "Taking my cock and wanting more. What more could you possibly want?" He leans closer to my ear. "Unfortunately, I didn't bring the dildo to shove in your ass on the rescue mission, but once we're home..." he trails off, making me moan with the unspoken promise.

My body responds to each filthy word that falls from his lips. "Please... Daddy," I whimper, my legs wrapping around his waist to pull him deeper.

With a chuckle, Remy obliges. "That's it, angel. Beg for me," he growls, increasing his pace, thrusting harder and faster. His words are a sinful soundtrack to our love-making, a torrent of praises that drive me closer to the edge.

"Daddy," I whimper, my body arches beneath him. "I... I'm going to..."

His thumb moves to my clit, rubbing small circles against the sensitive nub as he pounds into me. "Come for me," he growls, his pace increasing.

A cry rips from my throat as I tip over the edge, my body shaking from the force. His name falls from my lips on a broken moan as I come around his cock, my walls clamping down on him.

His thrusts become erratic, his rhythm faltering as he chases his climax. With a final deep thrust, he spills inside me, his hot cum filling me up. He grunts my name, his body rigid above me as he rides out his orgasm.

We lay there for a moment, breathless and spent. Remy pulls out slowly, rolling onto his back and pulling me into his side. His hand slowly traces up and down my marred bare back softly, his other hand brushing a few stray hairs from my face.

"Angel," he murmurs, his voice hoarse from his release. "You're amazing."

I snuggle into his side, a sense of contentment washing over me. "So are you," I murmur, feeling instantly exhausted.

His arms wrap securely around me, the rhythm of his heart under my ear lulling me to sleep. The last thing I remember is the soft kiss he presses to my forehead, his quiet "I love you" echoing in my ears as I drift off.

45

REMY

*T*he dank basement smells of mold, decay, and
fear. In the center, bound by heavy chains
and under the glow of a single light bulb, is Alex
Vishekov.

My men found him hiding only a few miles outside
Chicago. Unfortunately, they haven't found his father
yet. I know murdering his son will draw him out, and
we'll end him, too.

I approach with slow footsteps, savoring the expression of pure fear on his once arrogant face. It's marred
with cuts and bruises that he sustained while my men
captured him.

"Hello, Alex."

His jaw clenches, and his eyes narrow. "My dad will
kill you for this."

I laugh, the sound echoing through the basement. "I
intend to kill your dad, too. Don't worry. He'll join you
in hell as soon as we locate him."

Seeing the flash of terror in his eyes as he pales is

beyond satisfying.

"You touched what is mine. You took what belongs to me. Do you know what I do to men who are fucking stupid and cross that line?"

His lips curl into a snarl, but there's a hint of defiance in his eyes. "I didn't touch that trash. I never laid a finger on her. I have standards, unlike you," he spits out. The venom in his voice doesn't match the fear in his eyes, but his blatant insult toward Ella ignites a rage in me that's darker and more violent than anything I've ever felt.

I walk toward him and slam my fist hard into his face, filling his mouth with blood as he spits it out. "If you have any sense, you won't insult Ella in front of me." I clench my fists harder. "I know what you had planned for her because she told me. I intend to make you pay for even thinking it."

With a smirk, I pull the blade from my jacket pocket, its gleaming edge reflecting the dim light in the room.

Alex's breathing hitches at the sight. "You're making a mistake."

"Am I?" I circle him, allowing the silence to stretch through the space. The terror mounting in his eyes tells me he's beginning to understand the gravity of his situation, but perhaps he always knew. He was just in denial.

He won't leave this basement alive.

My boots echo on the concrete floor as I come full circle to face him. "Did you think," I murmur, leaning in close, the cold steel of my knife dancing dangerously near his throat, "you could take something that belongs to the Morrone Famiglia and not pay the price?"

I drag the blade's edge over his bare, sweat-soaked skin. I revel in how his body tenses under the cold steel, the fear in his eyes growing with each second the blade dances over him.

I don't cut, not yet.

Torture is an artistry, the fine line between fear and pain, and I'm the master.

"You know, Alex," I purr, "fear is a powerful motivator. You should've been more afraid of me before you crossed me. You should have believed the rumors about my reputation." Each word is punctuated by the movement of the blade, a whisper against his skin, promising a world of agony.

I'm furious at what he did to Ella. There was no world in which I would have let what he did go. Alex was dead the moment he stole her. However, the scars he inflicted on her skin sealed how he'd die. A slow, painful, and tortuous death.

The whip on the wall draws my attention. Alex may need a taste of his own medicine. I stow the knife back in my jacket pocket before retrieving the whip and uncoiling it behind him.

"W-What are you doing?" Alex stammers.

"Making you feel the pain you inflicted on Ella." I draw it back and whip him with all my strength, cutting the flesh on his back to the bone. He screams, and I continue, each strike harder than the last.

His back is a quivering mass of raw flesh when I'm finished. I stand back and survey my work with satisfaction.

"How does it feel?" I ask, walking around to gaze into his eyes.

He's barely holding onto consciousness. I wonder if that was the same for Ella, as she won't talk about it since we returned from Vegas. It will take her time to get over the trauma, but I convinced her to see a therapist she could talk to. She thought she would die and harbored deep-seated fears of dying because her mom and dad died so young.

A momentary flicker of dullness crosses his eyes, and I slap him hard across the face to jolt him back to the present. "Stay with me, Alex," I command, a smirk pulling at the corners of my lips. "I'm only just getting warmed up."

I retrieve the knife from my jacket pocket again. The terror in his eyes spikes as I casually trace the blade's sharp edge with my thumb.

"Now, let's continue, shall we?" I press the tip of the knife against his trembling, sweat-soaked chest and slowly slice through the skin, relishing the guttural scream that rips from his throat. The hot, fresh blood pools around the cut, dribbling down his stomach in rivulets. The sight of it, the smell of it, it's intoxicating.

Ella wanted to be here for this, but I refused. I can't have my angel see this side of me. This side of me she doesn't ever need or want to see. She knows darkness thrives inside me, but that's as far as it will go.

His pleas for mercy are music to my ears as I continue my grim work. Each scream, each whimper, is a symphony, a testament to the pain he's going through. The knife dances across his skin, leaving trails of crimson in its wake. His body jerks and convulses futilely to escape the agony, but there's no escape. Not from this. Not from me.

"You really shouldn't have touched Ella, should you?"

He jerks his head from side to side. "Please," he begs.

Pathetic.

His tears mix with the sweat on his face, his eyes completely black as the pain has dilated them. This is his hell. And I'm his devil.

"Please, what?"

His jaw is slack as he murmurs. "End me."

At least this idiot isn't asking me to spare him, as that was never on the cards.

"End you?" I echo my voice, a low rumble that reverberates off the cold, damp walls of the basement. "I'm not sure I've put you through enough pain."

He looks at me with resignation, knowing there's no escape from this reality.

I play with him more, making him scream and grunt as blood collects in a pool beneath him.

After another few minutes, I surprise myself and give him his dying wish. I drive the blade deep into his chest, right where his heart should be—if he even has one.

The sound that escapes him is almost a sigh, a release, his plea for mercy finally answered. His body convulses once, twice, before falling still. I watch as the light in his eyes flickers and finally dies out, replaced by the emptiness of death.

I step back and look at the carnage. My men will clear it up, so I wash my hands in the sink in the corner. Ella is upstairs at the bar, waiting for me to finish. She knows I'm getting revenge for what he did to her. Once I've got all the blood off my hands and face, I grab my jacket off the peg on the wall and walk out of the room to ascend the stairs into my club.

Ella looks nervous as she fiddles with her coaster on the bar. The glass of wine I ordered her is still untouched.

I approach her and put a strong hand on her back. "It's done," I breathe.

The tension in her shoulders eases a fraction, and she turns to face me. "You made Alex pay?"

I nod in response. "I'll make anyone that wrongs you pay."

Her eyes flash with admiration as I sit on the barstool beside her.

"You've hardly touched your drink."

She breathes in deeply. "I was too anxious."

"It's over now."

Her eyes dip to the blood painted across my shirt. "Shouldn't you change?"

I tilt my head. "I don't need to. No."

Her brows pull together. "But there are people——"

"This is my club, and people know who I am."

Ella's throat bobs as she swallows.

I've warned her many times about who I am and what I'm capable of, but how her face has paled suggests she's not okay with it.

She straightens and plays with the ends of her hair.

"Right. Shall we go home?"

I tilt my head, sensing her unease over the entire situation. "You're uncomfortable being seen with me like this?"

She shrugs. "I'm just uncomfortable in general. And tired."

I clench my jaw. "Fine. We can leave." I take her hand in mine, noticing the way she flinches. But I ignore it until we're seated in the back of the limousine.

"Is there a problem?" I ask, sitting opposite her.

Her eyes widen. "What do you mean?"

"You are acting like you are afraid of me, but you know what I'm capable of." I tilt my head to the side. "Hell, you even said you were glad I would make him pay. What changed?"

She draws in a deep, shuddering breath. "I'm scared of what I'm becoming."

"And what is that?"

"My mom."

I raise an eyebrow. "I knew your mom; believe me, you're nothing like her."

She nods. "I know, I just..."

I cup her face in my hands. "Why did your mom marry me?"

She bites her inner cheek. "For money."

"And why do you want me?" I ask.

Ella blows out a breath and shakes her head. "God knows why, but I love you."

"Clear fucking difference, Ella. Your mom was rotten on the inside. She never treated you like a daughter should be, putting money ahead of you. Not to mention practically using you as a meal ticket until she had a better option." When Ella got to talking about all her mom had done to her over the years, it made me so fucking angry. So angry that I would have killed her myself if she weren't already dead for hurting Ella like that.

A few tears escape, and I wipe them away.

"So stop putting yourself down."

Ella nods. "Thank you."

"Come here." I open my arms, and she rests her head against my chest, allowing me to hold her all the way home. Once we return, I'm unsure what kind of mood she'll be in.

"Are you hungry?" I ask as we enter the house.

She shakes her head. "No, let's go to bed."

I take her hand and lead her up the stairs to our room. Once we get inside, she grabs hold of the lapel of my jacket and pulls me into a kiss. I kiss her back, feeling so much emotion clawing at my chest. I want her to understand how much I love her. That there's nothing I wouldn't do for her. I'd die for her if I had to.

"I want you," I breathe against her lips. "Strip for me."

Her eyes light up as she steps back and strips her clothes off teasingly. "Yes, Daddy."

I wrap my arms around her when her panties drop to the floor, lifting her. Kissing her, I carry her to the bed and drop her in the center before fixing her wrists to the headboard and then her ankles, ensuring she's spread wide and at my mercy.

I take a step back. "The most beautiful thing I've

ever seen."

Her cheeks flush darker. "Don't be silly."

I'll never understand how she doesn't see what I see. A beautiful angel. However, years of her mom never showing her love and belittling her more than I ever realized have left her with issues with her self-esteem. I intend to fix that.

"I'm not being silly." I pull my tie off and throw it aside. "You're a fucking angel." I unbutton my shirt and toss it to the floor. "More beautiful than any woman I've ever seen." I pull off my belt and unfasten my pants, dropping them to the floor. "And I would go as far as to say that there's nothing on this planet or in this universe, you could show me that matches your beauty."

Ella licks her lips, eyes fixed on my cock. "I think I'm staring at the most beautiful thing I've ever seen." Her eyes drag up my body to my face. "You."

I shake my head. "There's nothing beautiful about me. I'm rotten and corrupted and will destroy you."

She groans, arching her back. "Good. I want you to ruin me."

I step toward her and place my hands on her knees. "Such a pretty little prize," I muse, forcing them open wider. "All spread open wide for me and soaking wet too."

"I'm always wet for you."

"I can see that," I smirk, sliding my fingers through her wetness, grinning as she squirms under my touch. "How about we roleplay?"

Her eyes flash, and she nods. "Yes, please."

I groan as she's beyond perfect. "Shall I get my

mask?"

She shakes her head. "No, I want to see you, but let's act."

I clench my jaw and nod. "Stay still," I growl, slipping into my role.

Please, no!" she pleads, her sapphire eyes wide. But there's nothing but excitement coursing through her as I slam three fingers into her cunt. "So wet and ready."

She whimpers. "Stop this. Please."

I chuckle, the sound echoing around the room. "Why would you tell me to stop when you are so wet you're leaking all over the sheets? Your cunt is begging for my dick." My fingers work in and out of her pussy viciously, and I lean down to bite her earlobe. "Begging me to stop just drives me wild."

She shudders, squirming from anticipation and desire as I slide the head of my cock through her entrance.

"No, I—"

"Please," she begs, a desperate whimper escapes her lips.

I shake my head. "We're only just getting started." The moment my cock bumps her clit, her hips rise from the bed. "And it looks like no matter how much you tell me you want me to stop, you love every moment."

Instead of sliding inside her, I rub the head of my cock against her clit over and over, driving her crazy. Her gasps turn into desperate cries, her body squirming beneath me. I love how responsive she is while she tries to pretend she doesn't want it, how every touch, every whisper ignites a fire within her.

"Please," she begs.

"Right now, I don't know if you are begging me to stop or fuck you," I drawl, my voice low and husky.

Her jaw clenches as she tries to maintain her part in our game. "I'm telling you to stop."

I press my fingers into her center, feeling her pulse around them. Her hands strain against the restraints as she tries to break free.

I pull back to look at her, her eyes shining with need, her lips parted as she pants for breath. "No one is going to help you." I grin, my hand sliding lower. "Let's see how much you can take because you are all mine." I slide my cock deep inside of her with one thrust.

"Daddy..." she half gasps, half moans, her eyes alight with desire.

Smirking, I lean down, my lips against her neck, trailing soft kisses down her skin. "Say it again," I murmur, my voice a low growl.

"Daddy..." she breathes, her voice a desperate whisper.

As I plunge into her, her body arches off the bed, a strangled cry escaping her lips. She can't maintain her role once I'm inside her. I pause for a moment, allowing her to adjust to my size. Her walls clamp down on me, pulsing and inviting. I can't help but groan, the sensation nearly overwhelming.

"You're so tight," I murmur, my voice a low growl.

She bites her lip, her hands straining against the restraints, her body squirming beneath me. "Fuck me," she pants.

I start slow, my thrusts shallow. Each thrust elicits a

moan from my angel as she shudders beneath me. Her reactions drive me wild, and soon enough, I'm picking up the pace. She cries out, her body writhing beneath me as I thrust into her relentlessly.

"Daddy... more," she pleads.

With a smirk, I angle my hips just right, hitting that sweet spot inside her. Her back arches off the bed, a scream tearing through her as pleasure washes over her. I continue to pound into her, our bodies slapping together.

"Oh God... I'm..." she whimpers.

I know she's close. I can feel her tightening around me, her body trembling. I kiss her, swallowing her cries as she shatters beneath me. Her climax triggers mine, and I spill into her, my body shuddering with the intensity of the orgasm.

As we come down from our highs, I pull out of her, untying her restraints. She whimpers, and I pull her into my arms and cradle her.

"You were amazing," I murmur, kissing her forehead.

She snuggles into my chest with a look of contentment on her face. "I love you," She murmurs, her voice barely a whisper.

"I love you too, angel," I say, kissing her hair. We fall asleep in each other's arms, content and satisfied. Ella has shattered my world and thawed out my cold heart. Love does exist. It just took this angel to come into my life and make me believe it.

46

EPILOGUE

ELLA

*T*wo *years later...*
I stand barefoot on a stunning Hawaiian beach dressed in a simple, flowing white dress. My stomach is big and round as I'm five months pregnant with our child. It took a little convincing, but Remy finally agreed to make my dreams come true, and we're having a baby.

I fiddle with the angel pendant around my neck. The pendant my dad bought me for my eleventh birthday. After some therapy, I got the courage to open the gift, which gave me closure. I always wear it now.

The ocean waves gently crash into the shore, providing a calming rhythm to this momentous occasion. Remy stands before me, his sun-kissed skin glowing against the setting sun, looking as gorgeous as the day I first saw him.

The guilt I'd initially felt about being with him has disappeared. I know Mom never loved him. He was her meal ticket. My love for him has only deepened in the two years since Remy got rid of Alex. He's pushed me to continue writing, and I've had three hit novels in those two years.

If it weren't for him and his belief in me, I'd still be stuck in a cycle of self-doubt.

The officiant tells us it's time for our vows, and Remy squeezes my hands. "Ella, since we met, you've completely captivated me. You became my obsession, and while it wasn't always easy, I'm so glad we made it here. I keep falling in love with you, over and over again, every single day. I promise always to cherish and respect you, to take care of you and keep you safe, to be there for you and our family, and to support and encourage you. I want to be with you until the day I die."

A lump forms in my throat as I respond, "Remy, you're my soul mate. I knew it the moment we met, even if our circumstances were a bit fucked up."

That earns a laugh from our guests.

"But I promise to always be there for you through the good and bad times. I promise to share life's happiest moments and toughest challenges with you. I promise to love and treasure you for as long as we live."

The officiant raises his hands, beaming. "By the powers vested in me and witnessed by all those here today, I now pronounce you husband and wife. You may seal your vows with a kiss."

Tears glisten in my eyes as Remy pulls me in for a passionate kiss. Desire ignites the moment his hands are on me.

Remy pulls away from the kiss, his eyes sparkling. "I love you, angel," he whispers.

"I love you too," I respond.

As the words leave our lips, Remy's family erupts in applause.

Ronan is five now, and he rushes up to me in his cute pageboy outfit and hugs me. "I'm so glad I've got a step-grandma and a step-aunt."

Remy and I chuckle as it's hard to explain to him that I'm no longer his step-aunt.

Mia approaches, smiling. "Just know, I'm not going to call you mommy."

I laugh, hugging her. "I should hope not."

Luca smirks. "I might." He winks, which earns him a clap on the back of his head from Remy.

Thankfully, he's only messing about as he's found his forever person, too. And even Leo is in a committed relationship now, something no one ever thought would happen, but I guess everyone has to grow up at some point.

Leo approaches me, eyes narrowing. "Congrats, Ella." He tilts his head. "It was obvious you always had eyes for Dad."

He did pick up on it early on. Camila has been the most reserved and judgmental of our match, but I don't think it's entirely because of our relationship. It doesn't help that her relationship with her dad is strained, anyway. Her husband, Gavril, is here. It's one of the few times I've met him. He's quiet and a little creepy, if I'm honest.

Paisley approaches and hugs me. "Congratulations." She holds her swelling stomach. "I can't believe our due dates are the same."

I chuckle. "I know. What are the odds?"

"Probably quite high considering the number of babies made a year and the fact there are only three hundred and sixty-five days a year," Massimo says.

I was so happy for them when IVF finally worked. Seeing how much it hurt Paisley over the last two years was heartbreaking. Once we finally met, we hit it off. Paisley joins Mia and me for drinks and dinner regularly. I don't know what I'd do without them.

Paisley glares at her husband. "Whatever. I think it's cool. Hopefully, we both go into labor at the same time."

"Unlikely," Remy says.

We both glare at him.

"What?" He shrugs. "The statistics say that most babies aren't born on their due date."

Paisley and I both shake our heads. "We can't even have a drink," Paisley says, sighing heavily. "But we can get some food. I'm starving."

I smile and nod. "Yeah, let's get to the restaurant."

Remy squeezes my hand as we walk alongside his son and daughter-in-law. We booked a nice little restaurant on the beach. The whole place is dedicated to our small party.

The sea-salt-infused air melds with the tantalizing aroma of freshly grilled fish and aromatic spices, a mouthwatering scent I can almost taste in the air.

"I must admit, I'm starving too."

Remy leans toward me to whisper in my ear. "Me too, but not for food..."

I whack his chest. "Behave." Even as I try to ignore his words, my thighs clench. I'm hungry for him, but we've got guests and need to eat something before we lock ourselves away in the honeymoon suite.

Remy and I sit in our seats next to Massimo and Paisley. The servers bring the first course, a platter of Poke, a traditional Hawaiian dish. Fresh cubes of ahi tuna served on a bed of warm jasmine rice.

My stomach rumbles at the sight of it.

"This looks delicious," Paisley says.

Both mine and Paisley's are grilled tuna since we can't eat raw fish while pregnant.

"Dig in," I say. Everyone starts to eat, chatting softly amongst themselves.

I gaze across the table at Remy, and my heart swells as he stares at me as if I'm the most beautiful thing he's ever seen.

"I'm so glad you guys chose Hawaii for your wedding. It's beautiful here, "Mia announces.

I arch a brow. "Well, we did have a lot of persuasion from someone."

She chuckles, knowing we wouldn't have picked Hawaii without her begging us to. Granted, she has good taste in wedding venues. The island and resort she picked are beautiful.

Luca clears his throat. "I'd like to say a toast."

Remy shakes his head. "We'd prefer if you didn't."

Everyone laughs, and Luca places a hand over his chest mockingly as if hurt. "I'll pretend you didn't say that to your favorite son."

Remy rolls his eyes.

"I just want to say that while it's pretty fucking weird that my stepsister is now my mommy." He winks at me, and I shake my head. "I'm so glad Dad has found someone he truly loves." His expression sobers. "It's been a long road to this point, losing our mom and then getting cancer, but I'm glad you survived to meet your soul mate."

He lifts his glass. "To the bride and groom."

Tears build behind my eyelids at his words. It's a short but beautiful speech.

"To the bride and groom." Everyone repeats and lifts their glasses.

I catch Remy's intense gaze on me as he stands to speak, too. "Thank you, son. I appreciate it."

Luca, for once, doesn't make a joke and bows his head, smiling. "You're welcome."

Remy clears his throat and straightens up, scanning the table. "Before Ella entered my life, I was dead inside, just going through the motions." His piercing eyes lock onto mine. "You're the reason I get up every morning. You're the laughter and light that fills my home. You're the love that fills my cold heart." He raises his glass. "And most importantly, you said 'yes' when I asked if you'd stick with me for the rest of your life."

A resounding chuckle filters through the air.

"To Ella." He raises his glass.

"To Ella," everyone says in chorus.

I swallow hard, realizing that I'm next to speak. "Thank you," I murmur, smiling. "As you all know, our relationship was not a typical one. It was complicated and messy from the beginning, but if I could go back and do it all again, I wouldn't change a thing." I pause and shake my head. "On second thought, I probably wouldn't run away and get captured by mobsters."

Everyone chuckles, and Remy rolls his eyes but with a smile on his face.

"All I need to say is that I love you." I raise my glass. "To Remy."

"To Remy," everyone says in chorus.

The rest of the evening is lovely, and it's the first time I've seen Remy's family relax together and just be. Even Camilla is at ease, and her husband doesn't seem too uptight after a few drinks.

Their kids are tucked up in bed in their suite, being looked after by the resort staff, as is Ronan.

As everything starts to wind down, Remy comes over to me. "Come with me. I have something to show you."

Leading me by the hand, Remy guides me down to a hidden cove separated from the main beach. The moonlight dances on the rippling water, casting a romantic glow on the blankets and cushions on the sandy floor.

The soulful melody of Ed Sheeran's "Perfect" drifts from a portable stereo and wraps itself around us, the lyrical promise of an undying love blending seamlessly with the gentle lapping of the sea against the shore.

Remy pulls me close, and we sway gently to the rhythm, lost in our own world. His dark eyes are filled with love and desire as he gazes into mine, sending a shiver of anticipation down my spine. Our bodies fit together like two missing pieces from a puzzle as if made for this moment, for this dance.

He leans in, his lips finding mine, and everything else disappears. Remy and I are locked in a dance as timeless as the universe. Our kiss deepens, fueled by the longing and love that have defined us.

"I love you, Ella," he whispers against my lips, his words swelling my heart.

"I love you more than you can ever know," I reply, my voice barely audible above the music.

We continue to dance, our bodies entwined, our hearts beating as one.

We celebrate our love in the cove's silence under the moon's watchful gaze. I found the love and acceptance I'd always craved in a man who was wicked toward me at first, but he turned out to be my true knight in shining armor.

THANK YOU FOR READING WICKED, the third book in the Once Upon a Villain Series. I hope you enjoyed following Remy and Ella on their journey.

If you enjoyed this book, you will enjoy the next one, Insane. It's on pre-order with a current release date of November 30th.

It's a dark captive cartel romance, and here is the cover and blurb.

Unhinged: A Dark Captive Cartel Romance

MADNESS IS HIS FORTE, and I'm entrapped in his chaotic world.

My life was good.

I was about to start my senior year at brown, so I took a last-minute getaway with my best friends to Mexico.

That's until we're snatched on vacation and thrown into a nightmare we could never have imagined.

Nothing could've prepared us for the darkness that awaited us.

We find ourselves in a dangerous world dominated by Ileana Navarro, a cartel leader whose power is matched only by her cruelty.

And that's when I met *Taren*.

They say he's as mad as a hatter, a man driven to

insanity not by nature but by the woman who raised him.

An enigma wrapped in riddles and cloaked with an aura of danger.

His madness is his charm, and to my surprise, I find myself drawn to him.

Taren intrigues me, scares me, and draws me in with a force I can't resist.

Despite the bars of our gilded cage, I find myself captivated by his madness.

He is a riddle I can't solve, a storm I can't weather, yet my heart can't seem to stay away.

Will I survive the darkness that awaits?

There's one thing that is painfully clear: once you step into Taren's world, there's no way out.

Insane is the fourth book in the Once Upon a Villain Series by Bianca Cole. Insane is a dark, captive mafia romance story with dark themes and certain subjects that may upset the reader. It has no cliffhanger, a happily ever after ending, and can be read as a standalone.

ALSO BY BIANCA COLE

Once Upon a Villian

Pride: A Dark Arranged Marriage Romance

Hook: A Dark Forced Marriage Romance

Wicked: A Dark Forbidden Mafia Romance

Unhinged: A Dark Captive Cartel Romance

The Syndicate Academy

Corrupt Educator: A Dark Forbidden Mafia Academy Romance

Cruel Bully: A Dark Mafia Academy Romance

Sinful Lessons: A Dark Forbidden Mafia Academy Romance

Playing Dirty: A Dark Enemies to Lovers Forbidden Mafia Academy Romance

Chicago Mafia Dons

Merciless Defender: A Dark Forbidden Mafia Romance

Violent Leader: A Dark Enemies to Lovers Captive Mafia Romance

Evil Prince: A Dark Arranged Marriage Romance

Brutal Daddy: A Dark Captive Mafia Romance

Cruel Vows: A Dark Forced Marriage Mafia Romance

Dirty Secret: A Dark Enemies to Loves Mafia Romance

Dark Crown: A Dark Arranged Marriage Romance

Boston Mafia Dons Series

Empire of Carnage: A Dark Captive Mafia Romance

Cruel Daddy: A Dark Mafia Arranged Marriage Romance

Savage Daddy: A Dark Captive Mafia Romance

Ruthless Daddy: A Dark Forbidden Mafia Romance

Vicious Daddy: A Dark Brother's Best Friend Mafia Romance

Wicked Daddy: A Dark Captive Mafia Romance

New York Mafia Doms Series

Her Irish Daddy: A Dark Mafia Romance

Her Russian Daddy: A Dark Mafia Romance

Her Italian Daddy: A Dark Mafia Romance

Her Cartel Daddy: A Dark Mafia Romance

Romano Mafia Brother's Series

Her Mafia Daddy: A Dark Daddy Romance

Her Mafia Boss: A Dark Romance

Her Mafia King: A Dark Romance

Bratva Brotherhood Series

Bought by the Bratva: A Dark Mafia Romance

Captured by the Bratva: A Dark Mafia Romance

Claimed by the Bratva: A Dark Mafia Romance

Bound by the Bratva: A Dark Mafia Romance

Taken by the Bratva: A Dark Mafia Romance

Forbidden Series

Filthy Boss: A Forbidden Office Romance

Filthy Professor: A First Time Professor And Student Romance

Filthy Lawyer: A Forbidden Hate to Love Romance

Filthy Doctor: A Forbidden Romance

Royally Mated Series

Her Faerie King: A Faerie Royalty Paranormal Romance

Her Alpha King: A Royal Wolf Shifter Paranormal Romance

Her Dragon King: A Dragon Shifter Paranormal Romance

Her Vampire King: A Dark Vampire Romance

ABOUT THE AUTHOR

I love to write stories about over the top alpha bad boys who have heart beneath it all, fiery heroines, and happily-ever-after endings with heart and heat. My stories have twists and turns that will keep you flipping the pages and heat to set your kindle on fire.

For as long as I can remember, I've been a sucker for a good romance story. I've always loved to read. Suddenly, I realized why not combine my love of two things, books and romance?

My love of writing has grown over the past four years and I now publish on Amazon exclusively, weaving stories about dirty mafia bad boys and the women they fall head over heels in love with.

If you enjoyed this book please follow me on Amazon, Bookbub or any of the below social media platforms for alerts when more books are released.

Printed in Great Britain
by Amazon

28689565R00256